WINNING THE MAIL-ORDER BRIDE

Lauri Robinson

MILLS &
BOON

Published in Great Britain 2017
by Mills & Boon, an imprint of HarperCollins*Publishers*
1 London Bridge Street, London, SE1 9GF

© 2017 Lauri Robinson

ISBN: 978-0-263-92605-7

Printed and bound in Spain
by CPI, Barcelona

A lover of fairy tales and cowboy boots, **Lauri Robinson** can't imagine a better profession than penning happily-ever-after stories about men—and women—who pull on a pair of boots before riding off into the sunset…or kick them off for other reasons. Lauri and her husband raised three sons in their rural Minnesota home, and are now getting their just rewards by spoiling their grandchildren. Visit: laurirobinson.blogspot.com, facebook.com/lauri.robinson1, or twitter.com/LauriR.

Books by Lauri Robinson

Mills & Boon Historical Romance

Oak Grove

Mail-Order Brides of Oak Grove
'Surprise Bride for the Cowboy'
Winning the Mail-Order Bride

Daughters of the Roaring Twenties

The Runaway Daughter (Undone!)
The Bootlegger's Daughter
The Rebel Daughter
The Forgotten Daughter

Stand-Alone Novels

The Major's Wife
The Wrong Cowboy
A Fortune for the Outlaw's Daughter
Saving Marina
Western Spring Weddings
'When a Cowboy Says I Do'
Her Cheyenne Warrior
Unwrapping the Rancher's Secret
The Cowboy's Orphan Bride

Mills & Boon Historical *Undone!* eBooks

Rescued by the Ranger
Snowbound with the Sheriff
Never Tempt a Lawman

Visit the Author Profile page
at millsandboon.co.uk for more titles.

Florence Jones.
Thank you for being such a dedicated fan!

Chapter One

The single fly that buzzed between the people sitting shoulder to shoulder in the pews in front of him annoyed folks. Not Brett Blackwell. When the fly finally landed on his shoulder, he let it be. The fly wasn't any more irritating than the sweat rolling down his neck, and the bug probably wasn't any happier than he was. Not usually prone to selfish thoughts, Brett wasn't sure what to do with the melancholy that sat inside him. It had to do with the ceremony taking place in the front of the church.

The folks up there were getting married. He'd paid money to have a chance that one of the brides the Oak Grove Betterment Committee had brought to town would pick him, but that hadn't happened, and there wasn't a whole lot of hope inside him to say he might have another chance at getting married anytime soon.

Only five brides had arrived instead of the twelve Mayor Melbourne had promised, and though the mayor claimed more would arrive soon, Brett was with the other dozen or so men who figured Josiah was just blowing hot air. The mayor liked to do that. Put Josiah Melbourne behind a podium and a person's ears would wear out before Josiah's voice would.

Brett figured the town should be glad that at least five gals had arrived on the train a month ago. There couldn't be a whole lot of women willing to travel to the center of Kansas to marry a stranger. Although Oak Grove was a nice little town, and growing as folks hoped it would, it was a long ways from everywhere else. Dodge City was a solid hundred miles south. Yet good people lived here. He liked most of them, and despite his own melancholy, he was genuinely happy for the men who were marrying the brides the Betterment Committee had brought to town.

Those men were some of his best friends. Steve Putnam had been the first to welcome him to town a few years ago, and he'd spent plenty of hours fishing in the Smoky Hill River with Jackson Miller, one of the other men standing up there. That was what he should do today, go fishing. It had a way of settling a man's thoughts.

However, his thoughts might never be settled again. Not until he found himself a wife like Steve and Jackson had.

As he was taller than most everyone else, his gaze easily surveyed the heads ahead of him, until it settled on Josiah Melbourne's. The mayor was sitting front and center as usual. Abigail White, wearing a hat full of flowers, sat beside Josiah, and Teddy, Abigail's brother and one of Brett's best friends, sat beside her. Teddy had been hoping for a wife too, as had several other men in the church.

Just last night he and Teddy had talked about that, about how they doubted the full dozen of brides Josiah had promised would show up, and how there wasn't a whole lot either of them could do about it.

The fly left his shoulder, and Brett watched as it circled a couple of people before it flew toward the window and ultimately buzzed out the opening. The fly's freedom sent Brett's thoughts in a different direction. That fly could have given up, or hit the glass and knocked itself out. But it hadn't. It had found a way to change its situation, and that was what he needed to do.

Change the situation.

He'd done that before. Had left Wisconsin to change his life and settled here in Oak Grove after completing his time with the railroad. He wasn't sorry he'd done either of those things. He wasn't sorry he'd chosen to set up his blacksmith shop here in Oak Grove or that he'd opened up a feed store to go along with his blacksmithing. He wasn't sorry for anything he'd done. That was how he chose to live his life. A sorry man wasn't good for anyone, including himself.

Brett sat up a bit straighter, listening as the preacher blessed the unions of the couples getting hitched, and when the preacher offered a prayer for the newly wedded couples, Brett bowed his head and added his own. Then, as an afterthought, he included a quick one for himself. That if God had a mind to, sending a few more brides to town would be appreciated, especially if one took a liking to him.

The services ended shortly thereafter, and he stood in line to shake each man's hand and give his congratulations to the brides. Then he stepped aside and waited for Teddy to exit the doorway.

It was time he found a wife of his own. On his own. Well, not completely, he needed a little bit of help.

While people continued to file out of the

church, congratulating the happy couples, Brett mentally went over the message he'd send his mother. Word for word so it didn't sound like he was desperate but that there was clearly an element of urgency He could send her a letter, but a telegram would be better. Short and to the point, a telegram would, in itself, tell his mother how speedily he'd like a response.

Teddy not only owned the local newspaper, he ran the telegraph office, and because of the festivities happening, which Teddy was sure to want to attend, Brett would offer a few extra coins to have the message sent today. He usually wouldn't ask for a favor when the office was closed, but seeing the new brides and grooms looking so happy—which they had a right to be—increased the urgency inside him.

When Teddy finally walked down the steps, Brett waved to catch his attention and was extremely glad when Teddy's sister, Abigail, remained behind. Abigail wasn't married, and at one time or another, almost every man in town had considered courting her, including him. Everyone had quickly changed their mind. For him, it wasn't because she was as thin as the pencil she always kept behind one ear or that the end of her pointed nose had a hook sharper than a hawk's, it was her voice. Its high-pitched

squeak was more irritating than a wheel needing grease and Lord but that woman was nosy.
As the town's one and only reporter, she felt
she had a right to know everyone's business
and that it was her duty to write about it. Every
picnic and stroll she embarked upon with a
possible suitor ended up in the newspaper.
His consideration of Abigail as a possible wife
hadn't gone that far for him. He had no desire
to read her thoughts about his size or accent.

"Say, Brett," Teddy said in greeting. "New
preacher did a good job, don't you think?"

"Ya, the brides and grooms sure look happy."

"Have a right to be, don't they?" Teddy said
with a bit of his own melancholy showing.

"Sure do." Glancing over to make sure Abigail was still busy talking to the preacher and
the mayor, Brett nodded for Teddy to follow
him a short distance away. "I have a favor to
ask."

"Sure, what is it?"

With another glance in Abigail's direction,
Brett said, "I need to send a telegram home.
A private one."

Teddy, who didn't resemble his sister in any
way other than the ink stains on his hands,
glanced over his shoulder before saying, "Your
privacy is safe with me, you know that."

"I do," Brett agreed. "And I appreciate it." Shrugging, he added, "I don't have a piece of paper handy."

"That's all right, just give me the gist of it. Abigail has a habit of reading any notes left lying around. Not that I'd leave yours lying around, but you know what I mean."

Brett nodded and leaned closer to whisper, "I need to send a message to my mother, Henrietta Blackwell, in Bayfield, Wisconsin."

Teddy nodded. "Got it. What's it to say?"

"I want her to send me a woman willing to marry me. Right quick-like."

"What's the woman's name?"

"I don't know," Brett admitted. "Whoever she can find."

Teddy sighed and then nodded. "So you aren't holding out any hope for Melbourne to produce the other women he promised?"

"No, but even if more do arrive, there's no guarantee they'll find me a suitable husband. There're a lot of men to choose from."

"Don't I know it," Teddy replied. "Think your mother knows two women?"

Brett didn't want to push his luck but could understand why Teddy asked. "Can't say," he replied, "but let's just start with one."

"All right." Teddy glanced over his shoulder

again. "I'll go send it right now. Abigail's heading straight over to the reception. She plans on writing a special edition of the *Gazette* about the weddings."

"I'll head that way too—keep an eye on her." Brett dug in his pocket. "How much do I owe you? I'll pay extra, this being so urgent and all."

"No charge," Teddy said, "with the understanding that if your mother sends you a suitable bride, I have your permission to ask her to send one for me. Abigail and I don't have any family we can ask, and she hasn't left too many friends in the wake of our travels either."

"Fair enough," Brett replied, shaking Teddy's hand. Rather than express his understanding that Abigail probably hadn't left any friends anywhere, he simply said, "I'll see you later."

"I'll let you know as soon as it's sent," Teddy replied, turning about.

Brett waited until Abigail walked down the church steps and then, keeping one eye on her, for she would surely question Teddy's absence if she noticed it, he fell in among the crowd of folks making their way to the open meadow where the reception of all five couples was to be held.

There, he made small talk with several folks and ate a plate of food from the tables the women of the town had laden with kettles and platters to go along with the side of beef that Steve Putnam had provided to be roasted over an open fire.

Normally appreciative of every meal he ate, Brett couldn't say he tasted much of what he put in his mouth. By the time he saw Teddy, who gave him a wave that said the telegram had been sent, Brett had had enough of the party and headed up the road toward home.

His mother would know exactly what type of woman would make a good wife. One who could cook and hopefully wanted a big family. Several boys for sure, but he wouldn't mind a couple little girls either. Actually, he knew he wouldn't mind the slightest if they were all girls. As long as he had others to share his home with, he really didn't care. His businesses provided enough income to feed as many children as his new wife wanted.

He'd closed down both shops in order to attend the weddings, and considering most everyone in town was still at the wedding reception, there was no sense reopening them. Therefore, after crossing the railroad tracks, he rounded the big building he'd built two years ago with lumber brought in on the railroad from his family back home and crossed the little field to the house that had also been built with solid northern pine. Kansas didn't have enough trees for all the lumber it needed, and after he'd left home, he'd let it be known his family had plenty of good Wisconsin lumber to sell and the railroads made getting that lumber to where it was needed far easier than it ever had been.

He'd set up plenty of accounts for his family's business back home before and after he hired on the railroad and started looking for a place to call his own.

Not all the lumber in Oak Grove had come from Wisconsin, but a good amount had. Just last month he'd helped unload a train car full of Blackwell Lumber. It had been for the town, so he'd gotten a good deal on it from his older brother. The town was building a few small houses just a ways past his. Hoping to sell them to new residents. Ready-made homes were one sure way to bring in new citizens. That was what the mayor had said, and the town council agreed with him. Just like they'd agreed when Josiah had suggested building the church and the schoolhouse and sending money back east to have brides sent out here.

Done worrying about those brides, Brett collected his fishing pole from the tool shed and headed back toward the tracks that ran along his buildings. A mile south was where he was going. To where the cool water of the Smoky Hill River flowed westward, leaving enough moisture behind for a few trees to shade the grassy banks. There was no better way for a man to collect his thoughts than to spend a few hours fishing.

As he stepped over the first rail of hardened steel, he couldn't help but remember the work that had gone into laying every inch, and the faint rumble beneath his feet had him looking eastward. A man could see for miles in this country, and though it was little more than a dot on the horizon, a westbound train was making its way into Oak Grove.

Knowing there was no need for him to meet it—there wouldn't be anyone needing a blacksmith or chicken or horse feed, he turned his gaze southward and continued over the tracks and past the few houses that sat on the east edge of town.

Jackson Miller lived in one of those houses. He'd been lucky enough to marry one of the brides. Maggie McCary. Steve Putnam had married the other McCary sister, Mary. Brett had hoped he'd stand a chance with Maggie or Mary, especially after tasting Mary's cooking.

That was what he missed most about home. Ma's cooking.

That wasn't completely true. Although he missed the tasty and plentiful meals Ma always had on the table, he'd learned enough from her to cook reasonably well for himself. Leastwise enough to satisfy his appetite. What he really missed was having others around the table to share meals with him. Being one of eight kids, his family home had never been quiet. Not like his little house was. Quiet and empty.

He was tired of the quiet. Tired of being lonely. And when he was tired of something, he took action. Just like he'd done today.

The music from the reception faded as he walked on, and by the time he arrived at the river, the only noise interrupting the afternoon air was a whistle announcing the train had arrived in Oak Grove. He smiled to himself. Soon that very train would be bringing him a bride.

The shrill sound of the train whistle had Fiona Goldberg closing her eyes and saying a brief prayer. She'd been praying since they'd left Ohio, and one more couldn't hurt. It wasn't as if she was asking for a miracle, just a bit of comfort to settle her nerves. Then again, that in itself might be a miracle. She was rather frazzled. The train ride had been a long one, and the boys weren't used to such confinement. Neither was she.

"Are we there, Ma?" Rhett asked with hope making his blue eyes shine.

"Yes." Giving her trembling hands something to focus on, she folded his collar back into place. "This is Oak Grove."

"Don't look like much to me," Wyatt said with as much disgust as he'd shown when they'd left Ohio.

Knowing there were times when it best served the purpose to ignore her seven-year-old's attitude, she stayed focused on straightening Rhett's collar. At five, he was looking at their move as an adventure rather than a necessity. "I'm sure it will be a wonderful place for us to live," she said.

"I'm not," Wyatt mumbled.

Fiona held her breath in order not to snap at her older son. All of their nerves were frazzled.

"Can we eat soon, Ma?" Rhett asked. "I'm mighty hungry."

She pulled up a smile just for him and kissed his forehead. "As soon as possible. I promise." Then she turned to Wyatt. "Gather the satchel from under the seat, please. And put your hat on."

Wyatt grumbled, as he'd taken to doing lately, but did as told. By the time the train rolled to a jerking and squealing stop, both boys were seated beside her and waiting for the conductor to announce they could depart. If she could have found her voice, she would have told the boys to be on their best behavior, but her own misgivings about marrying a stranger—with two children in tow—had her throat burning and her eyes stinging.

Refusing to let her children see her fears, she smiled at each of them and then nodded as the conductor waved them forward.

Wyatt was the first one out the door, followed quickly by Rhett. As Fiona descended the steps, joining them on the platform, Wyatt mumbled, "Told you it weren't much of a town."

She couldn't disagree, not at first glance, but she'd seen worse places. The town was small, but the buildings were nicely painted and the streets fairly well kept. The thing that struck her as odd was the lack of people. There weren't any, and the stores looked closed.

"There's the sheriff's office," Rhett said, grasping a hold of her skirt.

"It sure enough is," a portly man said, walking out of the depot and toward them. "You'd best behave or you'll be visiting it."

Her spine stiffened as Fiona gathered Rhett closer. "Pardon me, sir," she said to the stranger, "but there is no call—"

"Fiona Goldberg, I'm assuming," the man said, dabbing at the sweat on his forehead with a white handkerchief. "I'm Josiah Melbourne."

Chagrin burned her cheeks. "M-Mr. Melbourne," Fiona stuttered. "I apologize, I didn't—"

"Recognize me? Of course you didn't." He stuffed the kerchief in his pocket and then pulled the lapels of his suit across his thick chest as he said, "You sent me a picture. I, in turn, did not send you one."

Her stomach bubbled. The picture she'd sent had been the one taken of her and Sam shortly after they'd been married. She'd snipped the photograph in half before sending it and still felt guilty about doing that. Despite how his life had ended, how their lives together had been, Sam had been her husband and she still owed him the honor she'd vowed on their wedding day.

Swallowing around the lump that threatened to completely close off her airway, she said, "Hello, Mr. Melbourne, it's nice to meet you."

"I'm sure it is." Looking at the children over

the top of his wire-framed glasses, he continued, "And these are your two boys. Wyatt and Red, I believe."

"Rhett," she corrected. "Wyatt and Rhett. Wyatt is seven and Rhett is five and they—"

"Let's be on our way, shall we?"

Fiona glanced over her shoulder, wishing they could step back on the train and start over. Not only had she blundered their initial meeting, Mr. Melbourne's interruptions were not leaving a pleasurable first impression on Wyatt. His eyes had narrowed, much like Sam's used to do when he'd been irritated.

If she had the ability to change time, to start over, it would be before today. Before she'd had to make a choice about the new life they were embarking upon. Sam's death had left them penniless and homeless. She'd done her best to make a living, but feeding two boys cost more than she could make doing laundry and sewing, and she'd refused to ask the Masons to give her another month of reduced rent.

"I've instructed that your belongings be delivered to the house," Josiah said as he grasped her elbow and started walking along the platform. "This way. It's on the other side of the tracks. The house is owned by the town and with my permission you'll be allowed to stay there, rent-free, for this upcoming week, after which time we will be married. Next Saturday. At the church."

A river of fear raced through her, once again making her question what she was doing. "One week is not very long to get to know someone," she said quietly.

"I believe I'm being generous, Fiona. You agreed to marry me. I could have had that arranged for today. Furthermore, I just paid for three train tickets from Ohio to Kansas. That wasn't cheap."

It took considerable effort to get past the flare of anger that started to swirl inside her. She was here and would make the most of it, but she wouldn't be belittled. "I'm sure it wasn't, Mr. Melbourne, and yes, that is correct, I have agreed to marry you, but a small amount of time for the boys to get used to the idea would not be unfair to them, or me. It's only been six months since their father—"

"That is not my problem," Josiah said.

It wasn't his problem, it was hers, and her hope of this being a solution was souring quickly. After church one Sunday a few weeks ago, Reverend Ward's wife had told her about Oak Grove's willingness to pay for the westward passage of any woman who would agree to become a mail-order bride. Mrs. Ward had heard about the invitation for brides from her sister over in Bridgeport and had quite openly suggested that the best thing Fiona could do for her and the boys was to leave Ohio.

Understanding they'd worn out their welcome at the church—if they'd ever *been* welcomed— Fiona had gone home that night and penned a letter to Josiah himself. Mrs. Ward had conveniently given her the name and address. Fiona had included her picture, not wanting anyone to be disappointed, for she'd never claimed to be a beautiful woman. She was too tall for that and her hair too dull and lifeless. She'd also been completely honest in explaining she was a widow with two young sons, and that although she didn't live in Bridgeport, had never been there, she had heard about Oak Grove's need for brides and hoped she qualified.

The hold Rhett had on her hand tightened as they stepped off the platform. She looked down and smiled at him, wishing there was another way to ease the apprehension on his young face.

"The week I'm offering is not for you or the children," Josiah said as gravel crunched beneath their feet. "It is for me to see if you will make a suitable wife. Besides being the mayor of this community, I'm an attorney. A man as prominent as myself needs to have a wife who can be looked upon just as prominently. One who understands the importance of such a position."

Fiona bit her lips together and breathed through her nose. She'd never been looked upon prominently. However, she had her pride, and honor, and could hold her head up despite the worst of situations. She'd been doing that for the past six months in ways she'd never had to before. And would continue to, if for no other reason than the sake of her sons. "I explained the untimely and unfortunate death of my husband in my letter, Mr. Melbourne, and—"

"Yes, you did, Fiona, and let me assure you, if I deem you worthy of being my wife, neither your husband's death, nor his infractions, will ever concern you again."

She bit her lips together again and willed her anger to ease. He wasn't a tall man. The top of his head was about level with her chin, and his shoulders twisted back and forth as he strutted along beside her. He was rather rude and pompous, but those were all things she could and would overlook in order to see her children clothed, fed and living under a roof that didn't leak. She'd had to overlook worse things.

In fact, she'd been overlooking things her entire life. Having been taken in as a small child by family members who'd already had enough mouths to feed had instilled a certain amount of accepting things as they were.

Drawing a deep breath, she said, "I thank you for this opportunity, Mr. Melbourne. Perhaps once you've shown me the house, you can enlighten me with a list of your expectations." As long as she knew what had to be done, she could do it.

The smile he bestowed upon her made her insides gurgle, as did the way his chest seemed to puff outward.

"I knew you'd be trainable from the moment I read your letter, Fiona. I'm so glad I wasn't wrong."

Knowing full well it wasn't what he was referring to, Fiona couldn't stop herself from replying, "I've been housebroken for some time, Mr. Melbourne. All three of us have been."

Chapter Two

Content that his afternoon of fishing had been just what he'd needed to put things back in perspective, Brett hauled his catch home to clean and fry up. He took the same route back, skirting the boundaries of town. Even though his melancholy had lifted, he still had no desire to attend the reception continuing to take place. Actually, all his alone time had put him in a considerably good mood. The Olsens who lived several miles from his family's mill had as many girls in their family as his had boys. Two of his seven brothers had married Olsen girls, and he was mulling over the idea that his mother might investigate if another one of the Olsen girls would be interested in moving to Kansas. That might be easier. Already knowing the gal she sent him. Ma knew most every family in northern Wisconsin, so it could be someone other than one of the Olsen girls. That would be fine too.

It wasn't like him to ask for assistance. He'd rather give it than accept it, but writing home wasn't that much different than donating to the Betterment Committee had been. At least that was what he was telling himself. Most of the single men in town had anteed up the money the mayor had deemed necessary in order to have a chance for one of the mail-order brides to consider them a viable husband.

The idea he'd sent that telegram to his mother took on more solid roots as Brett cleaned the six catfish. Matter of fact, he'd bet she'd be right pleased to help out. That was how she was, always willing to help whoever needed a bit of assistance.

Once he had the fillets soaking in a dish of water on the kitchen table, he went to collect a shovel in order to bury the heads and entrails. Although his mother had raised only boys, she hadn't shied away from making them understand that keeping a clean house was just as easy as keeping a dirty one.

Stepping out his back door, Brett paused at the sight of two young boys examining the fishing pole he'd left leaning against the porch

railing. He glanced left and right before looking at the boys again.

Not recognizing the two boys as any he
knew in town, Brett asked, "Where did you
fellas come from?"

The taller of the two, and presumably the
older, pulled the smaller boy away from the
fishing pole. "Over there," he said while pointing toward the field that held the one house the
city had erected so far.

The smaller of the two dark-haired boys cast
a wary gaze at Brett as he scooted behind the
taller one.

"We didn't touch your pole," the older one
said. "Just looked at it."

Brett understood his deep voice and heavy
northern accent took some getting used to, so
he tried to speak more softly. "You can touch
it. It's a sturdy pole. I've had it a long time and
have caught a good amount of fish with it."

The younger boy peeked around the older
one, glancing from the pole to his brother, who
shook his head.

"That's all right," the older one said. "I can
tell it's a good pole from here."

"A fisherman, are you?"

The boy shrugged.

Brett would guess him to be about seven or

eight. "You must be. Only a fisherman knows a good pole by just looking at it."

"I like to go fishing," the younger boy said. He might have said more if the older one hadn't frowned at him.

"Me too." Brett then glanced across the field again. "Are your parents thinking of buying the house from the city?"

"No," the older one said. "The mayor's letting us stay there for a week."

"He is?" That didn't sound like Melbourne, unless there was a cutback in it for him, but that wasn't something Brett would discuss with a child.

"Yes, he is," the boy replied before asking, "Why do you talk like that?"

Brett wasn't insulted. There had been a time when he'd tried to alter his accent, but that was more work than it was worth. This was the way he'd talked his entire life, and he figured he'd go right on doing so. He patted the boy on the head while walking down the steps. "Because I'm not from around here. I lived up north, by Canada, until a couple of years ago when I moved here."

"We saw you carrying the fishing pole," the younger boy said as they both started walking beside him. "And some fish."

"Ya, I went fishing. Caught a fine batch of cats." He held out the bucket. "Gotta bury the innards."

The younger boy, most likely having figured out there was no need to be scared, pointed toward the bucket. "Ma used to bury those in the garden."

"That's what my ma would do too. Or have me or one of my brothers do it," Brett answered while stopping at the tool shed door. "But seeing I don't have a garden, I'll bury them out by that little tree."

"You don't have many of those around here," the older boy said.

Brett entered the shed, grabbed the shovel and stepped back out. "Trees?"

The boy nodded.

"No, we don't," Brett agreed. "I'd like to see a few more, that's for sure."

Both boys started walking beside him again. "There were lots of trees in Ohio," the younger one said.

"Ohio? Is that where you're from?" Brett asked.

"Yes."

The tone of the older boy said he'd rather be back in Ohio. Brett figured that was how most children felt when it came to moving away from their home and didn't begrudge the youngster whatsoever. "Never been to Ohio. But we had lots of trees in Wisconsin. Say, what are your names?"

"I'm Wyatt, and this here is Rhett."

"I'm five," Rhett supplied.

"Wyatt and Rhett, you say," Brett said while setting down the bucket near the small and only tree on his property. "Well, my name is Brett. Brett Blackwell."

"Hey, your name sounds like my name. Brett. Rhett."

"That it does," Brett answered the younger boy while jabbing the shovel into the ground. "But I'm a lot older than five."

"How long you lived around here?" Wyatt asked.

"More than two years. Oak Grove is a nice town. I'm sure your folks will like it." The hole was deep enough. Brett set aside the shovel and dumped the bucket's contents in the hole and then grabbed the shovel to replace the dirt. "You two will too once you get to know others."

"We already know others," Wyatt said.

There was so much anger in the boy's voice Brett had to follow the glare Wyatt was casting across the field. Right to the house the city had for sale. "Who?" he asked. "Who do you know?"

"The mayor."

Brett nodded. "Josiah Melbourne likes to hear himself talk, but he's not so bad once you get to know him."

"I don't want to get to know him any more than I already do," Wyatt said.

"Me neither," Rhett said. "He told us to go outside and not come back in until he leaves and that was a long time ago."

Carrying the empty bucket and shovel, Brett started walking back toward his house. "Probably because he has some important business to talk about with your folks."

"Like when he's gonna marry our ma."

Brett stumbled slightly. "Marry your ma? Where's your pa?"

"Got hisself killed back in Ohio," Wyatt said. "That's why we had to move here, and why Ma has to marry the mayor."

The mayor prided himself on being from Ohio, and it was an acquaintance of his rounding up brides from there—which made Brett ask, "Did your ma know the mayor when he lived in Ohio?"

"No. The preacher's wife told Ma she had to come out here and marry the mayor 'cause folks at the church didn't want us there no more."

That didn't sound like a thing any preacher's wife should say and Brett couldn't stop himself from asking, "She did?"

"Yes, she did." Wyatt had both arms crossed over his chest and his squinting eyes held enough anger to make a rattlesnake take cover.

Children shouldn't harbor such anger. Shouldn't have to. A good portion of anger was starting to well around inside Brett too—at the idea of more brides arriving and Melbourne harboring one for himself. That wasn't playing by the rules. The women were supposed to have a choice of who they wanted to marry.

"You gonna cook those fish you caught?" little Rhett asked.

They'd arrived back at the tool shed, and as Brett set the shovel inside, he answered, "I am. Do you boys like catfish? I got more than I can eat."

Rhett licked his lips while looking up at Wyatt. The older boy shook his head and reluctance filled his voice as he said, "Ma probably wouldn't like that."

"Well, I wouldn't want you to get into trouble with your ma, but knowing how long-winded the mayor can be, and seeing you two are hungry, and considering I invited you to eat, I don't see how she could be too mad. Do you?"

"No," Rhett answered while his older brother was still considering how to answer. "She promised we'd eat right after we arrived in town, and that was a long time ago."

"Let me rinse out this bucket, then we'll go cook us some fish," Brett said. "We'll leave the door open so we can hear if she hollers for you."

Wyatt appeared to agree with that and held out a hand. "I'll rinse out the bucket. Rhett's been hungry for hours."

Brett handed over the bucket, but not until he asked, "Didn't they feed you on the train?"

"Just once a day," Wyatt answered. "Last night was the last time we ate."

Brett grasped Rhett's little shoulder to lead him up the steps while gesturing toward the well for Wyatt to find the water to rinse out the bucket. "Come on, little feller. Let's get something in your stomach." He'd always liked helping others, but thinking about these boys not eating since last night had a powerful bout of sorrow rising up inside him. As children, he and his brothers ate nonstop because that was what boys did. His mother used to say they had hollow legs, but she'd never not let them eat. Never not had a pantry full of food. It wasn't until he'd gotten older that he realized how lucky that had made him. How rich, not in money, but in life, that had made him. That was part of what made him willing to share whatever he had with whoever needed it.

"Where'd you get so many eggs?" Rhett asked, pointing toward the wire basket on the counter.

"I bought them over at the mercantile." Seeing how the boy's eyes were glued on the basket, Brett said, "We'll fry some to go with the fish."

"We will?"

Brett nodded while starting a fire in the stove. "Sure enough will." When he was young and snatched a cookie or slice of bread before a meal, his mother would say he was going to spoil his appetite. That hadn't happened and he doubted it would for this little feller either. Brett shut the stove door and opened one of the warming oven doors to take out a plate of biscuits he'd purchased from the bakery yesterday. "Here, go ahead and snack on one of these while I get the fish and eggs frying."

Rhett needed no further coaxing. Neither did Wyatt. By the time the fish was frying, they'd each eaten two biscuits. While they'd been taking the edge off their hunger, Brett had been telling them about other children living in town, mainly the hotel owner's two rambunctious boys. He also told them about the school and how they'd meet many other children there.

Rhett seemed excited, but Wyatt was hesitant. At seven, he carried a big load on his shoulders, and Brett couldn't help but wonder what had put it there.

"You boys know how to set a table?" he asked while cracking an egg on the edge of the frying pan. With no sisters, he and his brothers had set the table many times while growing up.

"Yes, sir," Rhett answered.

"You'll find everything in that cupboard." He pointed toward the cabinet behind Wyatt. "Don't forget napkins."

He was setting the plate full of fried fish on the table when a woman appeared in the doorway. She was tall and slender, and wearing a dark green dress that was buttoned all the way up to her chin, but it was the dark circles beneath her eyes that made a knot form in Brett's stomach.

"Brett invited us to eat with him, Ma," Wyatt said.

"You said we'd eat as soon as we got to town," Rhett said at the same time.

She bit her bottom lip as she turned to look at him again. "I apologize, Mr. Blackwell—"

"No need to apologize, Mrs. Goldberg," Brett said while she glanced toward her sons once again. It was obvious Josiah had told her his name, just as Wyatt had told him hers. "I did invite Rhett and Wyatt to supper. As you can see, I have plenty, and feeding my new neighbors would be my pleasure." A second thought formed then, that of Josiah inviting them to eat with him. "Unless you have other plans of course. I'm afraid I didn't think of that."

The way she paused long enough to close her eyes briefly and swallow sent a tiny shiver up his spine. When she opened her eyes and he spotted the moisture she'd been trying to hide, he experienced a wave of melancholy that surpassed all he'd been feeling for himself the past few days.

"No, Mr. Blackwell, we don't have other plans, and I apologize for that, as well."

If there hadn't been little ears nearby, he'd have asked why. Melbourne should have planned something for their first night in town. Then again, if Josiah hadn't been aware they'd be arriving today, he might have been taken off guard, and considering Rollie Austin was one of the men who'd gotten married today, there wasn't any place in town open for them to get a meal.

"That must be why I caught so many fish today," Brett said while pulling out a chair for her. "I already told the boys the fish just wouldn't stop biting on my hook."

She glanced from him to the table and back at him. "This is so kind of you, Mr. Blackwell, but we couldn't impose. The boys shouldn't have—"

"No one's imposing, ma'am." Seeing her hesitation, he added, "I appreciate the company."

She glanced around the room. "And your wife?"

Brett laughed. "Don't have one." He gestured to the table. "It's nothing fancy, just fish and eggs, but there's plenty."

The indecision in her eyes had Brett holding his breath. Or maybe it was the way she was biting her bottom lip. Her face was like the rest of her, long and thin, and her eyes reminded him of a cloudy day—sort of sad and hopeless. Brett took another step closer. "You have to be hungry. Your boys sure are. Think of it as my way of welcoming you to Kansas. Once your bellies are full, you can get settled in your house and then get a good night's rest. Tomorrow will be a new day."

"That's what you always say, Ma," Rhett said.

The hint of a smile that formed on her lips put a faint shine on her face. "Yes, it is." Turning his way, she nodded. "I'd— We'd be honored to share a meal with you, Mr. Blackwell, and we sincerely appreciate the invitation."

"I'll get another plate," Wyatt said, displaying a full smile.

"I'll help him," Rhett offered.

The younger brother had smiled many times during their short visit, but Wyatt hadn't, and by the smile that grew on the woman's face, Brett would bet it was the first time she'd smiled in a while too. He wanted to know why. And he wanted to change that. Someone as pretty as she was should be smiling all the time.

"Thank you, Mr. Blackwell," she said, holding her hand out. "I hope the boys haven't made themselves a nuisance."

"Not at all, ma'am." He shook her hand, noting the soft skin on the back of her hand couldn't hide the calluses on her palm. "Welcome to Oak Grove."

"Thank you," she answered softly, sincerely. "Thank you very much."

Not quite ready to let go of her hand, he tugged her toward the table. Up close he noticed how unique her eyes were. They held no distinct color, but a mixture of gray, green and brown, and a light appeared in them as she bowed her head slightly.

With a timid smile, she said, "The fish smells wonderful."

He couldn't smell anything but flowers. Sweet-smelling flowers that gave off such a wonderful scent all he wanted to do was breathe it in.

"I bet it tastes just as good too."

Brought back from fields of flowers by little Rhett's voice, Brett let go of her hand to pull out the chair. "Let's eat while it's hot," he said. "Otherwise, it'll start to stink." Giving Fiona a friendly wink, he added, "Fish is like that."

Fiona pinched her lips to keep from giggling as the big man took his seat at the end of the table beside her. He was so friendly, so kind, her insides were practically dancing. This was the kind of welcome she'd hoped her sons would experience. Something that would assure them they were welcome here.

That their lives would forever be changed, forever be better than they'd been back in Ohio. If only Josiah Melbourne had been so welcoming to her and her sons. He'd been more concerned that she and the children wouldn't behave appropriately—and had gone so far as to write a list of things they could do and things they could not do. She'd nearly gnawed the end off her tongue while forcing herself to remain tolerant. And silent. As he'd suggested. Until she'd seen the boys encounter the blacksmith.

Josiah had stopped her on the way out the door, insisting that Brett Blackwell was harmless and would keep the boys busy while he and she continued to discuss their arrangement. A discussion she'd feared would never end. Her first impression of Josiah hadn't improved much, and she was already afraid she'd made a mistake in coming to Kansas.

She'd thanked whatever lucky stars she might have left when Josiah had finally taken his leave, only to remember she didn't have anything to feed them for supper. Arriving at Brett Blackwell's open back door and seeing her boys seated at the table full of food had been enough to bring tears to her eyes. But it had been his charm, the way he'd coaxed her into believing he truly wanted to share this meal with them, that had broken through the tough exterior she'd tried to hold in place.

He was right, the children were hungry, and thankfully he hadn't questioned why she hadn't had any other plans of how to feed them this evening. He couldn't possibly know how much this meal meant to her right now.

"Thank you," she said while taking the platter of fish fried to a golden brown. After forking the smallest piece onto her plate, she passed the platter on to Wyatt. Brett then handed her another platter full of fried eggs. There had to be more than a dozen. She took one, the smallest, and then passed that platter on to Wyatt, as well.

As Rhett, who now had the fish platter, slid a third piece of fish onto his plate, she opened her mouth to tell him that was enough, but a large hand gently touched her wrist.

"There's too much here for me to eat, so you boys best eat until you're too full to swallow another bite," Brett said.

He removed his hand from her arm and, with a nod, gestured for everyone to start eating. The boys needed no more encouragement than that, and as Fiona watched them begin eating with gusto, her own stomach flipped. She swallowed hard against the sensation that sent a lump into her throat. When she'd mentioned to Josiah that her sons were hungry, that they hadn't eaten since last night, he'd interrupted her to point out that if it had just been her on the train, she would have had three meals a day.

Anger had flared inside her, yet at that moment, she'd never felt more trapped. Mr. Melbourne had paid for their accommodations, and she had no means to reimburse him, so she'd forced herself to once again remain silent. Furthermore, in a moment when she'd believed there had been no other option, she'd given him her word that she would marry him. Therefore, she would. She had never gone back on her word and wouldn't now. Her children needed to know remaining true to one's word, although sometimes difficult, was the right way. The only way.

"Eat," Brett said quietly. "Before it gets cold."

She nodded, and though each bite swelled in her throat, she forced it down and took the next one. Just as she would each and every obstacle that came her way. Eventually it would get easier.

At least that was her hope.

When her plate was empty, she set down her fork. Within seconds, Brett handed her the platter that remarkably still held several pieces of fish. It made her think of Jesus feeding the masses, and that was enough to bring tears to her eyes. She hadn't asked for a miracle, yet it appeared one was happening. With tears stinging her eyes, she shook her head.

"You haven't eaten enough to keep a bird alive," Brett said, sliding two more pieces of fish onto her plate. He then added two more eggs to her plate before holding the plate over the center of the table. "Anyone else need more?"

Both boys eagerly accepted the offer, and the man, whose booming voice could startle birds from the trees in the next state, laughed so softly, she may have been the only one to hear it.

When little more than crumbs sat on all the plates and platters circling the table, Fiona said, "I do believe that was the best fish I've ever eaten."

"Me too," Rhett agreed. "I didn't even know I liked fish that much."

Laughter, including hers, filled the room. As it settled, Fiona set her napkin on the table. "Mr. Blackwell, we can't thank you enough for this fine meal. Therefore, I do hope you won't mind when I insist upon doing the dishes. It's the least I can do."

"That's not necessary, ma'am," he said while shaking his head.

"I believe it is," she said. "And I insist."

He jumped to his feet to pull her chair back as she prepared to stand. Hoping he understood that she had to repay him in some way, she looked up to meet his gaze.

There was tenderness in his blue eyes, but there was something more, something she wasn't sure if she'd ever seen before, but an inner, almost foreign instinct said it was respect.

"I will allow you to *help* with the dishes," he said. "I've been doing them for so long, I'd feel lazy watching you do them all by yourself."

"Well, I guess that's fair," she said, rising to her feet.

"We'll help," Wyatt offered.

Lately, there hadn't been many opportunities for her to feel pride, or be proud of her sons, but she was proud at this moment. The table was cleared in no time, and with her permission, the boys went outside to play. After scraping some soap into the tub of warm water, she started washing the dishes and, upon his insistence, handed them to Brett to dry and put away.

"I—uh—I'm sorry about your husband," he said when the silence grew a bit thick.

"Thank you," she said out of courtesy but then broached the subject she'd been contemplating since finding the boys at his house. "I can only imagine what my sons told you."

"Nothing bad," Brett said. "Just that their father had died and that you came here to marry Josiah Melbourne because some church lady told you to."

"That about sums it up," she admitted.

"Sounds to me like that woman needs to listen to what the preacher's preaching."

She couldn't help but grin. "That may be true, but it was what we needed—the boys and I. A fresh start."

"If you don't mind my asking, don't you have any family?"

"No. My parents died when I was young."

"Who'd you live with, then?"

"My aunt and uncle. They had several of their own children and were very glad when I married Sam." She bit the tip of her tongue. It wasn't like her to blurt out such personal information. If she hadn't stopped herself, she would have told him she and her sons wouldn't have been any more welcome with her aunt and uncle now than she had been twenty years ago.

"How old were you when you married your husband?"

"Seventeen. I thought I was old enough. Thought I knew what I wanted." Grabbing another plate, she clamped her back teeth together. One meal shouldn't make her feel as if she needed to share her entire life story. She must be overly tired and not thinking straight. Or nervous. Being alone with him had heightened her senses. She could feel him moving about to return the dishes to their rightful places. Knew the exact moment he stepped closer to her again. Like right now. Beneath the wash water, she squeezed her hands into fists to stop them from trembling.

"Oak Grove is a good town," he said. "You'll like it once you get to know everyone."

"I hope so," she said. "The boys need a place where they feel welcome." That was better. What the children needed wasn't a hidden secret.

"We all do," he said. "Big or little."

"That's true."

"That had to take a lot of guts," he said. "Courage, I mean. For all of you. Moving away from Ohio."

He was obviously as nervous as she was, and the idea of that—of a man his size, so capable of so many things, being uneasy—made her grin. Only because in some silly, unfathomable way, it made her relax a bit. "I wouldn't call it courage," she said.

"I would. That's what it takes. Some folks spend their whole lives wishing things would change but never once realize they have to do something to make them change."

She handed him the last pan and then walked to the table to wipe it down. "You say that like you've experienced it firsthand."

"I have, more than once."

The thoughtfulness of his tone had her turning around. He merely grinned before turning around to put the pan in the cupboard. Her heart skipped a beat and the swelling in her throat made her swallow, mainly because she couldn't think of anything to say, even though she'd like to know more. She wanted to know why a man so kindhearted, successful and handsome wasn't married. Were the women in this town blind? His back was to her, and even that was so fit, so muscular and shapely in how it narrowed from broad, thick shoulders to a trim waist, it awakened that feminine and primal part deep inside her that hadn't been awakened in a long time. A very long time.

She had to swallow again as he turned about,

and tightened her leg muscles to keep her from wobbling.

"I'll go dump this water," he said, picking up the tub.

Heart thudding, it was a moment before she trusted her legs to work. Then she crossed the room and draped the cloth over the edge of the counter. "I—I'll collect the boys. It's getting late, and…" Unable to think of more to say, she nodded. "Thank you again for the meal."

"It was my pleasure," he said.

Drawing another deep breath, trying to quell the awakening that continued to grow, she hurried out the door.

Chapter Three

The single bed in the house was small and the mattress so thin it fell between the rope stays. It shouldn't matter. Fiona was so tired and worn-out more than any other time she could recall—she should have fallen asleep as fast as the boys had.

Thankfully, her breathing had returned to normal and the throbbing in parts of her that shouldn't be throbbing had stopped. That had happened hours ago, yet sleep hadn't arrived.

As her gaze went to the window, to the quiet darkness emitting nothing except a single star in the faraway sky, Fiona knew she couldn't blame her sleeplessness on the bed, or even on her body's reaction to spending the evening with a handsome man.

She was scared. Scared she'd made the wrong choice.

Brett's kindness, how he'd shared his fish and eggs with them, should be looked upon as a sign of what the others in the community were like. How she and the boys would be welcomed. Instead, she was comparing him to Josiah. Weighing Brett's welcome against Josiah's. Everything inside her said the differences would continue, and that made her fear what was to come in the next few days. And the years after that.

She'd had practice in that area. Comparing men. As Sam had changed, she had too. She'd started to compare herself to other women— how happy and satisfied they were in their lives to how she felt. That was when she'd started to compare their husbands to Sam. Not just in attractiveness, but how they treated their wives. Her hope had been to find a man who would treat her and her sons with compassion and kindness this time, and she greatly feared that hadn't happened.

Would life be better for her children here? It had seemed that way in Ohio. That moving away was their only chance to find something different. She'd lost all hope back there and was having a hard time finding any tonight. Or of finding any peace in believing she'd done what had to be done, any optimism in believing she had the strength to continue upon this path she'd chosen.

She wasn't a weak or frail woman. Hard work had never worried her, and her faith had never failed her, yet it was none of those things that lingered in the back of her mind right now. It was her. She wasn't cut out to be the wife of a mayor. Of a man so prominent. More than that, though, was her worry of how Josiah would treat her children. He'd shown no compassion or understanding for what they had been through before leaving Ohio nor shown any concern about their arrival in a strange place. Not even when it came to their hunger.

She'd had to be strong her entire life and had hoped that would change here. That the man she'd promised to wed would be her shelter against the storm that had raged upon her for so long. Life had worn her out, and she was tired of being tired. Tired of fighting the battle by herself.

Perhaps she was just being selfish and just needed time to get to know Josiah better.

The bed creaked as Wyatt shifted.

Lying on her side in order to leave as much space for the boys as possible, Fiona twisted to look over her shoulder.

"Where are you going?" she whispered as he slipped off the bed.

"To sleep on the floor," he said.

"No, Wyatt, you—"

"It won't be any worse than the train," he said, gathering one of the blankets.

"I'll—"

"No, Ma, *I* will sleep on the floor."

He was stubborn, especially when he set his mind to something. Pulling the pillow out from beneath her head, she handed it to him. "Take this pillow too."

"No. You need that one. Rhett's using the other one. I'll be fine." A thump and shuffling sounded as he settled onto the floor. "I'll be right here, so don't worry, Ma. Get yourself some sleep."

Curled up near her feet, Rhett was using the other pillow, and tears burned her eyes as she replaced the pillow beneath her head. For all his orneriness lately, Wyatt was still a good boy at heart and had taken it upon himself to be the man of the family ever since Sam had died. "Good night, honey."

"Night." Silence barely had time to settle when he asked, "Do you think Brett would give me a job, Ma? He owns both the feed store and the blacksmith shop."

Brett did own both businesses, and she'd already witnessed enough to believe he was generous enough to give anyone a job. Yet she couldn't tell that to Wyatt. "You're too young for a job."

"No, I'm not, and if Brett gave me one, you wouldn't need to marry the mayor."

Fiona closed her eyes to gather any invisible strength still hiding somewhere inside her. "Yes, I would," she whispered. "I gave him my word. I can't go back on that." She pinched her lips together and dug deep enough to say, "Besides, I want to marry Mr. Melbourne."

"No, you don't."

"Yes, Wyatt, I do."

"Don't see how you can when he don't like none of us."

"He never said—"

"He didn't have to. I saw it in his eyes. He thinks we're thieves. Thinks Pa was a thief too. Just like the folks in Ohio did."

As hard as she'd tried to keep the children from hearing what had happened to their father, they had heard. Knew Sam had been with the Morgan brothers when they'd tried robbing the train. Knew he'd been shot while trying to get away. He'd made it home. Died in their bed. Therefore, everyone in town had thought she'd known what he'd been up to. Thought she could very well have been a participant. She hadn't been. Hadn't known what he and the Morgans had conjured up, but few had believed that.

No one had been more shocked by what had happened than she was. Sam had never stooped to such dire actions before. Things had never been easy, money had always been tight, but they'd managed. Somehow they had always managed. Losing his job at the refinery the year before had devastated Sam. Changed him. In ways she couldn't explain, nor had she liked who he'd become. Always angry. Always blaming others for things that truly hadn't mattered. Including her and the boys.

She swiped aside a single tear and drew a deep breath. "Your father was not a thief. He made a mistake. A terrible mistake. One he paid dearly for. You go to sleep now. And no more talking about jobs."

Fiona felt more than heard Wyatt roll over, face away from the bed, and she had to pinch her nose to stop from sniffling as tears rolled down her cheeks. A part of her hated Sam for the pain he'd caused them. Her and Wyatt and Rhett. And for the disgrace they'd encountered. The hatred and scorn that had been bestowed upon them had been unbearable. Leaving Ohio had been the best choice, her only choice, and without Josiah's offer, without his paying for the tickets, it would never have happened. If for no other reason than that, she would stand by her promise and marry Josiah Melbourne.

As usual, Brett rose at the break of dawn and set a pot of coffee to brew on the stove. It was Sunday, and the few chores he had to do—feeding and cleaning up after the team of horses he used to pull his wagon and kept housed in the barn connected to his black-smith shop—wouldn't take long. Never did. He missed having more to do in the mornings. Back home there had been cows to milk, hogs to slop, eggs to gather, chicks to feed, water to haul. All sorts of things. There was room in his barn and on his property to have more critters, but seeing he didn't need them with just him to feed, he figured he'd wait until he had a family before acquiring anything more than the set of buckskin horses.

After pouring a cup of coffee, he glanced around the room and sighed. Washing dishes had never been something he enjoyed. It was just a chore that needed to be done, but last night it had been more than a task. Drying the dishes while Fiona washed them had been enjoyable. Even though he wondered if he'd asked too many questions, especially when he'd enquired about her husband. He hadn't meant to pry but had been curious and had wanted to know more about her. Still did.

If he breathed deep enough, he could almost smell flowers again. And looking at her, well, that in itself was enjoyable. Especially when she smiled. It was like watching a bird take flight, gracefully opening its wings to catch the wind. Despite how beautiful her smile had been, it seemed almost rusty. Like she hadn't used it very often. If he could change one thing about her, that would be it. Actually, that was the only thing that needed to be changed about her—her smile. It needed to become well used. Never leave her face.

Maybe he could ask them over for supper again tonight. That had made her smile last night, and having her and Rhett and Wyatt sitting at his table had given him more joy than he'd experienced in a long time. Those boys had been hungry, and even though she'd tried to pretend that she hadn't been, she had been hungry too. Watching her eat, he'd wished he'd made more than just fish and eggs.

Their arrival should have been celebrated

with a full meal. A fancy one, complete with dessert. That thought caused a knot to twist in the center of his stomach. As soon as he figured Josiah would be awake, he'd pay the man a visit. There were several questions rolling around in his head. Questions Josiah needed to answer.

With his thoughts trailing straight back to Fiona, Brett carried his cup of coffee outside and walked around the corner of his house, to where he could see the little city-owned house. As he stood there, staring across the area covered with grass that wouldn't turn green again until it rained, he wondered what had happened to make Fiona agree to become Josiah's wife. She was a sensible woman and didn't seem like the type to take up with Josiah. Then again, she most likely hadn't known exactly what Josiah was like when she agreed to marry him.

The front door of the house opened, and Fiona emerged, wrapping a shawl around her shoulders before pulling the door closed behind her. She was wearing the same dress as yesterday, but her hair was loose. Long and brown, it flowed over her shoulders, down her back, fluttering in the wind as she walked down the two steps and then made her way toward the outhouse.

Giving her privacy, or perhaps because he didn't want to be seen staring at her, Brett turned and walked around the corner of his house. Taking a sip of his coffee made another thought form. The boys had said there wasn't any food in the house they'd rented. At that thought, he entered his house, collected a clean cup and filled it with coffee. He then grabbed the handle of his egg basket. There were only six left, but that should be enough to hold Fiona and the boys over until the mercantile opened.

Outside again, Brett peered around the corner until he saw Fiona walking back toward the house, and then he hurried in that direction.

"Good morning," he greeted, stopping her before she could open the front door.

Turning about, she released the hold she had on the doorknob. "Good morning to you too, Mr. Blackwell."

Her voice was soft, and he tried to lower his as he stepped closer, understanding the boys were still sleeping. "I brought you some coffee and some eggs. The mercantile doesn't open until eight."

The small smile on her lips didn't falter, but something about her did, and he wondered why. "The coffee is still hot," he said. Plenty of people didn't like cold coffee. Plenty of people didn't like coffee. "I'm sorry. I don't have any tea."

She shook her head slightly. "I prefer coffee, thank you, but I—"

"Here." He handed her the extra cup. Thinking of last night when he'd had to coax her into eating, he then set the basket on the top step. "Do you have a minute?"

"Why?"

"I want to show you something."

"What?"

"It'll only take a few minutes, but we have to hurry."

She frowned but nodded. "All right."

He would like to have taken her hand but settled for gesturing for her to walk alongside him. They walked around the side of the house so they were facing east. The land was flat all the way to where it met the sky, which was turning from pink to orange.

Stopping, he took a sip of coffee and watched out the side of his eye as she did the same. Without looking her way, he said, "Last night, I told you tomorrow would be a new day. Well, I thought you might like to watch it appear."

"Oh, my," she said so softly he almost didn't hear it.

"You don't like watching the sun rise?" he

asked, surprised. He thought everyone enjoyed watching the sun slowly creep into the sky.

She shook her head, then nodded. "I don't think I've ever watched one before."

"Never watched a sunrise?"

"No."

"Why?"

She shrugged. "I guess I never had time. Or maybe I thought others would believe it was a waste of time."

He thought that might be the saddest thing he'd ever heard. "It doesn't take long," he said. "And it's worth it."

Glancing down at the cup she held with both hands, she nodded before looking back up at him and smiling softly.

"Considering this will be your first full day in Oak Grove, I can't think of a better way for you to start it."

"I can't either." Her gaze shifted, straight ahead, to the center point where the earth met the sky.

A small hump of yellow had formed and was pushing the orange glow higher. They stood there, silently, sipping their coffee and watching as the yellow continued to rise and form a half circle that slowly grew into a majestic ball with a center so bright it looked white.

As happened every morning, yet still a miracle in itself, the sun soon rose completely above the ground, shooting its glorious rays in all directions. Then slowly, yet too fast to actually define precisely how or when, the sky in all directions turned a crystal clear blue. He'd seen many sunrises, but this one seemed to be the most beautiful one ever.

Hearing her sigh, Brett glanced her way. The full smile on her lips made his insides rise as gently as the sun just had.

"That was beautiful. Simply beautiful." She closed her eyes for a moment and then opened them to look directly at him. "Thank you."

In all his years he'd never suddenly been struck with a want so strongly, but right now he wanted to pull her into his arms to hug her. And kiss her.

Not sure how to make those desires disappear, he took a step back and glanced toward her house. After clearing the lump from his throat, he said, "Those boys of yours will be hungry again this morning. Boys always are. They'll want to start exploring Oak Grove too."

"How do you know so much about boys?"

"Because I was one," he said. "And I had several brothers. Seven actually. Four older and three younger."

"Your poor mother—she must have had her hands full."

"She did, but she also had a broom and wasn't afraid to use it on any one of us." Memories of home made him smile. "I guarantee none of us wanted to make her mad enough to use it."

"I'm sure you didn't."

He couldn't stop a short bout of laughter. "You've only heard a part of it. You see, if any one of us got Ma mad enough to use the broom, that meant Pa would use the belt on us for making Ma so mad."

"Oh, my."

"For the most part, she didn't use that broom for nothing but sweeping up the mud we hauled in on our boots, and Pa didn't use that belt for anything but holding up his britches."

"Learned early, did you?"

He winked one eye. "About the same time I learned to walk."

Her giggle was soft, but the sparkle in her eyes said he hadn't imagined it. He nodded toward the house. "You got two good boys in there, ma'am. Plenty to be proud of. Polite and well behaved."

She nodded and started walking toward the house. "Thank you. I sincerely hope they behaved yesterday, and I apologize again for their arriving so unannounced. For myself too."

"I won't accept any apologizing. There's nothing to be sorry about."

They rounded the house and she held up her cup while stopping near the steps. "Thank you for the coffee and the sunrise. You've made my—our arrival something we'll never forget."

Sensing there was more behind her words, things he shouldn't press her on, Brett gestured toward the basket on the back stoop. "I gotta go see to my horses, but if you need something to go along with those eggs, feel free to take what you need from my kitchen. The door's open."

"The eggs are more than enough, Mr. Blackwell, thank you." She then glanced at her cup, which was still half-full.

"The pot's on the stove," he said while turning about. "Help yourself to more coffee if you want." Although he knew she wouldn't help herself to more coffee or anything else, he wished she would. His heart was lighter this morning than it had been in a long time. A very long time. Because of her.

As he walked past his house, he set his cup on the porch rail and then headed over to feed his horses. It was during that time, while forking hay into the corral, that he realized the mercantile wouldn't be open today. Most every business in town observed the Sabbath. The town had passed a special ordinance for a few to be open, mainly Rollie Austin's hotel and eatery.

Brett set the pitchfork aside and then walked around the lean-to that held his forge. Wally Brown, who oversaw the feed store for the most part while Brett saw to the blacksmithing, usually gave the horses their grain, but not on Sundays. Besides working for him, Wally worked for the livery. He had living quarters in the barn loft over there and kept an eye on things overnight.

Brett unlocked the front door and, once inside, walked directly to the window that faced his house, and Fiona's a short distance farther away. He'd watched the sun rise with many people over the years. Family. Men he worked with at home and on the railroad. Friends while hunting. Companions while traveling. Yet never once had he appreciated sharing one more than he had with her this morning. It wasn't just because he'd had someone standing beside him. It was because it had been Fiona. He wasn't sure how he knew that, but he did.

If she was one of the women from Ohio the Betterment Committee had paid to come to Kansas, Fiona didn't have to marry Josiah. She should have the opportunity to get to know all the men who'd contributed, including him.

Except he wasn't in the running any longer, was he? Not if his mother sent him a bride. Maybe he should go see Teddy, have him send another telegram.

Turning away from the window, he crossed the space and sat down at his desk. His mother may not have gotten his first telegram yet. That was doubtful. One specifically for her would have been delivered minutes after it arrived.

There wasn't a whole lot he could do about that, but he could talk to Josiah and find out exactly how Fiona had come to agree to marry him.

No longer caring if Josiah was up or not, Brett exited the building, locked the door and headed up the street.

A peaceful quiet filled the streets, and as he walked past, he noticed a sign in the hotel's window that said the eatery was closed until after church this morning.

Josiah's law office was two doors down from the hotel. Like many other business owners in town, Josiah lived in the quarters above his office. Even before he built his buildings, Brett had been thinking about the time when he'd have a family. Not wanting them to live above a feed store, he'd gone ahead and ordered enough lumber for a house as well as the feed store and blacksmith shop.

Brett walked past the law office door with Josiah's name painted on it, turned the corner and then walked around to the back of the building, where he promptly knocked on the back door.

He knocked a second time before hearing movement inside the house, and then someone telling him to hold his horses.

It wasn't his horses he was trying to hold on to. His temper was rising far quicker than normal.

Josiah pulled aside the curtain to peek through the glass before he opened the door. "What are you doing here at this time in the morning?" Josiah asked, pulling open the door.

"We need to talk," Brett said, stepping over the threshold, forcing Josiah to step back in the process.

Straightening his vest, pulling it down over his thick waist once he'd caught his footing from jumping backward, Josiah asked, "About what?"

"Fiona Goldberg," Brett said, shutting the door with a solid thud.

Josiah's face and neck reddened. "Mrs. Goldberg and her sons aren't any of your business."

Fighting had never been Brett's way. He always figured it wouldn't be fair. He was much bigger and stronger than most men. However, using that size and strength for his own good, or the good of others, now and again didn't bother him. He took a step closer and laid both hands on Josiah's shoulders. Looking down upon the much shorter man, he said, "As I see it, she is my business. Any bride from Ohio is fair game to any one of us who donated to the committee."

It was July, and the morning air was warming quickly, but not so much that sweat should be trickling down the mayor's face. Josiah pulled out a kerchief and wiped his forehead. "Fi—Mrs. Goldberg is not one of the brides the committee ordered. She came upon hard times and contacted me personally, offering to be my bride. I agreed. Therefore, she is mine and mine alone."

Brett wasn't certain he believed Josiah, but he had no reason not to. Especially since just yesterday he'd taken it upon himself to order his own bride. Irritated by that as much as everything else, he said, "Seems to me you aren't treating your wife-to-be very well. You left her and those little boys alone to fend for themselves last evening."

"I promised her some time to get to know me," Josiah said. "Something only a gentleman such as myself would know about."

If there was any man in town who considered himself a gentleman, it was Josiah. Brett removed his hands and stepped back.

Josiah pocketed his kerchief. "I was just getting ready to walk over and check on them. See if they need anything."

Torn as to how much he should and shouldn't say about Fiona and her sons eating at his place last night, the air left Brett's chest with a huff.

"There will be other brides arriving, soon, Brett," Josiah said. "You'll have a chance at one of them."

Not wanting the mayor to know that wasn't his greatest concern, Brett asked, "When?"

"I can't say for sure, but my friend, who is the mayor in Bridgewater, Ohio, is gathering them up as we speak. He'll notify me as soon as they are ready."

"You've been saying that for a month," Brett pointed out. "And for two months before that you promised there would be a dozen women."

"There will be. This sort of thing takes time."

Brett let the frustration inside him ease out

on a long breath. "Folks are getting tired of waiting."

"I know," Josiah said, "and I'm working on bringing in all twelve brides as promised. Now, I really must head over to see Fiona before church this morning." He took a couple steps sideways and pulled open the door.

With little else he could say or do, Brett nodded and left.

Chapter Four

If she'd been mad before, this morning Fiona was furious. She and the boys were fully prepared to attend services, had already started walking toward town, figuring they'd easily find the church, when Josiah had stopped them. Not only stopped them, but forbade them from attending this morning. Said he wasn't prepared to introduce her to the town yet.

"They don't want us here any more than the folks back in Ohio," Wyatt said, looking out the window.

Keeping her fury to herself, Fiona hooked her apron over her head and then tied it in place behind her back. "As long as we are friendly and honest, people will like us."

"No, they won't," Wyatt disagreed.

Convincing him could prove impossible, so she changed the subject. "You two go change out of those clothes. No sense getting them dirty."

"Can we go visit Brett, then?" Rhett asked.

"No—"

"Can't," Wyatt interrupted. "He ain't home."

"How do you know that?" Rhett asked.

Turning from the window, Wyatt said, "I saw him leave a long time ago and he hasn't come back." Glancing at her as he walked toward the bedroom they'd all shared last night, he added, "Bet that mayor told Brett not to like us."

"He did not," Rhett declared. "Did he, Ma?"

"Of course not." Convincing herself about anything when it came to Brett would take far more than a few words. He seemed to have taken permanent residency in her mind. Watching the sunrise with him this morning had been utterly amazing. They'd barely spoken, yet she'd felt his presence, much like last night while washing dishes. This morning it had been more than a presence. His silent companionship had told her she wasn't alone in a way she'd never experienced before. Shaking her head to clear her thoughts, she gestured to both boys. "Go change like I told you."

Not done with his nastiness, Wyatt settled a glare on her from the bedroom door. "Don't know why you put an apron on, there ain't no stove to cook on. Ain't no food to cook either."

There was no stove or food—she'd built a small fire outside earlier to cook the eggs Brett had given them—but it was Wyatt's attitude she had to address. "Rhett, go change your clothes." As her younger son walked into the other room, she took Wyatt by the arm. "I understand this situation is very difficult for you. It is for me too. But no matter how hard it is for any of us, I will not tolerate rudeness. Not toward me, your brother or anyone else. Do you understand?"

Young enough so that a good scolding usually worked, Wyatt nodded. An inkling of dread entered Fiona at the defiance still living in his eyes. A scolding soon wouldn't work. Not with the load of anger harboring inside him. She had no idea what to do about that. How to help him get past it.

"This can be a good life for us, Wyatt. I sincerely believe that, but we'll have to work on it. And it may not be easy. Especially not at first."

"Life could have been good for us back in Ohio too," he said.

Not wanting him to know just how impossible that would have been, she said, "It could have been, but I thought we needed a new start. Try out a new place with new people."

"Where people don't know our pa died while robbing a train," he said softly, solemnly.

If her heart had been whole, it would have broken in two right then. As it was, the few pieces of her heart that remained intact crumbled a bit more. She couldn't deny what Sam had done, nor justify it. "He wasn't thinking right, honey."

"Why'd he have to start drinking, Ma? That's when he got mad at everyone."

Wyatt was only seven, yet it was amazing just how intelligent he was, and how much he remembered. She'd tried to hide Sam's drinking from him as much as she'd tried to hide everything else but had failed there too.

"I don't know, Wyatt. I honestly don't know."

"Hey, Ma?" Rhett asked, coming out of the bedroom. "Could we go fishing? Catch us some fish like Brett did. Those sure were good last night."

"We don't even have a fishing pole, dum—"

Wyatt stopped when she gently squeezed his arm.

"Those certainly were good fish we ate with Mr. Blackwell last night," she said, using the moment to bring up another subject. "You boys mustn't call him by his first name. He is Mr. Blackwell."

With a nod, Rhett said, "Maybe Mr. Blackwell will let us use his fishing pole."

"And please don't bother him," she said. "He is a busy man."

"We won't bother him, just ask to use his pole," Rhett said.

She shook her head. "That would be bothering him. Perhaps he wants to go fishing himself today."

"Maybe he'd take us with him!"

Rhett's entire face had lit up, and it hurt to squelch his excitement. "I'm sure Mr. Blackwell is far too busy for that." Other than the small bed, the house held no furniture, so she sat down on the top of one of the three trunks they'd brought with them from Ohio. "But Mr. Melbourne said he'll be back after church." Expecting Wyatt to reply, she gave him a warning look before saying, "Perhaps he has something fun planned for all of us."

"Like what?" Rhett asked.

"I'm not sure." Hoping Josiah would consider their needs, she said, "A picnic maybe?"

"Ya think?" Rhett asked.

She shrugged but included a smile to keep

his hopes up. All of their hopes up. Yesterday Josiah had said he was going to let others know at church this morning that she had arrived in town. She'd assumed that meant they were to attend church with him, but this morning, when he'd told them to remain at the house, he'd said he would plan a time for her to meet the townspeople. He hadn't mentioned the boys, but surely he must plan on introducing them all at the same time.

"Do you think there will be fried chicken?" Rhett asked, licking his lips.

Guilt at getting his hopes too high struck her. "I truly have no idea." Standing, she said, "This morning I had to gather dried grass to fry the eggs, so in case Mr. Melbourne brings something I need to cook, let's go gather some more. I'll show you how to twist it tight so it'll burn longer."

"How do people live without wood to burn out here?" Wyatt asked as they all walked to the door.

"I'm not sure," she answered. The only reason she knew about twisting grass was from a woman back in Ohio whose sister had gone west on a wagon train and wrote her about such things.

"Bre— Mr. Blackwell has a bunch of wood

stacked over at his place," Wyatt said. "And another pile by his blacksmith shop. Maybe he can tell us where he got it."

"I'm sure Mr. Melbourne will be able to answer all your questions," Fiona said. "Just so long as you don't make a nuisance of yourself by asking too many at once."

The new preacher, Connor Flaherty, the same one who'd performed the weddings yesterday, was almost as long-winded as the mayor, Brett considered, but the preacher's words about the ten commandments were worth listening to. A reminder of those was always good for the soul.

His needed some reminding right now. Fiona and the boys were not in church. Josiah had arrived, alone, shortly after Brett had. Knowing he was too curious not to watch her place this morning, he'd headed over to the livery, where he could keep an eye on things inconspicuously. While doing just that, he'd shared a pot of coffee with Wally before the church bells had rung. Wally had forgone services, as usual, and had grumbled, complaining that the single men in town would starve if Rollie closed his eatery every Sunday morning.

Thinking of that made Brett's stomach

growl. He'd skipped breakfast, choosing to give the last of the eggs to Fiona. He didn't regret that. Nor did he begrudge Rollie for closing his eatery this morning. Rollie had married one of the brides yesterday, and the couple was in church this morning. Along with Rollie's two young sons.

When the services ended, Brett exited the building, shaking the reverend's hand on his way out. He'd just stepped off the bottom step when movement behind one of the few trees caught his eyes.

Teddy stayed as hidden as possible while waving at him.

Brett glanced left and right, making sure no one else had noticed Teddy, before he walked to the tree.

"What are you doing?"

"Staying out of Abigail's sight," Teddy said. "I told her I wasn't feeling well this morning."

"Why? What's wrong?"

"Why? So I could watch for your mother's message. Nothing has come in yet, and I'm heading back over there. Just thought I'd let you know. Abigail's having lunch with the new reverend at the eatery in order to interview him for her special edition, so I'll have the office to myself most of the afternoon."

A good portion of guilt rolled around in Brett's stomach. Teddy was so eager over the prospect of a new avenue to acquire brides, Brett didn't want to squelch it, even though the idea was no longer exciting to him. "Thanks," he said. "I appreciate it."

"Just remember our deal," Teddy said, ducking as he left the coverage the tree had provided.

Brett watched until Teddy made it all the way across the road and into the newspaper office before he turned and walked up the road.

The hotel was indeed open, and the smell of fried chicken filled the air. Brett entered the building and, noting all the tables were full, went over to the hotel desk. "Rollie," he greeted.

"Hey, Brett, how are you?"

"I'm good. You?"

"Fine, better than fine, actually," Rollie said as a woman stepped up beside him. "You know my new wife, Sadie."

"Sure do," Brett replied, nodding toward the woman with pink cheeks. She was a tiny gal and sort of cute with her reddish hair all piled up on top of her head. He'd met her several times since she'd arrived along with the other brides, mainly right here at the eatery. Shortly after her arrival, Rollie's cook had taken ill for a few days and Sadie had stepped in to help. Along with several others, Brett had figured she'd end up marrying Rollie, so he hadn't pursued her. Besides, he couldn't say he'd heard her speak other than a few whispered *you're welcome*s. "Ma'am," he said, tipping the brim of his hat.

She smiled and bowed her head slightly.

"What can I do for you, Brett?" Rollie asked while tugging his wife a little closer to his side.

"Looks like you have a full house. Think I could get a meal to take home?" He and Wally did that often enough, especially when both shops were too busy to shut down long enough to go eat.

"Of course," Rollie said. "The special is fried chicken today, with beans, fried potatoes and sweet pickles."

"Sounds good." Fried chicken was one of his favorite meals. Someday he'd buy a whole flock of chickens so his family could have fried chicken every Sunday if they wanted.

"I'll get it," Sadie said quietly.

"Make it a double order, my dear," Rollie said. "Brett's a hearty eater and one of our best customers."

The new bride nodded and said something to Rollie. Brett didn't hear what because a

shrill laugh had dang near split his eardrums
in two. He recognized the laugh came from
Abigail and leaned back to look around the
corner and into the dining room. There she sat,
along with the preacher and the mayor.

The mayor? As Josiah ordered food from
one of the young girls who also worked at the
eatery, Brett's spine stiffened even more than
it had from Abigail's laugh. A good bout of
disgust heavily laced with anger filled him.
As Sadie walked around him, Brett reached
out and touched her arm. "Make that order
enough for four people to eat," he said. "Four
hungry people."

She glanced at Rollie, and so did Brett, but
didn't say anything.

"You heard him, dear, enough for four."
While his wife walked away, Rollie added,
"The fried chicken smells so good you're buy-
ing enough for tonight too, are you, Brett?"

"Something like that," Brett answered.
"How much do I owe you?"

Rollie told him the amount, and while Brett
counted out the payment, anger roiled harder
and faster inside him. He had half a mind to go
pull Josiah off his chair by his fat neck and tell
him that while he was stuffing his face, there
was a fine woman and two little boys who

hadn't eaten a decent meal in weeks. Months mayhap considering they'd left Ohio penniless. The boys had inadvertently told him that and he believed it.

He knew for certain Josiah hadn't taken her any provisions. While visiting Wally, he'd seen Josiah walking toward her house empty-handed. Those six eggs he'd given her weren't enough to keep them going for long.

"I sure do hope Abigail White doesn't scare the new preacher off before he gets to know anyone else," Rollie said. "The sermon he gave was wonderful this morning. Sadie and I discussed it on the walk home. He even held the boys' attention. They barely squirmed in the pews."

Close to fuming, Brett didn't dare do much more than nod.

"I hear tell he's from California," Rollie said. "Answered an advertisement the mayor sent out to newspapers in that area. Abigail helped him with those. That's what she claims. I'm sure we'll read all about it in the special edition this week."

Brett nodded again and couldn't stop himself from saying, "Seems the mayor is hauling quite a few people into town."

Rollie frowned and then grimaced as he

asked, "You aren't angry at me, are you, Brett? For marrying Sadie? I know you contributed to the Betterment Committee and all, but—"

"No," Brett said, stopping the man. "I'm not angry at you, Rollie. You needed a wife and you got one fair and square. I hope the two of you are happy."

"Oh, we are. We are. And I'm glad you feel that way, Brett. You are one of my best customers. I consider you a friend too."

"I consider you a friend too, Rollie." Brett let out a sigh, but it didn't help his anger toward Josiah and how he was treating Fiona. "And like I said, you deserved a wife. Some men in this town don't."

Rollie frowned, but it didn't last long. His wife appeared, carrying a large basket covered with a blue checkered cloth.

"Here you are, Mr. Blackwell," she said quietly.

"Thank you, Mrs. Austin," Brett said. "I'll return your dishes and basket tomorrow." After a nod toward Rollie, he turned and walked out the door.

As he made his way toward his place, his disgust for Josiah didn't fade. Fiona deserved better than the likes of Melbourne, and so did Wyatt and Rhett. They needed someone they could count on, all day, every day. That would never be Josiah. Though he might be a fine mayor, he wasn't much of a man. Not in Brett's eyes right now anyway.

"Hi, Brett—I mean Mr. Blackwell, what's in the basket?"

Good thing a train hadn't been coming. He'd crossed the tracks and rounded his blacksmith shop without glancing left or right once along the way.

"Mr. Blackwell?" he said to the boy sitting on the top rung of the corral holding his big draft horses. "I told you yesterday you can call me Brett."

"I know, but Ma says we can't," Rhett said. "Says we have to call you Mr. Blackwell."

Manners were important for children—and adults—so he shouldn't discount what Fiona had told her son. Laying a hand on the boy's shoulder, he asked, "How are you today, Mr. Rhett?"

The boy laughed. "I'm not a mister."

Leaning down, Brett whispered, "I'm not much of one either. Especially to my friends."

"Am I your friend?"

"You sure enough are."

"Wow."

Brett laughed at how he could almost see

himself in the little feller's eyes. They were sparking as brightly as his freckled face was shining. That was how little boys should look. Happy. He ruffled Rhett's thick crop of brown hair. "Like my horses?"

"Yeah. They're big. Like you."

"Yes, they are. Climb down. I have to find your brother and your mother so I can show all of you what's in this basket."

Rhett obeyed, and seeing how the boy had to run in order to keep up with his long strides, Brett slowed down.

"You wouldn't have a fishing pole in that basket, would you?" Rhett asked.

"I don't think a fishing pole would fit in this basket," he answered. "Besides, I have plenty of fishing poles."

The boy nodded, but disappointment had his little shoulders dropping.

"Why?" Brett asked. "You want to go fishing?"

"Yes, but I don't have a fishing pole, and Ma said we couldn't ask to borrow yours." Rhett sighed. "Those fish last night sure were tasty."

"They were," Brett agreed.

"Ma says the mayor might take us on a picnic today, but Wyatt says that's not going to happen. He says Mr. Melbourne doesn't care if we're hungry or not."

For only being seven, Wyatt was a smart boy, and that made Brett a bit sad. Wyatt was still young enough he should be more like Rhett. Carefree and sitting on corrals admiring horses. "Where are your mother and brother?"

"In the house," Rhett answered. "Wyatt's getting a talking-to for being a smart mouth. He told Ma she lied. That the mayor ain't coming and we're going to starve. That there will be no picnic. No fried chicken."

"Fried chicken?"

Rhett nodded. "That's what I wanted. It's my favorite. I like it so much I can almost smell it right now. That and fish. I like fish too. And fishing. And catching frogs. You ever catch frogs?"

"Sure have. Lots of them." They were near his house, so Brett said, "I have to set this basket inside, then we'll go find your mother and brother."

"But I thought you were gonna show us what's in the basket," Rhett said.

"I did and I will. We just have to gather up your mother and brother first." And a fishing pole or two, Brett added silently.

Chapter Five

Sitting on the trunk, head down, Fiona was berating herself. Not only for scolding Wyatt again for talking negatively about Mr. Melbourne, but for not saving a couple of the eggs Brett had dropped off this morning. If she'd known they wouldn't have anything for lunch, she wouldn't have eaten any eggs this morning, saved them instead for the boys to eat now. This, this worry of never having enough to feed them, had been a major reason why she'd agreed to marry a man she didn't know. Had never even met.

If only Josiah could be more like Brett. If only—

The door opening startled her. She jumped to her feet as Rhett barreled through the doorway, and she instantly swiped at the wetness on her cheeks as Brett stepped over the threshold.

Pressing a hand against the quickened beat of her heart, she shook her head. "Oh, Mr. Blackwell, I do hope Rhett wasn't disturbing you again."

"Nope, not at all. He's helping me find you and Wyatt."

Her gaze shot to the bedroom door. The one Wyatt had slammed shut a short time ago, shouting that he hated her. He hated everything. It had reminded her so much of Sam the past few months he'd been alive, it had brought her to tears.

Pulling up a false smile, she asked, "Whatever for?" Her stomach fell. "Did Rhett take your fish—"

"This little feller didn't do anything." Brett then pointed toward the bedroom. "Wyatt in there?"

She nodded.

"Would you mind if I had a word with him?"

Her instincts said she shouldn't ask more of this man, but she was beyond knowing what she should and shouldn't do. Truly at her wit's end in so many ways, she shook her head. "No, I wouldn't mind."

Brett patted Rhett's head and then touched her arm gently as he walked toward the bedroom. After a single knock, he entered the room. Fiona didn't consider following. Brett was so kind and trustworthy, she had no fears he might harm Wyatt, and she'd know soon enough what was said. Wyatt would most likely come running out, shouting of all the things he hated all over again.

"I'm thirsty," Rhett said.

She collected a glass from those she'd unpacked and led him to the door. "We'll draw some fresh water from the well."

It was a short walk to the well that had been dug and enforced by a short rock wall. Josiah had said it would be shared by all the houses the town was building in this area. After pulling up the bucket, she filled the glass for Rhett. She took a couple swallows too and then refilled the glass to carry into the house for Wyatt.

To her surprise, as she turned around, Wyatt was walking out of the house.

Brett was behind him and paused long enough to shut the door while saying, "Rhett, come here."

Rhett took off in a run. Fiona stood still, watching Wyatt approach. His face was sheepish, but also sad.

He stopped a few feet away. Shuffling his feet back and forth, he hung his head. "I'm sorry, Ma. Sorry I yelled at you. Sorry for being so ornery."

Fiona didn't know if she'd ever been so close to dropping to her knees. New tears stung her eyes, and she couldn't stop herself from glancing toward Brett. He wasn't looking at her or Wyatt, instead he was showing Rhett something on the ground, keeping her younger son's full attention off what was happening. His actions gave birth to a form of respect she might never have witnessed before, and that did weaken her knees.

Her steps wobbled slightly as she stepped closer to Wyatt and knelt down. Taking both of his hands in hers, she said, "Thank you for apologizing. That's very big of you." Tears burned hotter. "I know none of this is easy. Not for any of us. But if we stick together, the three of us—you, me and Rhett—we'll make it. Someday we'll be so happy, we won't even remember how sad we were at times." Feeling her words fell short of his apology, she squeezed his hands a bit tighter. "I want you to know, it's all right to be mad, it's all right to be sad, but it's not all right to be bad or misbehave. That only hurts others and that's not what we want to do, is it?"

He shook his head. "No."

"I also want you to know I'm proud of you. You're a wonderful son and have been a big help to me. I'm proud to be your mother."

His face scrunched up as he rubbed one eye and she pulled him forward for a solid hug. If she could have a miracle right now, it would be to offer him something special. Like the picnic she'd suggested earlier. A basket of fried chicken couldn't appear out of nowhere, so she stood and guided him to the well, where she handed him the glass of water.

"Have you two had enough water?"

She turned to look at Brett and Rhett as they walked closer, both grinning. A smile tugged on her lips, and she gave in to it. "Yes, Mr. Blackwell. Would you care for a glass?"

"How about a jarful?"

"A jarful?"

He nodded.

"Well, yes, I have several empty jars in the house." She'd brought along her canning jars from Ohio, hoping to someday have a garden again.

"Would you mind filling up, say, three or four jars and bringing them over to my place?"

The simple request shocked her, yet simple or not, she would not refuse. Whatever he'd said to Wyatt had made more of an impact than all her scolding. "Of course I wouldn't mind."

"Good. We'll meet you there." Looking at Wyatt, he asked, "Care to join us?"

Wyatt looked at her. She nodded. "Go. I'll be right along."

While Brett and the boys went in one direction, she went in another. Back to the house, where she gathered four jars, his egg basket and a cloth to wrap around the jars so they wouldn't jostle against each other while she carried them in the basket. Back at the well, she filled the jars, secured their lids and packed them back into the basket. Then she made her way across the short field to Brett's house.

The back door to his house was open, and stepping in only to see the stove, icebox, pie cupboard and other furnishings had her wondering once again why he wasn't married. Whoever did marry him, whenever that happened, would be a very lucky woman.

"We can go, can't we, Ma?"

Her gaze settled on her sons, each standing at Brett's sides, holding fishing poles. She couldn't have stopped a smile to save her life. Feigning to not understand, she asked, "Go where?"

"Fishing!" both boys yelled.

"And on a picnic," Brett said as he lifted his arms. One hand held a large basket. The other held a folded colorful quilt. "Complete with fried chicken, beans, potatoes and sweet pickles."

This man was a miracle worker. She had to pinch her lips together to keep a sob of joy from escaping. Then, pretending to have to consider his offer, she asked, "Sweet pickles?"

He nodded. "The sweetest."

Glancing toward the boys, she grinned, "Well, who on earth could say no to sweet pickles?"

"Not us!" the boys squealed, and despite all the sadness she'd known the past months, she laughed. Truly laughed.

"Let's go, then," Brett said. "I'll show you the way to the Smoky Hill River, where we'll catch enough catfish to feed the entire town of Oak Grove."

"I believe you could do that, Mr. Blackwell, feed this entire town."

"If it needed to be done, then we'd have to find a way to do it, wouldn't we?"

His attitude was so positive, so admirable, she had to laugh again, and nod. "I suspect so."

With him carrying the basket and quilt, the boys carrying fishing poles, a small shovel and a can, and her with an egg basket full of jars of water, they left his house and headed south, across the tracks and along the edge of town.

"This is the fastest way," Brett said. "When I walk through town, people stop me to talk and it can take more than an hour to get to the river."

Briefly contemplating yet another insight into his character, she said, "But you don't mind, do you?"

"No, I don't," he replied. "But these boys would. They want to go fishing and eat fried chicken."

"That they do, Mr. Blackwell, that they do."

"And you don't mind if we take the quickest route."

She shook her head. "No, I don't mind."

"Good. Then I hope you don't mind if they call me Brett. I told them it's all right, but if you insist, I'll abide by your rules."

In no place to deny him anything, she said, "I don't mind."

"Good. I'm glad we agree on that, Mrs. Goldberg."

"Me too, Mr. Blackwell." It felt as if they were playing a game, where neither of them said they could call each other by their given names, but each wanted to. She thought of him as Brett. Had since last night. Yet that wouldn't be right. She would soon marry someone else and—

"Oh." She stumbled slightly as her mind finally caught up.

"What is it? You step on a rock?"

"No." She glanced toward the town that was now beside them. Josiah had said he'd be back this afternoon. "We—" Lowering her voice so the boys trotting along in front of them wouldn't hear, she said, "I probably should have remained at the house."

A sternness formed on his face. "The mayor is having lunch with the new preacher and the newspaper reporter. He'll be busy for some time yet. The reporter is very thorough."

"Oh." That could explain why Josiah didn't want her to go to church with him. He could have told her. She would have understood.

"Come now," Brett said. "There's no frowning allowed on picnics."

He was once again smiling and his eyes looked bluer than the sky. Mesmerized for a moment, she wasn't sure how to respond.

"It's against the law."

Confused, she asked, "What is?"

"Frowning while on a picnic."

"Against the law where?"

"Here. It's my picnic, so I set the laws. And I say it's against the law."

"Oh, are you a lawmaker?"

"I must be."

She laughed at his silliness.

"That's better." He laid the quilt over the arm holding the basket and took her elbow with his free hand. "We're being left in the dust."

The boys were several yards ahead of them. Her legs were long, and for most of her life, she'd gotten used to slowing her stride in order for others to keep up. That wasn't so with Brett. Their strides matched as they both increased the lengths of their steps to catch up with the boys.

In hardly any time, the town was far behind them and the sounds of flowing water could be heard. Brett led them to an area downriver that had several tall shady trees. After he set the quilt and the basket down, he told her he'd be right back and then encouraged the boys to follow him. A short distance away, he heaved a large rock onto its side and gestured toward the can and the shovel.

Upon returning to her side, he said, "They'll have the can full of worms by the time we get the picnic set up."

Using the privacy of the moment, she whispered, "Thank you for whatever you said to Wyatt. I—" She shrugged. "I'm afraid I was at my wit's end with him."

"He's a little boy trying to wear a man's boots, but the boots are too big, too heavy for him to walk with, and that has him flustered. He just needs to be told it's all right to take those boots off once in a while."

Fiona's throat constricted a bit more. She'd recognized how Wyatt was trying to take over Sam's position of the man of the family, but Brett's explanation gave her an understanding she hadn't recognized. How hard it was for Wyatt to do what he felt he needed to do. As a fresh bout of guilt rose up inside her, she whispered, "You're right. You are so right."

He grabbed the quilt and flipped it across the ground. Kneeling down, she helped him unpack the basket that held bowls full of all the things he'd mentioned, and a large apple pie, as well.

"Well, she didn't say anything about this," he said, setting the pie on the quilt.

"Who?"

"Mrs. Austin at the eatery. That's where I got the food." He pointed to the plates and forks. "I remembered the plates and forks at the house but forgot serving spoons."

"I'm sure we'll get by." Then a bit over-whelmed by all of his kindness, she closed her eyes against the burning in her throat. "I don't know how to thank you for this. I'm sure Rhett told you he was hungry."

With a laugh, he said, "He may have men-tioned that, but I'd already bought the chicken. I told you, I know how hungry little boys can get."

"So do I," she said, looking toward the boys. "There hasn't been a day since Wyatt was born that I haven't worried about feeding him, and then Rhett too."

The touch of his hand on her arm was gen-tle. "Why?"

"Because feeding children is expensive," she said without thinking. "My uncle made sure I understood that from the moment I moved into his house and reminded me of that again when I got married. Sam promised me we'd always have food, but—" Here she was again, telling him things she shouldn't be telling anyone.

"But?"

Swallowing the fire in her throat as she watched Rhett and Wyatt happily filling the can with worms, she said, "The night Sam died, Rhett and Wyatt went to bed hungry. There was no food in the house. No flour. No beans. Not even an egg. I'd butchered the last chicken the week before. I'd tried taking in laundry and sewing, but that only angered Sam. He said he was going hunting that morning and would be back with food. But he went to rob a train with the Morgans instead." The pain of the days following that night burned hot inside her. "A person can't understand what it's like to know your children are hungry and have no way of feeding them until they live through it themselves."

Warm fingers folded around her wrist. The hold wasn't hurtful, but it was solid, strong. "Look at me," Brett said quietly.

She did and saw fortitude and honesty in his eyes as his gaze met hers.

"I don't have to tell you I'm a big man, you can see that. I didn't get this way by going hungry. Therefore, I can't imagine what you've been through, or those boys. Now, I don't make promises lightly, but I can, without a doubt, promise you one thing. No friend of mine, big or little, will ever go hungry as long as I'm around."

Fiona blinked at the tears blurring her vision. "I didn't mean—"

"You simply told me the truth, Fiona, and that's what I'm telling you. No matter what today brings, or tomorrow or next year, you have my promise. All I want in return is for you to remember that promise."

No man could ever have vowed something as reverently as he just had. She shook her head because she couldn't fathom how or why she'd told him the painful secrets she'd guarded for so long. She'd never even told Sam that going without food had been her worst fear since childhood.

"Promise me you'll remember it," he said.

Pinching her lips together, she nodded.

"Say it," he coaxed.

"I promise."

His hold on her wrist tightened slightly before he let go and turned around. "Hey, you two, this food looks awfully good over here and smells even better."

Fiona quickly wiped both eyes, making sure no tears had slipped out as the boys, emitting delight-filled squeals, ran toward them.

"We got a whole can full of worms," Wyatt shouted.

"That means we'll catch lots of fish, don't it, Brett?" Rhett asked, thrusting the can toward Brett as they arrived.

"It sure enough does," Brett answered, taking the can and setting it down by the shovel.

"But we have to eat first. You fellas go rinse the dirt off your hands."

There wasn't a single complaint about washing as the boys ran to the edge of the river.

"Wash up good," Brett shouted in their wake. "Get all that worm grime off!"

Feeling as if her insides had been miraculously cleansed, Fiona giggled. "You are one of a kind, Brett Blackwell."

He laughed. "That's a good thing. This old world couldn't handle two of me."

Fiona wished that there were two of him, and that the other one was named Josiah Melbourne.

The boys each claimed a corner of the quilt, as did Brett, and in between bites of food, the boys showered him with questions about fishing. She might have hushed them if he hadn't seemed to enjoy answering them so much. He told them about his home in Wisconsin, about fishing with his father and brothers, and about working in the woods. How men cut down the big trees and floated them down the river to the mill. She was enjoying the conversation as much as the boys and was just as enthralled by his antics as he embellished the stories with humorous descriptions of saws so long it took four men to carry them and trees taller than the river was wide.

His boisterous laugh was contagious. Rhett and Wyatt were laughing like they hadn't in a very long time. So was she. The bright sun overhead paled in comparison to the shine on Brett's face. He'd taken off his wide-brimmed hat and the black hair falling across his forehead made him look as young and carefree as her sons.

He was a handsome man. Far more so than Josiah Melbourne.

Although she hadn't said the words aloud, Fiona bit the end of her tongue as if she had. They shouldn't be here. She and the boys. She was promised to another man. Had made that promise herself. Yet there was a part of her that simply couldn't deny Rhett and Wyatt this little bit of fun. Or herself. Being here, it was almost as if she'd left her old life behind.

She started stacking the empty bowls, including the pie pan. "Well, if you three plan on fishing today, you better get at it."

"She's right," Brett said. "Gather up your plates, boys, we'll rinse them off before we start fishing."

"No," Fiona said. "I'll rinse off the dishes. You three go fishing." Sensing a protest, she shook her head. "It's the least I can do, Mr. Blackwell."

He gave her a single nod and then picked up his hat. "Come on, fellas, let's do as your ma says."

Fiona waited until they'd gathered the fishing poles and can of worms and started walking toward the riverbank before she rose to her knees to gather the empty plates left on the corners of the quilt. An odd sensation had her pausing and placing a hand on her stomach. It was a moment before she realized just what she was feeling. She was full. Her stomach was completely full. She hadn't experienced that in so long, she'd forgotten what it felt like.

She glanced toward the riverbank, where Brett knelt between her sons, helping them bait their hooks with worms from the can. She and the boys probably should have stayed at the house, waited for Josiah, but that didn't stop her from saying a prayer of thanks that they were here. The boys would remember this day for years to come. So would she.

Rationalizing that they all deserved a happy memory to replace many not-so-happy ones, Fiona collected the dishes and carried them down to the river to rinse off before she packed everything into the basket, stacking the plates and forks from Brett's house on top. She'd just tucked the blue checkered cloth across the top of the basket, when excited shouts drew her attention. She jumped to her feet in time to watch Rhett reel in a fish. Brett was beside him, encouraging him the entire time, and then instructed him how to remove the hook and secure the fish on a stick.

Once that was all done, Rhett looked up the bank. "Did you see that, Ma? I caught a fish. A big one."

"I saw," she answered. "It is a big one."

Brett waved a hand. "Come join us. We have a pole for you."

"Ya, Ma, come join us!"

By the time she arrived at the river's edge, Brett had baited her hook and tossed the line into the water. He handed her the pole at the same time Wyatt yelled that he had a fish on. That started a round of fishing like she'd never encountered. As soon as Brett finished helping Wyatt, Rhett hollered that he had another one. Then Wyatt again, and so on, until there were a good number of fish on the stick stuck straight up in the mud.

While Brett was still helping Rhett put another worm on his hook, her line went tight. She'd caught fish before, and knew what to do, but when the pole was almost yanked out of her hold, she squealed.

Brett was instantly next to her, telling her to keep the line tight.

"It must be a whale," she exclaimed. "I've never had a fish fight so hard."

"It's a catfish," Brett said. "They put up a good fight. Keep reeling to keep the line tight."

"I'm trying," she admitted as each rotation got harder. The end of the pole was bowed and the dark water swirling a few feet away.

"I do believe you have a monster," Brett said as both of his hands covered hers. One holding on to the pole, the other helping her turn the crank.

Fiona's heart leaped inside her chest so unexpectedly, she stumbled slightly.

"Whoa, there." Brett released the pole long enough to wrap an arm around her and grab the pole again. "Don't let him pull you in."

His massive arms trapped her as he continued to reel the crank while steadily pulling up on the pole. She tried to concentrate on catching the fish, but her mind and body were thinking about other things. No, one thing. Brett. And how impossible it would be to fear anything with a man this big and strong for protection.

"Keep reeling," Brett said, "he's getting tired."

The water was still swirling, so she highly doubted the fish was getting tired. Brett was doing all the work on their end. Her hands were simply beneath his, absorbing the warmth of his touch and sending that warmth throughout her body.

"Let's take a few steps backward," Brett said. "Drag him into the shallow water so I can grab him before he breaks the line."

She nodded but in truth had no say in the matter. Brett was already walking backward and her position of being caught between his arms had her following his footsteps.

The pressure of his hand as it turned the crank told her it was getting harder and harder to reel in any more line.

"Keep your hand on the reel and the line as tight as you can," Brett said as he eased his hands away.

"What are you going to do?"

"Catch your fish." The next instant, he ran past her and into the river.

The boys started cheering as Brett stood in the knee-deep water, trying to grasp the fish making the water swirl and splash. Fiona couldn't stop herself from joining in, cheering him on, especially when Brett let out a victorious yell and stood up straight with his arms wrapped around a huge catfish.

She hurried forward, reeling line in as she moved.

"That's the biggest fish I've ever seen!" Wyatt shouted.

"Ma was right, it is a whale!" Rhett added.

"It's a dandy for sure," Brett said, walking toward shore. "I'd guess it weighs close to fifty pounds."

"Fifty pounds? Surely not." Yet as she said the words, her mind was calculating the fish probably did weigh more than Rhett. It was huge. Even compared to Brett, who was the largest man she'd ever seen. The fish was as wide as Brett's chest and its tail hung down past his thighs.

"That's my estimate," he said, stepping out of the mucky water and onto the muddy shoreline. "You pickle him up and you'll have enough jars to last through the winter."

"I've never pickled fish," she replied, already calculating if she had enough jars.

"My ma did all the time, I can show you how," Brett said as he walked past her. "Gotta carry this guy up the bank, he's big enough to dive right back in from down here."

The riverbank wasn't overly high, but it was steep and lined with plenty of rocks and sticks. She was just about to tell him to watch his step, when Rhett, running to catch up with Brett, tripped over the line that still connected the fish to the pole in her hand. In the split seconds that followed, several things happened. The pole was jerked out of her hands as Rhett tumbled forward. Brett dropped the fish in order to catch Rhett before he fell on a large rock, and she dived on top of the flopping fish.

Its tail slapped her in the face before she managed to trap it under one hand while maneuvering about to plant one knee on the fish's back and the other behind its head. With the fish secured, she glanced up. "Is he all right?"

Brett was holding Rhett in one arm, and they were both staring down at her. Wide-eyed. So was Wyatt.

"I'm assuming you mean Rhett," Brett said.

"Yes." A touch of chagrin burned her cheeks. "I didn't want the fish to get away."

Grinning, he nodded. "I see that. And Rhett's fine."

Wyatt pointed to the ground. "You broke Brett's pole, Ma."

She'd heard a snap when she'd landed on the fish but hadn't given it any notice. "Oh, no," she mumbled. "I'm so sor—"

"Don't worry about the pole," Brett said,

setting Rhett down. "I have several more. Are you all right?"

"Perfectly fine," she said while glancing down toward the muddy slime covering the front of her dress. "I guess I got a little muddy."

"I'd say a lot muddy, Ma," Rhett said. "Muddier than me, even."

Looking at each of the boys and Brett, she laughed. "I guess that's true, but I didn't let this monster get away, did I?"

"No, sirree!" Wyatt exclaimed. "You jumped right on. I didn't know you could move so fast."

That made her laugh again, and the others joined in.

"What is going on here?"

Fiona froze and coughed and had no need to look up the bank to know Josiah stood there.

Chapter Six

The laughter in Brett's throat turned to a growl as he turned toward the bank. After what Fiona had told him earlier, Josiah's neglect of her yesterday and today instantly curdled his stomach. "Catching fish, Melbourne, haven't you ever seen that done before?"

"Get up here, Fiona," Josiah shouted. "Right this instant."

She didn't move, other than to glance his way, and Brett doubted he'd ever seen such pleading in a person's eyes before. Or such regret. He planted a foot on the fish's tail, next to her hand, and grasped her arm to help her up. Once she was standing, he started to tell her she didn't have to leave but held his silence when she shook her head.

She bent down and picked up the pole that had snapped in half. "Boys, gather up the fishing poles."

The fun they'd been having had completely disappeared and left a gloom hanging heavily in the air. With sad eyes, both boys looked at him, and having no other choice, he nodded, "Do as your mother says."

Brett hoisted the fish off the ground, which seemed to weigh more now that excitement no longer surged through him, and carried it up the bank. Fiona had already climbed up the embankment. Her head hung low as Josiah barked how she should be embarrassed.

Although he shouldn't step in, Brett couldn't stand by and watch her being chastised. "She doesn't have anything to be embarrassed about."

"Women," Josiah snapped, "especially those concerned about their reputation, do not go fishing, and you stay out of this, Blackwell. I told you this morning to stay away from her." He grabbed Fiona's arm and forced her to start walking. "And I told you to stay at the house. I've wasted over an hour looking for you."

Brett considered dropping the fish in order to grab Josiah by the arm and give him a good solid piece of his mind, but, as if reading his intention, Fiona shook her head again.

She also stopped walking and pulled her arm out of Josiah's grasp. "I apologize for not being at the house, but the boys were hungry and bored."

Josiah mumbled beneath his breath before he gestured toward the boys. "Gather up those heathens so you can go change your clothes."

Brett squeezed the fish so hard it struggled in his arms, but he held his tongue as Fiona's eyes narrowed.

She lifted her chin and calmly said to Josiah, "We will meet you at the house. Right after we help Mr. Blackwell carry all this back to his place."

"He doesn't need any help," Josiah protested.

"Yes, he does." Wyatt ran up to stand in front of his mother. "And we're gonna help him."

This wasn't his fight, but Brett was having a hard time not stepping in. With a steady glare, he let Josiah know what would happen if he lifted a hand toward either Fiona or the boy.

Josiah must have understood at least a portion of how that might turn out for him because he took a step back. "All right, the boys can help Brett if they must while you and I return to the house, Fiona."

Fiona's eyes said all Brett needed to know. He could accept she and Josiah needed some time alone to settle a few things, and he gave her a single head nod to let her know the boys would be fine with him.

"Very well, Mr. Melbourne," she said. "I will return with you, but I will carry the baskets and quilt."

Josiah didn't argue, nor did he offer to carry anything for her.

Brett's jaw hurt from biting his back teeth together and he had a hard time pulling his eyes off Fiona and Josiah as they walked away.

"I don't like him," Wyatt said.

"Me neither," Rhett mumbled.

Brett was of the same sentiment, but letting the boys know that wouldn't be right, so he hefted the catfish higher into his arms. "This here cat is getting heavy. Can you boys handle the poles and the rest of the fish?"

"Yes," Wyatt said. "I'll go get the other fish and the worms too."

Setting the poles down, Rhett said, "I'll help him."

Turning his attention fully on the boys, Brett followed them back as far as the riverbank. "You fellas sure are good help. I'd have to make three trips without you."

Wyatt gathered the stick full of fish, while Rhett collected the shovel and can of worms.

As the younger brother climbed up the bank,

Brett leaned down. "Hook that shovel handle over my fingers. It'll come in handy if this old cat starts flopping about."

"How?" the boy asked while holding up the shovel handle.

Teasing, Brett replied, "I'll give him a thunk with the shovel."

That made Rhett laugh, but Wyatt was once again occupied by staring toward where his mother and Josiah walked along the trail far ahead.

"Is that stick strong enough to hold all those fish?" Brett asked.

"Yes," Wyatt answered.

"Tell me if it gets too heavy," Brett said. They'd caught around a dozen fish, and some were good-sized.

"It won't get too heavy for me," Wyatt said stubbornly.

"Then let's get these fish home," Brett said, "because this one's getting heavy for me."

He'd hoped his teasing would make them smile.

It didn't.

Their walk home was solemn, and though Brett tried several times to engage the boys in conversation, it was apparent their earlier excitement wasn't going to return. His either.

Upon arrival at his place, he said, "Just put everything down by the porch."

Once everything, including the big cat, was on the ground, Brett stretched the cramps out of his arms. The apprehension in their eyes as the boys looked at each other gave him a sense of what they were thinking. "Do you boys know how to clean fish?" he asked.

"No, sir," Wyatt answered.

Brett couldn't miss the hope in the boy's eyes. "It's time to learn, don't you think?" Noting the hesitation, he added, "Your ma will let us know when she wants you to come home."

"Do you think so?" Wyatt asked.

"Yes, I do," Brett replied. "Because I'm going to go ask her." He not only thought the boys were better off staying at his place, he wanted to make sure that Fiona was safe. "Put the fishing poles in the shed. I'll be right back."

Fiona waited until they'd entered the house and the door was firmly closed before she spoke. She had promised to marry Josiah and she would, but she would not tolerate any more of his rudeness. Not to her or her children. Spending the afternoon with Brett made her determined her life here wouldn't be a repeat of what life had been like for them in Ohio.

"My sons, Mr. Melbourne, are not heathens." She had to continue while her courage was up. "As I said, they were hungry and bored. They had been cooped up on the train for days, eating barely enough to ward off hunger. Mr. Blackwell was not only kind enough to offer them yet another meal, something you have not concerned yourself with since our arrival, but he also provided them with a bit of enjoyment. Something else you have not concerned yourself with."

Josiah's face turned redder, but she wasn't done. Not by any means.

"I understand you paid our way here, and that it was expensive, but that does not give you the right to be rude and inconsiderate to us. I made it perfectly clear in my letter that I have two sons. If you were not willing to accept them, to provide for them, you should not have agreed to my offer."

It wasn't like her to be so bold, but she had to be for her children as much as she had to marry Josiah for them.

"I was going to bring you a meal, but—"

"When?" she demanded with all the anger she'd harbored during their walk to the house. He'd berated her the entire time, for not behaving nobly, as the wife of a mayor must.

Well, if he was noble, she wanted nothing of it. She spun about and gestured toward the door. "My sons were hungry last night and again this morning. If not for Mr. Blackwell, they would have gone to bed hungry. And that, Mr. Melbourne, is not tolerable. It wasn't yesterday or today and it won't be tomorrow either."

He sighed heavily. "Now, Fiona, there's no need to be so upset."

"Yes, Mr. Melbourne, there is." The anger peaking inside had her shaking. "If I'd wanted my sons to starve, to be ridiculed and shamed, I would have stayed in Ohio. You either agree to provide my sons with food, three meals a day, every day, or this marriage is off."

He stepped forward and waggled a finger at her. "You can't call this wedding off—only I can. Now, you either—"

"Oh, yes, I can, and I will."

His face was beet red and his nostrils were flaring. "How? You have no money, nowhere to go."

He was right. She had no money, no idea where she and the boys could go, but she wasn't about to back down. "I'll figure something out." Recalling the reason she was here, she added, "You're not the only man in this town in search of a wife."

That seemed to knock some of the air out of him, because his shoulders drooped slightly, and that gave her hope.

"I've agreed to all of your demands," she said. "Now it's your turn. You either agree to provide for my children, beginning immediately, or the marriage is off."

A thud on the front porch interrupted anything he'd been about to say, which concerned her because the glare in his eyes said she may have gone too far. She pinched her lips together as he moved toward the door. She'd hoped it would take the boys longer to arrive home. Having them witness this argument was not something she could allow.

"Oh, Brett," Josiah said, rather friendlier now. "Do come in."

Not seeing her sons, Fiona moved closer to the door.

"I don't need to come in," Brett said. His somewhat cautious gaze landed on her. "I just want to make sure it's all right that the boys stay at my place long enough to clean the fish."

Before Fiona could open her mouth, Josiah was already talking.

"That would be fine. Thank you for providing them with such activities," he said to Brett. "After being cooped up on the train for so long, they are in need of some fun. I wanted to say thank-you for seeing that they were fed last night and today, as well. I had every intention of getting back here last night and this morning, but my mayoral duties didn't allow that to happen. With the weddings yesterday and the new preacher's first sermon this morning, I found myself running from one thing to the next."

Fiona could understand that being the mayor held a lot of responsibilities, but she couldn't imagine him running and had a distinct feeling that Brett felt Josiah was lying. She did too. Perhaps not lying so much as making excuses.

Looking at her, Brett asked, "Is it all right if they stay at my place for a while longer?"

A new wave of regret at how their wonderful afternoon had ended filled her as she nodded. "Yes. Thank you."

He glanced at Josiah and then back at her. Understanding he was concerned about her, she said, "I'll come get them in a little bit."

He nodded. "They'll be fine."

She didn't even have to search to find a smile. "I know they will, Mr. Blackwell. Thank you."

Without another word, Brett turned around.

Josiah immediately shut the door. "As I told Brett, duties filled my weekend, but now that the weddings are over, things will be slower.

I'll still be extremely busy but will find the time to dedicate to you and your sons."

Staring at the closed door, Fiona wasn't overly sure those were the words she wanted to hear from Josiah. She drew in a breath and held it for a moment, trying to get past how he had to *find* the time.

"Fiona? Did you hear me?"

She'd given her word and couldn't go back on it. "Yes, Josiah, I heard you."

"Good, now that that's all settled, would you mind changing your dress? I'll take you over to my place and then to dinner at the hotel."

Fiona wilted slightly as her conscience spoke to her. *Be careful what you ask for, because you may receive it.*

"And your sons of course," Josiah said.

"Of course." Without another word, Fiona walked into the bedroom and closed the door. There was still water in the pitcher she'd unpacked and filled this morning, and as she poured some into the chipped but matching basin, she sighed at how disappointed the boys would be. After catching and cleaning the fish, they'd want to eat it for supper. When it came to their happiness, she seemed to be thwarted at every corner.

Perhaps that was her fate in life, and try as she may, she couldn't change it.

She removed her dress and hung it over the open windowsill to dry so she could scrape off the mud before washing it and then put on her second best dress. A sense of frustration told her Josiah would notice if she put on her best dress again—the one she'd worn yesterday—and that he wouldn't approve of her meager wardrobe.

This dress was dark brown and too heavy for the warm weather, but it would have to do. She then brushed her hair and twisted it back into a bun. Though they were a distance away, and Brett's house was on the other side of this one, she could hear the boys. Their laughter, along with Brett's deep voice, carried on the wind and seemed to swirl around her. Mocking her in some unintentional yet deeply emotional way.

"Fiona? Are you almost done?"

She closed her eyes for a moment, willing the strength and determination she so greatly needed to appear, before she said, "I'm coming."

Josiah was standing in the open doorway, and the somewhat critical stare that went from her head to her toes made her walk past him and down the steps before saying, "I'll go get Wyatt and Rhett."

"I'll join you," he said, catching up and taking a light hold on her arm.

Unlike Brett's, Josiah's touch made her skin crawl. She told herself to ignore the sensation. That in time she'd come to accept it. And him. She wasn't going to tell herself that she would also love him. That could prove impossible. Furthermore, love had nothing to do with their relationship. Their marriage. Respect would be enough.

"It's certainly a warm day," Josiah said.

"Yes, it is." Accepting he was trying, she decided she should too. "Is July your warmest month here?"

"I dare say yes, but August can be just as hot. As can June," he answered. "However, January is most certainly the coldest. I've seen some of the shallower creeks freeze clear to the bottom in January. Of course, you've seen that too. There's nothing strange about that in Ohio."

"No, there's not," she replied. The boys had seen her and Josiah walking around Brett's house but acted as if they hadn't. Though it bothered her, for they'd always been happy to see her, she couldn't blame them.

They flanked Brett near a long and wide board stretched between two barrels. Several bowls sat on the table, full of water and fish fillets, and the bucket near their feet was full of entrails.

"These boys are as good at cleaning fish as they are catching them," Brett said as he wiped the board clean with a cloth that he then dropped into another bucket of water.

"It's time for them to go get cleaned up," Josiah said. "I'm taking them to my place and then to dinner at the hotel."

"But we're gonna eat the fish we caught," Rhett said, first looking at her and then Brett. "Aren't we?"

Fiona stared at the bowls of fish. Four in total. Big bowls. It was impossible for her not to think about how many meals she and the children could have out of those fillets. Food had been scarce most of her life, and those full bowls appeared to be the bounty she'd prayed for more than once.

"I'll tell you what," Brett said, kneeling down to look Rhett in the eyes. "I'll take some of this fish over to Rollie Austin and ask him to put it in his icehouse. That way it'll stay good and cold and you can eat it tomorrow."

"But I don't want to eat it tomorrow," Rhett said. "I want to eat it today."

"Tomorrow will be wonderful," Fiona said, stepping forward and placing her hands on Rhett's shoulders. "Thank you, Mr. Blackwell."

Rhett's little eyes were full of pleading when he glanced up at her, and though she could empathize with her son, her nod told him what she expected.

He complied. "Thank you."

"You're welcome," Brett said as he ruffled Rhett's hair. "Now you have something to dream about." With a wink, he added, "Eating fish. Tomorrow morning you'll wake up hungrier than an old dog trying to find where he buried a bone."

"I guess so," Rhett said sadly.

Fiona had kept one eye on Wyatt, expecting him to argue as well, but he hadn't. In fact, he stepped around Brett and took a hold of Rhett's hand. "Come on, I suspect we need to go wash our hands and faces before we go anywhere."

"Yes, you do," Fiona said. "And change your shirts." She also reached over and squeezed Wyatt's shoulder. "Thank you."

He nodded and led Rhett away.

"Well, I gotta bury these innards," Brett

said, picking up the bucket. "You folks enjoy your dinner at the hotel."

Somewhat taken aback because he'd never been so abrupt with her before, it was a moment before she could respond.

In the meantime, Josiah said, "Of course, we won't keep you."

"No," she said. "We won't. Thank you again, for everything, Mr. Blackwell."

Brett nodded and walked away, carrying his bucket. She felt as if a part of her was in that bucket. Her happiness. Which had appeared for a short time today, and a part of her feared she might not experience it again anytime soon.

"Fiona," Josiah said. "You need to make sure your boys are presentable."

Pulling her eyes off Brett, she sighed. "Yes, I do."

Brett forced himself not to turn around, but when he stopped at the shed for a shovel, he couldn't help but look. Fiona and Josiah were almost back to her place. A mighty bout of sorrow for those little boys welled up inside him. They'd been looking forward to eating the fish they'd caught. Poor fellas. He felt sorry for Fiona too. More than the boys, even.

Josiah wasn't known for his ability to make friends, but Brett had never found a reason to completely dislike the mayor. Until now.

Mad because there wasn't a whole lot he could do, he grabbed the shovel and headed toward the edge of his property to bury the fish guts. His mind kept going back to Fiona and how the shine had disappeared from her eyes. It was as if someone had blown out a candle inside her.

That led his mind down another route— marrying a stranger. He hadn't given that much thought before. Not even while attempting to get to know the brides that had arrived last month. He certainly hadn't been drawn to them like he was to Fiona. Couldn't imagine any one of them would have been content watching a sunrise with him, or jumping on a huge catfish to make sure it didn't get away.

He had to wonder if Josiah was that drawn to her, or if he just wanted a wife.

Jabbing the shovel blade into the ground, Brett cursed beneath his breath. Yesterday, he'd thought a woman—any woman—could be the wife he wanted, but now he wasn't so sure. There might be a whole lot more to getting married than he'd thought.

Brett finished burying the fish guts and

walked back toward his house—purposely not looking next door. He couldn't shut off his ears, though, and clearly noticed there wasn't much talking, other than Josiah, as he and Fiona and the boys headed toward town.

After putting away the shovel and rinsing out the bucket, Brett stood next to the make-shift fish-cleaning table he'd thrown together for the boys to have plenty of space during their first attempts at fish cleaning. They'd done a good job, and he'd been proud of them. Helping them had brought back a lot of memories. Good ones of fishing with his father and brothers. It also made him think of the future.

The heaviness that settled in his chest had him staring at the bowls full of fish fillets.

Rollie wouldn't mind storing the fish in his icehouse, he did that for plenty of people, but this was a lot of fish. Back at the river, he'd told Fiona he'd show her how to pickle it, but he'd need a lot more vinegar and crocks, which couldn't be bought today.

With few other options, Brett carried the smallest bowl of fish into the house to cook for supper and retrieved the basket he needed to return to Rollie, figuring it would work to haul the fish over to the hotel.

As he set the basket onto the boards, Teddy

walked around the edge of the blacksmith shop and waved.

Brett returned the wave and waited until the man was closer before saying, "Hey, Teddy."

Letting out a low whistle as he stopped next to the boards spread between the two barrels, Teddy said, "Went fishing, did you?"

"What makes you say that?" Brett answered drily.

Teddy chuckled. "Did you leave any for someone else to catch?"

"Actually, we didn't catch that many. One of them, a catfish, had to weigh close to fifty pounds. I'd show you the head, which was about the size of yours, but I already buried it."

Teddy laughed again, as Brett knew he would. Teddy was a good sort.

"Too bad. I could have drawn a picture of it for the paper." Teddy frowned then. "We? Who went fishing with you?"

Brett shrugged slightly, knowing Teddy would soon know. "My new neighbors."

With his frown growing so deep his dark brows met above his round glasses, Teddy asked, "Neighbors? Do you mean the woman I just met? The one with Josiah?"

"Yes. Fiona Goldberg and her sons, Rhett and Wyatt."

"Where'd she come from?" Teddy asked. "Josiah wasn't very forthcoming with that information."

"Ohio. Seems Josiah ordered her for himself. Claims she isn't one of the brides ordered by the Betterment Committee."

"What? The Betterment Committee? You mean she's one of the brides?"

"No, I just said Josiah ordered her for himself."

"But she is a bride?"

"Yes. For Josiah."

"That doesn't seem right. We're all supposed to have a choice of every bride—or they were to have a choice of all of us. Now he's changing the rules. Bringing in one just for himself?"

Brett shrugged again. "That's Josiah for you."

"Yeah, well, I know plenty of men who won't like it, and they'll tell Josiah just what they think about it. I've got half a mind to write—" Teddy stopped and then set both hands on the boards and leaned a bit closer. "I guess we can't say much about it, can we?"

Brett had already figured plenty of men would speak their mind, but something about the gleam in Teddy's eye had him asking, "Why do you say that?"

"Because of what you had me do," Teddy answered. "Don't tell me you've forgotten." Reaching into his pocket, he pulled out a slip of paper. "Your ma must be one fast worker. She replied to your telegram. Says to expect your new bride to arrive midweek."

A shiver shot up Brett's spine as he glanced at the slip of paper Teddy handed him.

Chapter Seven

The disappointment inside was hard to hide, yet Fiona had to hide it. Bury it. She'd gotten used to doing that over the years, but it never got easier. "You have a lovely home, Josiah," she said, biting the tip of her tongue. It was a lie, and lying would never come easy for her. Not that it should, but try as she might, she hadn't been able to find anything about Josiah's home that was welcoming. Parts of it might be considered lovely. Just not to her eyes. She'd hoped for a house, with a yard for the boys to play in and room for a garden, perhaps a few chickens…

"As you can see, I take pride in everything I own and will expect the same from you and your children," he replied.

She withheld a sigh as she glanced around, hoping things would begin to look more hospitable. They were on the second floor of the building. The lower level held his office and a large room he called the waiting room— for the customers of his law practice. There had also been a narrow back room that ran the width of the house. It held little more than a small woodstove and the staircase that had brought them up here. There were two large rooms. The one they stood in was a parlor of sorts. It housed a sofa and a couple of stuffed chairs and several small tables holding glass lamps and other breakable items that made her nervous. Children had accidents, they broke things, no matter how careful they tried to be.

The other room held a large bed and dresser. The furniture was attractive, she suspected to some anyway. It was made of dark wood and the cushions were covered with thick black leather like those downstairs in his office and waiting room. The walls were bare, other than a large mirror in the bedroom and a painting, of a woman lying upon a rock with the wind blowing her hair and dress about, that hung over the sofa in the parlor.

There were curtains over the windows, long burgundy-colored drapes that fell to the floor and were tied back with gold ropes. Both windows faced the road and she couldn't understand the reason for the balcony on the outside of the windows. There was no door to walk out of, and in her mind she could see Wyatt and Rhett climbing out the windows to explore that additional area.

"I see you take pride in your surroundings," she said, walking across the room to take another look out the window. "It's very tidy and clean."

She leaned over slightly as Rhett tugged on her skirt.

He'd been looking out the window and quietly asked, "Where will Wyatt and I sleep?"

She'd been wondering the same thing, and hoping Josiah had an appropriate answer, she turned to cast him an enquiring gaze.

His smile did seem sincere as he said, "I'll show you."

She allowed the boys to precede her as they followed Josiah into the bedroom. On the far side of the room, next to the dresser, he reached up and pulled on a rope hanging from the ceiling.

A small set of ladderlike stairs descended to the floor, and Josiah waved for the boys to climb the steps. She followed.

Josiah didn't, but he did say, "I'll ask Jackson Miller if he has time this week to put in a floor. Don't want them falling through the ceiling."

The boys had stopped on the top steps, and peeking over their heads, she understood why. It was not only dark, it was hotter than an oven. "They'll need a window or two too," she said. Until that happened she wouldn't be able to tell if the area would make a sufficient bedroom or not.

"I'll have to think about that," Josiah said. "Don't want too much heat escaping during the winter months."

The stairs were too narrow for her to turn around, so she backed down them and assisted Rhett as he did so, as well. She refrained from assisting Wyatt. There was already enough disgust in his eyes.

"Speaking of heat," she said to Josiah, "is the stove downstairs the only one you have?"

"Yes, it puts out sufficient heat," he answered.

That stove was not only short, barely up to her knees, it was too narrow to hold much more than a coffeepot. "What do you cook on?"

Josiah frowned slightly. "I take all my meals at the hotel, as do most of the single men in town."

"Isn't that expensive?" she asked.

"No…" He glanced at her and the boys. "I see your point. It wasn't expensive for one, but it will be for all of us to eat there every day."

Understanding an unmarried man may not have thought of such things, she offered, "I can cook on the one downstairs, baking will be a bit of a challenge, but I'm sure I can figure something out."

He nodded thoughtfully.

"We'll need a table and chairs, though, and perhaps a cupboard or two."

"I'll talk to Jackson about that too," he said. "But I must warn you, I don't like clutter."

That was obvious. There certainly wasn't any clutter. Nor was there anything to clutter. Sparse was a better description for his home. "Have you lived here long?" she asked.

"Five years, ever since moving out here from Ohio."

"Do you plan on building a house?"

"Build a house? No. Why would I? If I did that, I'd have to travel to my office every day, and that would make no sense." He once again pulled the lapels of his suit coat together—an act he seemed to do rather consistently. "As the mayor, I need to be accessible at all times, and as a lawyer, clients need to know where to find me."

"I'm sure they do," she answered, once again holding in a sigh. Something she found herself doing rather consistently!

"I'm hot," Wyatt said. "Can Rhett and I go outside?"

"Yes."

"No."

Josiah had spoken at the same time she had, making her ask, "Why can't they?"

"Because they can't be running around town."

"They won't go running around town, but surely they can go out back—"

"There's nothing out there but the outhouse and the railroad tracks, and they can't ever play by those tracks. Trains roll by here every day."

She stopped herself from saying they couldn't remain holed up inside all day, mainly because she'd been about ready to include herself in the statement. Furthermore, Josiah was already walking toward the steps that led downstairs.

"We might as well go to the hotel and eat," he said.

She waved for the children to follow him. Rhett did so, but Wyatt stopped beside her.

"Our place in Ohio was a whole lot better than this," he said.

It had been. They'd had two bedrooms and a parlor and a kitchen complete with a stove. And a yard, with trees and grass for the boys to play in. It hadn't truly been theirs. It had belonged to someone else. Yet it had felt more like home than this one might ever do.

Chiding herself for having such uncharitable thoughts, she whispered, "Can we give it a chance? Maybe it won't be all that bad."

Wyatt opened his mouth but then closed it again. "Yes, we can give it a chance."

As he started down the steps, she smiled, glad he was at least willing to try. She also knew why. Because of whatever Brett had said to him this morning. Her heart took a slight tumble then. The entire time they'd been exploring Josiah's home, she'd purposely refused to allow herself to compare anything about it to Brett's. Or him to Josiah. However, that was getting exceedingly hard.

The four of them, her and Josiah walking in front and the boys behind, as Josiah had instructed them to do, followed the boardwalk to the hotel. Only one building separated his law office and home from the hotel—a dry goods store with a closed sign on the door.

"The hotel is the only business open on Sundays," Josiah said. "It's a town ordinance." He gestured across the road, where a northbound road met the west to east one they were walking alongside. "The school is down that way. There's plenty of grass around it for the kids to play in. No need for any of them to be running the streets."

"Perhaps after we've eaten, we can go there, show it to the boys," she suggested.

"No need to," he replied. "It's closed."

"For the summer?"

"Yes. We'll have a new teacher come fall. Abigail White, she runs the newspaper along with her brother, Teddy, has nearly every newspaper in the state running ads to find us a new teacher."

"What happened to the last teacher?"

"She married Art Cresswell a few months back," he answered. "I was against it, but others persuaded me to let the marriage happen. Summer arrived just in time."

"What do you mean?"

For the first time since she'd met him, he lowered his voice to a whisper. "She's of the condition. Can't have a woman in that state teaching the children of Oak Grove." Before she could reply, he pulled open a door. "We're here."

"Evening, Mayor," a tall man said while looking at her with a curious gaze.

"Hello, Mr. Austin," Josiah greeted. "Allow me to introduce you to Fiona Goldberg and her children, Red and Wyatt. Fiona, this is Rollie Austin, he owns the hotel and restaurant. He also has two boys."

"Hello, Mrs. Goldberg," the hotel owner said. "It's nice to meet you. I'm assuming you are new to our community."

"Nice to meet you too, Mr. Austin," she answered, and looking for a way to correct Josiah's blunder of Rhett's name, she continued, "We arrived yesterday. How old are your boys? Rhett is five and Wyatt is seven." She made a point of pronouncing Rhett's name with strong *t*'s at the end as she set a hand on his shoulder and the other on Wyatt's.

"Kade's ten and Wiley's six." Glancing around, the man added, "They're around here somewhere and will be glad to meet some boys around their age. With school being out for summer, they don't have many friends in town to play with them. Most of the boys their age live out of town."

"It'll be nice to meet them, won't it, boys?" Fiona asked her sons.

As she expected, Rhett smiled and nodded, while Wyatt's somber expression never changed.

"I think they're in the kitchen with Sadie, my wife."

Although he didn't have very much hair on his head, his face had plenty. Muttonchop sideburns met a thick dark mustache over his upper lip. She noticed all that because of how his cheeks turned red.

"I'll go find them," he said.

"We're gonna sit down," Josiah said.

"Of course, the evening regulars haven't arrived yet." Nodding toward her, the man said, "I'll be right back."

"He just got married yesterday," Josiah said as they walked into a room holding a dozen or more tables covered with blue checkered tablecloths.

The table coverings reminded her of the cloth over the picnic basket Brett had shared with them. That seemed like it had been days ago rather than merely hours.

"His wife was one of the brides the Betterment Committee brought into town," Josiah said as he sat down.

Once both boys were seated, Fiona sat down too. Curious, she asked, "How many brides were there?"

"Five arrived last month, the other seven are still being rounded up—haven't secured transportation yet." Scooting his chair closer to the table, he said, "The special today is fried chicken. I had it for lunch. It's good."

"So did we," Wyatt said.

Fiona was surprised. Since they'd left the house, the few times Josiah had said anything to the boys, Wyatt had seemed content to let Rhett answer.

"Which is your favorite," she said to Wyatt, with a smile.

He shrugged.

"It's my favorite too," Rhett supplied. "Along with fish."

"Mrs. Goldberg," Mr. Austin said, escorting a pretty young redheaded woman toward their table. "This is my wife, Sadie, and sons, Kade and Wiley." The two black-haired boys arrived at the table first.

"You moving to town?" the taller one asked.

"Where do you live?" the shorter one said at the same time.

"I told you they'd be excited," Mr. Austin said.

"The only kid my age in town is Becky Brooks, and she's a girl," the shorter one said.

The disgust in his voice made Fiona smile. She kept it on her lips as she greeted the woman, "Hello, I'm Fiona."

"I'm Sadie," the woman said quietly. "The special today is fried chicken."

"We know," Josiah said. "We'll take three meals. The boys will share one."

Fiona took a moment to consider her response. Sadie Austin appeared very shy and the way she nodded and turned about said she appreciated not having to make small talk. And Josiah was trying. She had to give him that. Furthermore, she wasn't overly hungry and, for the first time ever, thought the boys might not be either.

After Mr. Austin and his sons followed Sadie to the kitchen, Fiona said to her sons, "Kade and Wiley seem like nice boys. It'll be fun to have friends your age so close."

Josiah cleared his throat. "The Austin boys have been known to be wild and out of control at times. It would be best if Red and Wyatt don't associate with them overly much."

"Rhett," Wyatt said. "His name is Rhett."

"It rhymes with *Brett*," Rhett said.

"I must warn you boys to stay away from Mr. Blackwell too," Josiah said. "See you don't bother him."

"We don't bother him," Rhett said. "He's our friend."

"Grown men are not friends with little boys," Josiah said.

"I'll see they don't bother Mr. Blackwell," Fiona said.

"Did I hear you mention Mr. Blackwell?" Mr. Austin asked as he set a plate before her and one before Josiah while his wife set plates before Rhett and Wyatt. "Brett Blackwell?"

"Do you know him?" Rhett asked excitedly. "We live in the house by his. He's our friend."

"Yes, I know him. He's my friend too. Is that what brought you to Oak Grove? Brett?"

"No," Josiah said. "Mrs. Goldberg and her sons are here because I invited them to consider moving to our town."

"Oh," Mr. Austin said. "So you're thinking about buying the house the town built? That's the only house near Brett's place."

He was looking at her, but Fiona wasn't sure how to answer. It appeared as if Josiah didn't want it known that she'd agreed to marry him. Perhaps because providing for her and her sons was not as easy as he'd imagined it would be. She couldn't blame him for changing his mind, for it didn't appear as if he had much experience when it came to having a family, but it would leave her in a precarious situation. Unless of course she took advantage of Brett's promise, which she most certainly couldn't do. Although, it certainly would be the easiest thing she'd ever done.

"They have my permission to stay there for a few days," Josiah said. "Thank you for the meals, Rollie."

The man gave a nod, and Fiona noticed a frown form as he turned away from the table. He also glanced over his shoulder to look at them before opening the door to the kitchen for his wife. If Josiah noticed, he didn't comment on it.

After he'd taken several bites, Josiah set his fork down to take a drink of water. "There's something you should know about Brett Blackwell, Fiona."

The entire meal was the same as what they'd shared with Brett, other than the apple pie, yet it didn't taste as wonderful as it had this afternoon. It wasn't the cook's fault. It was hers. She set her fork down too. "Oh, and what is that?"

"He's a drinking man." Josiah took another bite as he settled a solid stare on her.

Brett had never resorted to spying on people, yet he couldn't convince himself to move away from the window. Fiona and her boys, as well as Josiah, were walking across the field toward her house and Brett found himself wondering how they'd spent the afternoon and evening.

When he'd delivered the basketful of fish to the hotel, Rollie had asked about her. From the sound of what he'd said, Rollie didn't know Josiah had ordered Fiona as a wife for himself. Brett didn't offer that bit of information, and now he wondered if he should go tell Teddy to keep it under his hat for a time. Maybe Josiah was having second thoughts.

Brett wasn't sure what he thought about that. Probably because he shouldn't be thinking about anyone getting married, other than himself.

He turned away from the window and crossed the room to pick up the telegram Teddy had left. Hannah Olsen. That was who would arrive on the train midweek. He couldn't say he remembered which one of the Olsen girls she'd been. All those girls looked alike to him.

The telegram was short and to the point. Much like his mother. It merely said he should expect Hannah Olsen to arrive midweek.

After reading the words again, he set the paper on the table. It was what he'd wanted, yet it didn't feel that way. Not inside, and he wasn't sure why. Other than he couldn't quite believe Hannah Olsen would smell as sweet as Fiona, or that her smile would be as bright, or that she'd spent most of her life worrying about having enough to eat. He couldn't stop thinking about that either. It not only made him mad at Josiah, it made him mad at her first husband. When a man married a woman, she became his responsibility in all ways.

Walking back to the window, he thought about how it had felt to have his arms around Fiona while reeling in that big catfish. And how cute she'd looked covered in mud after jumping on the fish to make sure it didn't get away. And how a mass of colors had taken over her eyes while she'd been laughing, and the glow of contentment on her face while she'd been sitting on the quilt and eating fried chicken.

Hannah would probably like picnics and sunrises—most women did—but he couldn't believe he'd enjoy them with her as much as he had with Fiona.

Brett thought about all those things, and more—namely if Hannah would be anything like Fiona—for the rest of the evening and throughout most of the night, finding it hard to sleep. The next morning as he watched the sun come up, he considered taking coffee next door again but then decided against it.

A smart man would keep his distance and mind his own business.

A short time later, he was glad he hadn't taken coffee next door when he saw Josiah walking toward Fiona's house, carrying one of the baskets from Rollie's restaurant.

That was how it should be, he told himself as he gathered his hat and headed toward the blacksmith shop. Maybe Josiah had been telling the truth, that up until yesterday he'd been too busy to provide for Fiona and her sons. Brett hoped that was the case, for Fiona's sake.

Wally arrived at the same time Brett did, and they greeted each other as usual before Wally went to open the feed store and Brett the blacksmith shop.

The morning started out as any other Monday would, but within an hour, more men were gathered inside his lean-to than ever before.

Don Carlson had been the first to arrive, claiming his plow horse needed a new shoe. Brett had been checking to see which shoe when the others started to arrive.

"There's nothing wrong with these shoes, Don," Brett said, walking around the horse.

Don nodded, as if not surprised, while asking, "Is it true?"

"Yes, it's true, I just checked, and—"

"He means is it true that Josiah ordered himself a bride?" Bill Orson said from where he stood against the wall. "Without giving any of us a chance at her?"

Bill and Don had donated to the Betterment Committee, hoping to obtain brides. Don's wife had died last year, leaving him with several children in need of a mother. Bill had moved to town last year and opened the saddle shop.

Brett glanced between Bill and Don and then leveled his gaze on Teddy as he walked into the group.

With a shrug, Teddy said, "Word was bound to get out. Josiah took her to supper at the hotel last night, and this morning he ordered pancakes for her and her boys. He even delivered them himself to the house the town owns that she's staying in."

Jules Carmichael let out a low growl. "You don't say. I never did trust that man. Said more than once he's a swindler. You can tell by his eyes, they're beady." He looked around the group expecting others to agree with him. When few nodded, he added, "Ever notice how he talks a lot yet never really says much?"

While others nodded and mumbled their

agreements and thoughts, Wally said, "I doubt he donated to the Betterment Committee."

"Did he?" Don asked Otis Taylor, the barber, who was also on the town council.

"I can't say," Otis answered. "Josiah kept track of all the donors, and he oversees the bank accounts. But I do know he never asked the council if anyone could stay in the house we built."

The last thing Brett wanted, or needed, was for this group to get all riled up and go off half-cocked. "The council only meets once a month, doesn't it, Otis?" Not only on the council, Otis was married, and his wife, Martha, had a dress shop in town, so he wasn't as vested in the mail-order-bride idea as some of the other men. Brett hoped that would help in this situation.

Otis nodded. "Aren't due to have another one until next week."

"Maybe Josiah is waiting until then to ask if F—Mrs. Goldberg and her children can use the house," Brett said, hoping no one would notice his almost slip of the tongue. "No sense having it sit empty."

"That could be," Otis replied.

"The other gals stayed at Rollie's," Don said. "I think that makes more sense."

"Me too." Jules frowned as he settled a steely

stare on Brett. "How do you know her name, Brett?"

"She's his neighbor," Teddy supplied as he elbowed his way through the men to stand next to him. "Only makes sense that he'd have already met her."

"How old is she?" Bill asked. "Is it true that she has two sons? Where's she from?"

For a man who didn't share much about himself, Bill was full of questions. None of which Brett wanted to answer.

"She has two boys," Teddy answered. "And I thought she was fine-looking."

"You've met her too?" Jules asked. "When?"

"Yesterday," Teddy answered. "Josiah introduced her to me, but Rollie told me her name is Fiona and that her sons are Wyatt and Rhett."

That brought up a full round of questions that flew about so fast Brett couldn't keep up. He stuck two fingers in his mouth and let out a fast, sharp whistle. When silence ensued, he shook his head. "Fellas," he started, "I'm sure Josiah will introduce Mrs. Goldberg and her sons to most everyone as soon as possible." He didn't feel sorry for what Josiah might encounter, but he certainly didn't want Fiona to have a steady line of men knocking on her door.

"Until then, I think you all should go about your business."

"You sure don't seem upset about all this," Jules said. "And I know for a fact you wanted a bride as badly as the rest of us."

"He does," Teddy said. "But he's already spoken to the mayor about Mrs. Goldberg and was told she isn't part of the Betterment Committee. Josiah said he paid for her and her sons' tickets out of his own pocket and that he's still working on bringing more brides to town. I think that's what the rest of us should consider doing too, finding our own mail-order brides."

"How are we supposed to go about doing that?" Jules asked. "I gave any spare cash I had to the mayor to bring one to town for me."

"Me too," Don agreed. "He promised twelve and only delivered five, not counting his own."

That brought on another round of questions. Brett was about to whistle again when Otis banged a hammer against the anvil. "I'm going to go talk to Josiah right now and get to the bottom of this. You can all meet me in my shop in an hour."

With boisterous agreement, the others followed Otis out of the lean-to, leaving only Brett, Wally and Teddy standing side by side in the opening of the lean-to.

Brett was scratching the side of his head, wondering if he should tell them to wait here for Otis, when Teddy slapped him on the shoulder.

"That went well, don't you think?" Teddy asked.

All Brett could do was cast a stare that said no, he didn't think it had gone well at all.

Chapter Eight

The breakfast dishes were washed, dried and packed in the basket. Fiona had set it near the door with every intention of taking it to the hotel and thanking the owner and his wife for the meal of pancakes and honey, but she had sat down to repair the loose buttons on Rhett's shirt instead. If not restitched, the buttons would soon fall off. Rhett had a habit of pulling his shirts off before unbuttoning them. Furthermore, she had a distinct feeling Josiah wouldn't want her to return the basket. He hadn't told her not to. Or to stay at the house like he had yesterday; however, he had said he'd return the basket to the hotel later today.

She kept telling herself that he was trying and that she had to be happy about that. And had to be happy about how he'd taken her seriously when she'd demanded he see to the welfare of her children. It was only right.

Then why did it feel so wrong?

She could demand such things until she was blue in the face but knew deep in her heart that all the demanding in the world would never make Josiah truly care about Rhett and Wyatt's welfare. That had to come from inside him, and she feared he might not have that capability.

Another burning sigh escaped as she removed her glasses to rub her eyes. She needed the glasses only to thread a needle, therefore she carefully folded the wire frames and put the glasses back into their leather carrying case. Sam had bought the glasses for her shortly after they'd gotten married, when he'd noticed her struggling to see the eye of the needle.

It shouldn't be, but it was hard to remember and cherish memories like that. Times when she and Sam had been happy. For they had been. In the beginning, when they'd gotten married and work was plentiful. The bad times of the years that had followed, when he'd lost job after job, and things had changed, seemed to take precedence in her mind, and her heart.

Money had always been tight and she'd

blamed the changes in him on the pressures of how quickly their family had grown. Having four mouths to feed was expensive, and she believed that was what led him to associating with the uncouth men he met while drinking. Yes, she blamed the drinking on those pressures too. At one time she hadn't wanted to believe Sam was a weak man, one who would bow to such behaviors when he had a wife and children who depended upon him, but after his death, she'd had no choice. No choice but to believe it was the pressures and then the drinking that had stolen the man who'd once been a loving husband and father from her and the boys.

Her eyes settled on the front door as if she could see through it, see the house that sat a short distance away. Brett didn't seem like the drinking type, but neither had Sam at one time.

"If I could go see Brett, I'd ask him if I could borrow a fishing pole," Rhett grumbled as he struggled to write the letters of his name on the slate board. "Then I'd go fishing. Catch another one of those big cats."

"We've already discussed that Mr. Blackwell is busy working today," she said quietly.

"I wouldn't stay long," Rhett insisted. "Just long enough to ask if I could borrow a fishing pole. He wouldn't mind. I'm sure of it."

This type of grumbling was what she'd expect from Wyatt, yet he hadn't even looked up from the arithmetic she'd instructed him to complete on his slate board.

"You have schoolwork to finish," she said. "And afterward the three of us are going on a walk."

"To the river?" Rhett asked with a spark in his eyes.

She shrugged. "You'll have to wait and see." She wasn't used to sitting around any more than the boys were. The few chores it took to keep the house tidy had taken very little time, including washing a few clothes that were now draped over the windowsills to dry. The washing basin had been large enough for the boys' clothes, but not for her mud-splattered dress. Without anything larger to use, she'd determined a walk to the river was in order. The children could play while she washed her dress, but she wouldn't tell them that until after their homework was complete.

"I sure do wish I had a fishing pole to take with us," Rhett said as he held up his slate for her to see his finished work.

"That is very good." She took the slate. "You're getting so good at writing *r*'s and *t*'s. I think two more times and your *e*'s will be perfect too." As Rhett took his slate, she asked, "Wyatt, how are you doing?"

"Done. Got them all right too."

She took his slate and quick surveillance proved he did have them all right. "Perfect," she said. "You're so good with numbers, Wyatt. I'm very pleased. Feel like completing a set of threes now?"

"Sure." He took the slate and set it on the floor in front of him.

As he erased his work, another bout of something Fiona couldn't quite describe washed over her. They were good boys and needed to be loved, appreciated for who they were, and that was something she'd never be able to demand someone provide.

By the time the boys were done, she had all the buttons sewn on securely. While the boys put away their slates and chalk, she gathered her dress and a handbasket to carry it to the river and back, then she and the boys left the house.

The sun was shining brightly and that felt like a reprieve. Casting a smile upon the boys, she said, "This way."

"We are going to the river!" Rhett shouted. "I knew it!"

"Yes, you did. You are a very smart boy."

Holding up her basket, she winked at him. "I need to wash the dress I got muddy yesterday. It smells like fish."

Both boys laughed, and that caused a shimmer of joy to tickle her insides.

"Hey, look," Rhett squealed. "There's Brett. Can I go ask—"

"No." Biting her lips for speaking so abruptly, Fiona took a deep breath. She also held it for a moment, hoping to settle the flutters inside her stomach. Even from a distance, he looked big and strong, and handsome and kind. Things she hadn't wanted to concentrate on but had been thinking about ever since meeting him. So opposite from Josiah. Which was something else she shouldn't be concentrating on. Or admitting. Or thinking about. "Mr. Blackwell is a busy man. We mustn't interrupt him while he's working."

"We'd need to borrow more than fishing poles," Wyatt said. "We'd need the shovel and can for worms too." Looking up at her, he added, "We still need to eat the fish we caught yesterday. Brett said he'd have the owner of the hotel store it in his icehouse for us."

"So he did," she answered. "Perhaps on the way home, we'll stop and see about that."

"Yippee!" Rhett shouted. He then waved at

Brett. "We're taking a walk to the river, but we'll stop and see you on the way back!"

"I meant we'd stop at the hotel," Fiona muttered.

Brett was returning Rhett's wave, and the flutters in Fiona's stomach increased as his eyes settled on her. Late last night, while trying to convince her body it was time to sleep, she'd remembered what it had felt like to have Brett's arms around her. How strong and solid they were, and how secure they'd made her feel. That comfort had been what had finally lulled her to sleep.

"Be careful," Brett shouted.

"We will!" Rhett shouted in return.

Fiona set a hand on Rhett's shoulder to steer him back on the path she was set on taking— around the backside of Brett's building.

"I sure do like Brett, Ma," Rhett said, looking up at her. "Don't you?"

She drew another deep breath, but it wasn't any more stabilizing than the other one she'd taken. "Mr. Blackwell is a fine neighbor."

"Yes, he is," Wyatt said. "We could have done worse."

"I suspect you're right," she told Wyatt. "And I'm certain we'll meet many more nice people. The hotel owner seemed nice too, as did his wife and boys."

"Too bad we won't be able to play with them very often," Wyatt answered without a glance her way.

"Why do you say that?"

"That's what Mr. Melbourne said last night at supper, at the hotel, don't you remember?"

"Well," she started, giving herself time to answer, "perhaps Kade and Wiley appear a bit wild at times, much like you two, because they are cooped up in the hotel most of the time. Maybe we could ask their father if they could come over to our house, and the four of you could play outside."

"That would be fun," Rhett answered. "We could show them where Brett buries the fish guts. I bet they'd like that. Don't you think?"

Knowing little boys as well as she did, Fiona laughed a little inside. "Yes, I think they would like that." Somewhere deep inside her, a place she kept trying not to respond to, she knew Brett would like that too. He'd enjoy watching the boys run around exploring things and, well, just being little boys. She kept trying to keep all that hidden because there wasn't anything she could do about Josiah being so different from Brett. Or how she kept questioning her ability to marry Josiah. It had all seemed so easy back in Ohio.

Maybe not easy, but her only option. And now that she'd made the commitment, she had to follow through with it. She certainly didn't have the funds to repay Josiah for the money he'd already spent on her and the boys. Furthermore, despite all her misgivings, she still didn't have another option. From her understanding, there were plenty of other men who wanted a wife, but that didn't mean any of them would want her. Or her sons.

At one time, on the train mainly, she'd imagined Josiah would be someone her boys would come to like, someone they would look up to and learn from. They might, but she wasn't sure she wanted them to. Not unless Josiah became more like…

She sighed and let the thought finish. Like Brett. A man she could fall in love with. A man who was good and solid and dependable. One who made promises and kept them, no matter what.

That described Brett.

Except for his drinking. She wouldn't tolerate that again. Couldn't put her boys through that again.

The thought had no sooner crossed her

mind when the man himself appeared, having walked around the other side of his building.

"Hey, Brett!" Rhett greeted. "You coming to the river with us?"

"I can't right now, buddy," Brett said, ruffling Rhett's hair while looking at her. "I'm just wondering why you're heading to the river so early in the day?"

Fiona had heard his question but was too busy looking at him to reply. Why did he seem to get more handsome each time she saw him? His eyes were so blue and clear, and honest. She could see the concern in them. The worry. No one had worried about her and the boys in a long time.

"Ma has to wash her dress," Rhett said. "It smells like fish."

"I have a washtub at my place," Brett said. "And a stove to heat up the water."

Fiona shook her head, mainly to toss aside further thoughts that weren't doing her a whit of good. "We can't keep imposing upon you, Mr. Blackwell."

"Who says you're imposing? Not me."

Lifting her chin, hoping that gave her fortitude, she replied. "I say."

Brett didn't say a word, but his eyes, the way they glanced to both Rhett and Wyatt before

they searched her face, said his mind was thinking of plenty of things. So was hers. She wanted
to ask him if Josiah was lying about him being
a drinking man. She also wanted to ask him if
he was interested in having a wife. Tell him
that she'd do everything within her power to
be a good wife to him.

Knowing her thoughts were out of despera-
tion and were sure to cause trouble, she said,
"Please excuse us. I need to get this laundry
done. Josiah will be coming back shortly and
I wouldn't want him to have to look for us
again."

It was a moment or more before Brett re-
sponded. "I'm sure you wouldn't," he said.
"Just be careful down there. The water is
deeper than it looks."

"We will be." Sidestepping him, she said,
"Come along boys."

"See you later, Brett," Rhett said.

"Don't worry, Brett. I'll make sure he
doesn't go in the water," Wyatt said.

"I know you will," Brett answered. "You're
a good big brother. One of the best I know."

Fiona's heart didn't know whether it wanted
to swell or break, and it took all her efforts to
keep walking forward. A part of her felt as if
she was making a mistake. A very big one.

"Why are you mad at Brett, Ma?" Rhett asked.

"I'm not mad at anyone," she assured.

"It sounded like you are."

She withheld a sigh in order to say, "I didn't mean for it to sound that way. I have a lot to do today and don't have time to stand around visiting."

"'Cause Mr. Melbourne will be coming back."

The amount of disappointment in his tone made her insides curdle. The boys couldn't know that. "Yes, he will be," she said with as much excitement as she could muster up.

They'd crossed the railroad tracks and rounded the livery stable. The trail to the river ran along the outskirts of town and was dotted with a few trees. Looking for something to engage the boys, she scanned the area. "Look," she said. "It's a cat."

"I see it," Rhett said. "Look, it jumped up on that tree. It's climbing it."

"Yes, it is," she agreed.

"It's probably after a nest of baby birds," Wyatt said.

When Rhett's face crinkled with sadness, she said, "I'm sure he's not after baby birds. He's just exploring. Cats are curious by nature."

"And hungry," Wyatt said drily.

Fiona tapped him on the top of his head and gave him a look that he knew well. One she hadn't had to use in almost twenty-four hours, but that in itself was progress.

"But not for baby birds," he told Rhett as he started walking again. "Cats would rather eat mice. He probably saw one up in that tree."

Rhett ran to catch up with his brother. "Do mice live in trees?"

"Mice live wherever they want," Wyatt answered.

Fiona caught up to both of them and gave Wyatt a look he hadn't seen often enough. One that said thank you. His grin made her smile and gave her a bit of hope.

They were walking past the last house when a lady stepped out of the back door. "Hello!" she greeted with a wave. "You must be Mrs. Goldberg. I'm Maggie Mc—Miller. Forgive me, I keep forgetting I'm married now. Well, not forgetting, I'm just not used to having a new last name."

The woman had to be one of the most beautiful ones Fiona had ever seen. Shiny black hair hung in waves all the way to her waist, and her face was not only angelic, her eyes shimmered with merriment as she hurried forward while speaking. She held out a hand in greeting as she stopped next to them.

"I was hoping to meet you soon," the woman said, including the boys in her grin. "All of you."

Not wanting to appear standoffish, although she was nervous, Fiona gently shook the proffered hand. "I'm Fiona Goldberg, and these are my sons, Rhett and Wyatt."

"Such handsome young men. It's so nice to meet you. All of you. As I said, I'm Maggie. I married Jackson Miller on Saturday. Do you have time for a cup of coffee or tea? I just made some."

A short and stout older man wearing a fancy suit and tall top hat stepped out of the house and asked, "Are you gonna invite them in to sit a spell, lass?"

Fiona couldn't help but wonder if this beautiful woman was married to the man who had to be more than three times her age. She knew Jackson Miller had married one of the brides that had arrived a month ago but had expected him to be much younger.

"Of course I invited them in." Turning back to her, the woman said, "That is my dear friend Angus O'Leary. He's a bit eccentric, but simply wonderful." Lowering her voice, she said,

"The first time I met him, he nearly scared me to death by sitting up in a coffin, but now I consider him one of my best friends. Please do come in even if it's just long enough for me to introduce you and your sons to him. You'll love him as much as I do."

In most circumstances, Fiona would have gladly accepted the invitation, but Josiah's behavior so far led her to believe he wanted her to wait until he'd formally introduced her before she met too many community members.

The other woman must have taken her pause as a rejection, because she said, "My husband, Jackson, he's with the mayor right now, seeing about putting a floor in the attic."

An ease washed over Fiona. Josiah must have mentioned her and the boys to the Millers. The opportunity to visit with one of the other women who'd arrived as a bride was something she'd hoped would occur.

"Well," Fiona said, "if we won't be imposing, Mrs. Miller."

"Of course you won't be imposing, and you must call me Maggie." With a wave, she invited the boys forward. "Do you boys like cinnamon rolls? I have some fresh out of the oven."

"They certainly do," Fiona said as both boys

looked to her for permission. "Thank you so much for the invitation."

"Oh, it's my pleasure," Maggie replied as they started walking toward the house. "You're my first official visitors since becoming Jackson's wife." She giggled slightly. "I simply become giddy when I say that—Jackson's wife. I'm half-afraid I may wake up at any time and it won't be true."

"Why?" Fiona asked, truly curious.

"Because Jackson hadn't contributed to the Betterment Committee, so he wasn't eligible to choose one of the brides," Maggie said. "The committee set some very strict rules."

"And the contract had some very fine print at the bottom of it," the man on the porch said. He then removed his big top hat and gave a sweeping bow. "Angus O'Leary at your service, ma'am."

"Angus, this is Fiona Goldberg and her two handsome sons, Rhett and Wyatt," Maggie said. "I do hope you've left room for one more cinnamon roll. I'm sure Fiona, Wyatt and Rhett will enjoy your company as they eat one."

"I will always have room to eat your cooking, lass," Angus replied while replacing his hat. Looking at her, he said, "You are in for a pleasant surprise—not only is Maggie beautiful, she can cook too. I dare say, if I were a wee bit younger, Jackson would never have had the chance to marry her."

Maggie grinned while patting the man on the shoulder. "You hadn't donated to the committee either."

"That wouldn't have stopped me any more than it did Jackson," Mr. O'Leary said with a laugh and another sweeping bow, inviting them all to step into the house.

It was a nice house, neat and tidy, but it was the furniture that stood out. As if she knew that was the first thing people noticed, Maggie said, "Jackson is an excellent carpenter. There's nothing he can't build, and make beautifully."

"Including the church's new bell tower," Angus said. "Brett Blackwell helped him erect it."

"You know Brett?" Rhett asked, instantly interested in the conversation.

"Of course I do," Angus answered. "Everyone knows Brett. He's a fine man. And the best blacksmith in all of Kansas. Maggie might have married him if she hadn't met Jackson first."

"You would have?" Fiona bit the tip of her

tongue, but it was too late—the question had already been asked.

"No," Maggie answered as she lifted cups and plates out of a lovely handcrafted cupboard. "Brett only visited me so often for more bottles of my tonic."

A lump formed so fast in Fiona's throat she sounded like a croaking frog when she said, "Tonic?"

"Yes. It's a family recipe," Maggie supplied. "But Jackson helped me understand it wasn't as medicinal as I'd always thought. It does little more than get a man drunk."

Chapter Nine

"You gonna walk over and see what's happening at Otis's shop?"

"No." Brett answered Wally's question before asking his own, "Are you going to do any work today? You've been staring up the street all morning."

"You see any customers?" Wally asked. "No. 'Cause they're all over at Otis's." With a wave in the general direction he'd been watching all morning, he added, "There's so many of them they can't all fit in the building. Half the men in town must be over there." Shifting his stance, as if that would help him see better, he continued, "What do you think is happening?"

"I'm sure we'll hear soon enough," Brett answered as he peered out the window over his desk toward Fiona's house. That had been the direction his mind had been on all morning.

His stomach was acting up too. It felt as if he'd swallowed a rope that had taken to coiling itself tight in his gut. He only felt that way when something wasn't right. Something serious.

Fiona and the boys had been gone a long time. Longer than it took to do laundry. The water was deep in some spots and snakes were known to hang out in the taller grass. Snakes. He should have warned her about rattlers. They were thick this year. If something happened to her or one of the boys, no one would hear them shouting. Not with the commotion over at Otis's.

Brett lifted his heavy leather apron over his neck. "I'll be back shortly."

"You going to Otis's?" Wally asked with excitement.

"No." Unable to come up with a believable excuse, Brett said, "I have an errand to run."

"What?" Wally asked. "It's not lunchtime yet." Glancing up the road again, he asked, "Want me to run the errand for you?"

"No," Brett replied, walking out the door and past Wally. "I won't be long."

"Don't bring me back any lunch," Wally shouted in his wake. "I'll go myself after you get back."

Brett didn't bother saying he wasn't going

to lunch. As he walked around the building, he wondered if Fiona and the boys had met up with Josiah. That was a possibility, if Josiah had made it past Otis's. But Wally would have noticed that. And mentioned it. He would have mentioned if Josiah had gone into Otis's shop too.

Deciding none of that mattered right now, Brett crossed the tracks and started for the trail that would lead him to the river. He would simply make sure they were all right. Just sneak up on them and leave again—if all was well—without them even noticing.

Without anyone noticing. He didn't need the men at Otis's shop hearing about it.

He walked past the livery stable unnoticed, but there were only a few trees along the edge of town, leaving him out in the open. He continued on his way, focused on the trees that started again after Jackson Miller's place. His mind ventured momentarily to the carpenter who had not only built furniture and other necessities for many of the townsfolk but had married one of the mail-order brides. Maggie McCary, or Miller now that she'd married Jackson, was a fine-looking woman.

So was her sister, Mary. At one time Brett had considered trying to win their attention but had given up on that idea before the wedding bells had rung in the church tower. He'd given Mary a ride out to Steve Putnam's ranch when she'd first arrived in town—Steve had hired her as a cook.

Maggie had remained in town and participated in all the picnics and parties the town put on in favor of the brides. He'd visited with her several times, purchasing several bottles of her tonic in the process.

The other three gals had been at the picnics and parties too. Sadie, the gal who'd married Rollie, was so shy and quiet, Brett had been sure his voice alone would have sent her running for the hills. The one who married Micah Swift, the banker, was named Rebecca and was clearly looking for more than a husband. She wanted money. Brett hoped she wouldn't be overly disappointed in her marriage to Micah. He might be the banker, but the Oak Grove bank was only a small branch of the one in Dodge. The one Micah's father owned, and he controlled every dime that went in or out of both banks.

The third woman named Anna had married Wayne Stevens, the depot agent. In that marriage, he hoped Wayne had a good set of earplugs. Brett had never met a woman who talked so much. Then again, maybe Wayne liked that. And Anna must have liked Wayne's dog. It was half wolf and the size of a two-year-old bear.

It hadn't taken him long to figure out none of those women would have made him a good wife. But that hadn't made him stop wanting one. If Fiona had been in that bunch of brides, he'd have claimed her the moment she'd stepped off the train. He couldn't put his finger on exactly what drew him to her, but he was drawn and would like to tell every other man in town to keep their distance.

But he couldn't do that.

She wasn't up for claiming. Josiah had seen to that.

Usually slow to anger, this time was different. He was certain Josiah wasn't playing by the rules, despite what the other man had already told him.

The gathering in his shop this morning proved others felt the same way, and Brett had to wonder how Josiah was going to turn things in his favor. It wasn't going to be easy.

Brett wasn't as worried about Josiah's hide as he was about Fiona. Some of the men were downright desperate for a wife. They had children who needed a mother, and they weren't going to simply stand on the sidelines. In fact, Fiona was more in line with what most every one of them needed. A mature woman who knew the ins and outs of marriage. Those other young gals hadn't.

Maybe that was why he'd taken an instant liking to Fiona. She was the kind of woman a man wanted to come home to every night. The kind a man wanted to watch the sun rise with too.

"Hello, Brett."

Lost in his musing, he hadn't seen Angus until the man was standing directly before him.

Dressed as always in his fancy black suit, Angus tipped the brim of his tall black hat. "How are you today?"

Brett nodded in response. "I'm good, Angus. How are you?"

"Mighty fine. Simply mighty fine." After releasing a deep sigh that said all was right in his world, Angus continued, "A matter of fact, I was just on my way to see you."

Considering the man didn't own an animal or anything that would need his blacksmithing, Brett asked, "Why?"

"Because I just met your new neighbor." Lifting one of his bushy brows, he added, "The Mrs. Fiona Goldberg."

Brett's heart thudded harder than if he'd just unloaded a wagon full of grain. "Where?"

"At Maggie Miller's house. I do say, Fiona and her children are delightful. Simply delightful."

"Are they still there?"

"No, they went on down to the river to wash clothes." With a nod in the general direction of the river, Angus added, "Walk with me. My legs stiffen when I stand in one place."

Brett agreed with a nod and forced his stride to remain slow to accommodate Angus's. The feller was old but had the spirit of a much younger man. However, to hear Angus say it, he already had one foot in the grave. In a way, he did. Angus had already had Jackson build his coffin. Two of them actually. Brett couldn't recall what had been wrong with the first one, but the second one, made of specially ordered cherrywood, was too short. That was what Angus claimed, anyway. Said it was long enough for him, but only if he took his top hat off, and that was not going to happen. However, he'd decided he'd wait for a while before ordering a third coffin.

The old codger had come into some money last year. A lot of it from the way he talked and spent his money—on certain things. Like coffins. He said it was all in preparation for when his time came. He wanted to go out in style. Staying true to his word, he got a shave every morning and never went anywhere without wearing a three piece suit and his beloved top hat.

Recalling all that gave Brett a clear insight. "You talked to Otis this morning, didn't you?"

"Of course. I talk to Otis every day. Even on Sundays. Of course, I pay extra in order to get a shave on a day his barbershop is closed."

"So you know that Fiona is here to marry the mayor," Brett said.

"I heard something along those lines," Angus admitted. "If I was a few years younger, Josiah wouldn't stand a chance with Fiona. I'd sweep her right off her feet. Those two little lads of hers too. I'd have myself a whole new family in one sweep."

"What if that wasn't what Fiona wanted?" Brett asked. He'd asked himself that question several times lately and still hadn't come up with an answer.

"Well, to start with, I'd ask her." Angus nodded. "That's what I'd do all right, I'd just ask her. She wants to get married again. Wants to have a loving man to help her raise those boys, and maybe make a couple more. But she's smart. I can tell by her eyes. If the right man asked her, she'd tell him the truth."

"What if that truth was that she wants to marry Josiah?" Brett asked aloud even though he hadn't meant to.

Angus chuckled. "I wander around this town every day. Don't have much else to do. And I can tell you that the only reason Josiah Melbourne wants to get married is because of Donald Swift."

"Micah's father?" Brett asked.

"Yes. Poor Micah." Angus shook his head. "A man's gotta feel sorry for that lad. Even before he married that money-loving bride of his."

"Micah seemed happy on Saturday," Brett pointed out.

"Of course he did—it was his wedding day, and he'd accomplished what his da told him to do."

"Donald told Micah he had to get married?"

"Sure did," Angus said. "I heard it with my own two ears. The two of them were arguing over donating to the Betterment Committee. Micah didn't think his father would approve of it, so Josiah wired Donald, asked him to come to town and talk to his son. Donald did, and he told Micah to make a large donation and to make sure he married one of the women. He claimed it would be good for business. That married men are more respectable and people believe they are more honest. Josiah agreed with every word."

"So Josiah thinks marrying Fiona will make him more respectable and trustworthy," Brett repeated mainly for himself.

"What's more respectable than marrying a widow and helping her raise her children?" Angus asked.

Brett had to nod in agreement. Yet at the same time he wondered about what the cost of that would be for Fiona and her sons.

"The trouble that I see," Angus continued, "is that until Josiah figures out he has to treat people the way he wants to be treated, he'll never figure out that respect doesn't just appear. It has to be earned." Then rather abruptly Angus stopped walking and turned around. "The hotel is serving ham for lunch today. I best go have myself a plateful before it gets dried out. There's nothing worse than dried-out ham. I'm sure you don't need my help carrying those things back to her house, do you?"

Having turned about when Angus had, Brett glanced over his shoulder. The river was only a few yards away, where Fiona wrung water out of a garment and, farther down the bank, Wyatt and Rhett chased each other around trees. Brett's heart swelled at the sight of all of them.

Afraid of being caught staring, he turned back to Angus, only to discover the old man was now several feet away, walking back to town with far more speed than he'd used while they'd walked toward the river.

Brett turned back around. Fiona hadn't noticed him, neither had the boys. He could turn around and follow Angus back to town. That was what he should do. They were fine. In no danger. He should go back to work and mind his own business.

The rope was still in his stomach and started coiling up again. He glanced around. Nothing was out of the ordinary. The boys were running about, but not in the long grass or near the rock cropping. Fiona was standing in the shallow water. It wasn't his favorite fishing spot—where he'd taken them yesterday. That was farther downriver. There wasn't much of a bank here. The land just sloped into the water. There were also several large rocks. Other townsfolk used those rocks to wash their clothes just like she was doing.

Her boots were sitting several feet away

from her, and that was enough to make him take a step forward, in order to tell her she shouldn't do that. The water was too muddy to clearly see what was beneath it.

He'd no sooner thought of what could happen when movement in the water caught his attention. It looked like a stick floating around the rock, but the way the rope in his stomach suddenly formed a knot told him that wasn't a stick.

"Snake!" Brett yelled and ran forward, his heart in his throat. "Fiona! There's a snake in the water!"

She spun around and, still running toward her, Brett saw the snake disappear under the swirl of her skirt. Her scream of pain shot through him like a bullet and gave him a bolt of speed.

He arrived as she stumbled out of the water. As Brett swept her into his arms, he shook the folds of her skirt before he glanced at the river, where he noticed the snake skimming across the top of the water. Recognizing the diamond shapes on its back, he cursed beneath his breath.

"It bit me," she said. "Brett, it bit me."

"I know, but it's going to be all right." Holding her tight in his arms, he bolted up the bank. "Rhett. Wyatt. Follow us. Stay close."

The boys ran toward them. "What happened, Brett?" Rhett asked.

"Ma got bit by a snake," Wyatt answered his younger brother.

Still running, with them at his sides, Brett assured both boys. "She's going to be fine. We just gotta get her to Doc Graham. His house is next to Jackson Miller's. We gotta run. Run fast."

"We can run fast, Brett. Real fast," Rhett said, shooting forward.

Without missing a step, Brett asked Fiona, "Are you doing all right?"

"Yes, but it burns."

Brett held her tighter. "I know. But don't worry. We're almost to Doc's place."

Rhett, running ahead of them, started shouting at the first sight of people, "Ma got bit by a snake!"

Several people ran toward them, leaving their houses and businesses. Questions abounded, but Brett kept his focus on Nelson Graham's house, hoping the doc was home. When the door of the doctor's house opened, Brett barreled through the forming crowd to leap up the steps.

"It's was a rattler, doc," he said. "I saw it."

"Bring her in here," Nelson said, pulling aside a curtain to reveal a room with a waist-high table. "Where did it bite her?"

"My calf," Fiona said. "It's burning and throbbing."

"Put her on the table, Brett." Nelson then shouted over his shoulder, "Mrs. Miller, close that door please. Tell everyone to stay outside."

As Brett set Fiona down, he glanced through the curtained doorway to see Maggie Miller shut the door and then gather Rhett and Wyatt to her sides. Meeting his eyes, she then moved forward and pulled the curtain closed, keeping her and the boys on the other side. A heavy bout of respect for the young woman filled Brett. He then looked at Fiona. "Mrs. Miller will watch the boys—don't worry about them."

She nodded and took a hold of his hand. "I'm scared."

He squeezed her fingers. Over the years he'd been injured plenty and seen many others hurt and injured, and not a single time had any of those events affected him like this one. The fear in her eyes, the tears dripping down her cheeks, gutted him. At this moment, he'd gladly trade places with her. "No need to be scared. You're in good hands."

"I haven't had the pleasure," Doctor Graham said, never looking up from his examination of her leg. "But I believe you must be Fiona Goldberg."

"Yes," Fiona answered.

"How bad is it, Doc?" Brett asked.

"It's a nasty bite," the doc answered as he looked toward Fiona. "Did you get bit just the once?"

Her swallow was visible. "I think so."

Nelson took a hold of her other hand. "There's a fang in there that I'll have to dig out, then I'm going to douse it with alcohol. It's going to sting, but it'll counteract the poison."

Tears fell from her eyes. "A fang?"

Squeezing her fingers again, Brett used his other hand to wipe the hair away from her forehead. "Every critter loses a tooth now and again. That old snake won't be biting anyone else until he grows a new one. He should have thought twice about biting you."

The hint of a smile that fluttered over her lips increased his heartbeat, but then so did the commotion that started on the other side of the curtain—just in a different way.

A shout from Maggie Miller saying, "You can't go in there!" filled the room as the curtain shook.

"Get out of my way!" A thud sounded and then a rending rip that was followed by a clatter as the curtain fell from its rod.

"Josiah!" Doc Graham shouted. "Stop right there!"

"I will not!" Josiah's face was beet red as he stormed forward. "What's going on here?" Waggling a finger at Fiona, he continued, "I'm tired of finding you at the river with Brett Blackwell every time I turn around!"

Brett would have rounded the table, but Fiona squeezed his hand harder. "He wasn't—" she started.

"Josiah, Brett may have saved Fiona's life," Nelson said, pushing Josiah backward. "Now get out so I can do my work."

"What were you doing down there with her?" Josiah shouted.

"She was washing clothes," Brett shouted in return. He would have grabbed the mayor by his shirt collar but couldn't release Fiona's hand. Her hold said she needed him and that was far more important. "If you'd provided her with the supplies she needed, she wouldn't be lying here now."

Another man entered the room and grabbed Josiah by the shoulders. Spinning the mayor around, Jackson Miller demanded, "You owe my wife an apology, Josiah. And those two little boys!"

"What did he do to Rhett and Wyatt?" Brett asked furiously.

"Gentlemen!" Doc shouted. "This is not the time or place! Mrs. Miller, step in so you can help me. Brett, you see to Fiona's sons. Jackson, rehang that curtain, and, Josiah, you get out before I send for the sheriff and have you arrested for destroying my property. Now, out! All three of you!"

Brett wasn't about to go anywhere until the pleading in Fiona's eyes melted the anger inside him. Even hurt, her first worry was her sons. He gave her hand a final squeeze and then let it loose. As he walked to the end of the table she was lying on, he grabbed Josiah by the back of his suit coat. Hoisting him up, he hauled Josiah over the crumpled curtain. "You heard the doc. Get out," he said, giving Josiah a solid shove, sending him in the direction of the door.

"You'll hear about this, Brett Blackwell!"

Brett didn't give Josiah's threat an ounce of concern as he gestured for Wyatt to open the door. He had plenty more that he'd like to say to Josiah, but none of it should be said in front of children. Brett scooped Rhett, who'd glued himself to his leg, into his arms.

"I'm charging you for these repairs, Josiah," Jackson said as he gathered up the curtain. "And you will apologize to my wife for pushing her and those little boys out of the way."

Josiah glanced at each of them and then out the door, where a large crowd stood, and then back again.

Brett had half a mind to plant his foot on Josiah's backside, but the arrival of Sheriff Tom Baniff made it unnecessary. A commonsense man who was highly respected, the sheriff gestured for Josiah to join him on the stoop, and then he pulled the door shut.

Brett laid his free hand on Wyatt's shoulder. "You boys all right?" he asked, including both of them in a glance.

They nodded, and Wyatt asked, "Is Ma all right?"

"She's going to be fine," Brett said. He had to swallow against the lump that formed in his throat as a muffled scream came through the curtain Jackson was putting back in place. He and Jackson made eye contact, and Brett had to swallow again. "It's just one little bite." He'd never heard his own voice shake, but he knew it was. "Doc will have her fixed up in no time."

Chapter Ten

Fiona had never known such agony, and though the hand holding hers wasn't nearly as strong or comforting as Brett's hand had been, she was incredibly thankful for Maggie remaining at her side through the slow and painful procedure. The doctor was very kind and explained things as he went along, but the pain had her wanting to tell him to hurry up and get it over with.

"You're going to be bedridden for a few days, Mrs. Goldberg," he said. "Have to keep all weight off this leg and keep it clean. The bite wasn't a deep one, but I had to make a fairly deep incision to get the fang out."

Sweat had started streaming down her face and Fiona couldn't stop trembling. Unsure what to say, to do, she looked up at Maggie and then had to squeeze her eyes shut at how the other woman's face was covered with tears. What would happen to Wyatt and Rhett? What if she died? Who would—

"You're going to be fine," the doctor said. "Brett got you here in plenty of time. You're sweating and shaking because of the poison. That'll subside, I promise. Just stay calm and breathe in and out nice and slow."

"What can I do for her?" Maggie whispered.

"Just what you're doing, Mrs. Miller," he answered. "I'm almost done."

Trying to follow his orders, Fiona focused on breathing in and out but had to hold her breath in order to squelch a scream as pain once again flared in her calf, shooting fiery agony up her leg.

"I've put a poultice on," the doctor said. "I'm sorry, but it's going to continue to hurt for some time, and the swelling will continue to make your leg throb. There's nothing I can do about that. Once we take the poultice off, we can cover it with a cool towel, but that won't be for hours." He patted her hand. "The good news is, you got bit on the leg, which means although the next couple of days are going to be painful, you'll then be on your way to a full recovery."

As relief washed over her, Fiona whispered, "Thank you."

"You're welcome," he said. "I have something for the pain I'll give you now. And just like you tell your sons, I'm telling you to get some rest. Just go to sleep." He was looking at her with a friendly and consoling smile. "That is what you tell your boys when they are hurting, isn't it?"

"Yes, it is," she answered.

"And it works, doesn't it? They wake up feeling better."

She nodded.

He smiled again, then looked at Maggie. "There are pillows and blankets in that closet."

Maggie squeezed her hand before she let it go. "I'll be right back."

Fiona closed her eyes again but opened them a moment later when the doctor told her to open her mouth. He fed her several spoonfuls of a bitter and thick liquid that stuck in her throat.

"I can't give you any water right now," he said. "It might make you throw up and we don't want that."

She was too busy trying to swallow to answer, and then Maggie arrived and placed a pillow under her head and covered her with a thin blanket.

"I'll let your boys step in for a moment,"

the doctor said. "Just so they know you are all right."

Fiona was still shaking. Try as she might, it wouldn't stop. Knowing that might frighten the boys, she gathered the edge of the blanket in both hands, hoping that would help, before she nodded to the doctor.

Her heart started to race, and she found it harder to breathe when the curtain parted and Brett walked in carrying Rhett in one arm and holding on to Wyatt's hand with his other hand. She'd found him handsome before, and caring and kind, but today, after how he'd come to her rescue and how he was providing her sons with such care, she couldn't imagine a more wonderful, perfect man. A fresh bout of tears formed and all the blinking in the world wouldn't stop them from slipping out of her eyes.

Rhett's bottom lip started to shiver as he asked, "Are you cold, Momma?"

He hadn't called her momma in some time, and that was enough to make more tears fall. Pinching her lips to gain enough control to speak, she nodded. "I guess I have a case of the shivers."

"Her dress got wet," Brett said to Rhett as

he put him down to stand beside her. "That must be why."

The way he was trying to ease Rhett's fears also touched her deeply. "That must be it," she said. "I'll warm up soon."

"You're gonna be all right, aren't you, Ma?" Wyatt asked. "Brett says you are."

"He's right," she answered. "I'll be fine in no time at all." The realization that might not have been the case if not for Brett had her pinching her lips together again to hold in a sob. Her children wouldn't have had anyone if that had happened. That thought was unbearable and she squeezed her eyes shut.

The moment she felt the warmth, she knew it was Brett's hand atop of hers. An overwhelming desire to feel his arms around her, holding her, had her clutching the blanket even harder.

"I'm going to take these two back to my shop for a few hours," he said. "I have some work I need done, and they are mighty fine workers. We'll be back to see you after a bit."

Afraid if she opened her eyes she'd start crying all over again, Fiona nodded. "Thank you," she whispered. Then, knowing she had to for their sakes, she opened her eyes and mustered up a smile for her sons. "You two be good."

"They always are," Brett said.

She nodded again, and then, wanting them to know how she felt, she said, "I love you, boys."

"We love you too, Momma," Rhett said as Brett picked him up again.

"Yeah, we do, Ma," Wyatt said as he patted her arm. "We love you."

A strangling sigh escaped as she watched them walk back through the curtain.

"They'll be fine," Maggie said, stepping up beside the table. "Brett's a good man. One of the best."

"I know," Fiona answered. That was also what made her so sad. Knowing how good of a man he was. And knowing she'd made the biggest mistake of her life when she'd agreed to marry Josiah.

Brett was glad to see the crowd had dispersed as he left the doctor's office, carrying Rhett and holding on to Wyatt's hand. The boys were worried. So was he. But Doc had said getting bit in the leg was the best place to get bit if you had to get bit. That it was the farthest away from the heart. Brett hoped that was true. He'd known plenty of folks who'd lived through a snake bite. Adults almost always did. However, most adults didn't have hearts as big as Fiona's.

"What do you need us to do for you, Brett?" Wyatt asked as they walked toward his shop.

"Well," he said, giving himself time to come up with something, "you two have seen my horses, Hickory and Birch?"

"Yes," Rhett answered. "Which is which?"

"Birch has the white blaze down his face, and he loves carrots. He'll do most anything for one. I just got a batch delivered to my place this morning and haven't had a chance to give either Birch or Hickory one." John Benet had brought a bag of them to the shop this morning, his excuse for coming to town when he'd heard about Josiah ordering himself a bride. "I'm hoping you two can do that for me."

"We sure can," Wyatt answered. "I'll make sure Rhett doesn't get too close to them."

"You don't have to worry about that," Brett answered. "Those two horses are as tame as baby bunnies."

"Could we ride them?" Rhett asked. "I've never ridden a horse afore."

"Sure," Brett said, knowing the boys would be perfectly safe with Hickory and Birch. "Just lead them to the fence with a carrot and climb on. They'll walk you around the corral until your rump is sore."

"My rump won't get sore," Wyatt said. "I've been on a horse before."

Brett smiled at the boy and nodded, but his attention had been snagged by something else. The crowd gathered around his shop. There had to be twice as many folks as this morning. Including women.

He set Rhett down. The boys had already seen enough people squabbling today. "You two run around the backside of the building. You'll find the bag of carrots in the lean-to."

Wyatt took a hold of his little brother's hand. "I'll keep an eye on him."

"I know you will," Brett answered. "You're the best boys I've ever known."

The boys were both grinning as they took off running. Brett wasn't. From the looks of things, this crowd was more worked up than the one this morning.

"It's deplorable, I tell you. Simply deplorable!"

That was Otis's wife, Martha, talking. She had the dressmaking shop in town but obviously wasn't sewing today.

Spying him, she rushed forward. "Oh, Brett,

how is Mrs. Goldberg? And where are those adorable sons of hers?"

"Doc says she'll be fine," Brett answered. "And her boys are 'round back with my horses."

"Oh, thank heavens," Martha said, pressing her hands to her chest. "The poor thing. How frightening." Whipping her head around so fast her red curls bounced, Martha pointed toward several other women. "I've gathered quilting club members to nurse her around the clock. We'll take turns, but we can't do it in that house. It's deplorable. There's nothing more in that house than a few belongings and a single bed. One bed for all three of them."

"Josiah should be horsewhipped," another woman said. "Expecting a woman and two children to live there with nothing. There's not even a stove to heat water."

"Our town is better than that," Joyce Chadwick said. "If he'd have told us, we'd have gathered the things she needs."

"Josiah didn't want anyone to know," Don Carlson said. "He was trying to keep her a secret."

"Some fine mayor, that is," Jules said.

Brett had to agree with both of them and turned to Wally. "Where is Josiah?"

"Over at the sheriff's office," Wally answered. "I think Baniff is trying to keep him from getting tarred and feathered."

"He can't keep him there all day," Angus said, stepping up beside Wally. "Unless he arrests him."

"He didn't do anything worthy of getting arrested," Brett said.

"Are you sticking up for him, Blackwell?" Jules asked.

"No," Brett answered. "I don't agree with what he's done, but he hasn't broken any laws." Figuring someone needed to be the voice of reason, he stepped into the center of the crowd. "Now listen here, folks. It's F—Mrs. Goldberg and her sons we need to think about now, not Josiah. It's mighty kind of you women to step up to help. She's going to need looking after. I have a couple spare beds in my place, so we can—"

"That'll be perfect, Brett. We can move her to your place," Martha said. "There'll be room there for the children and Mrs. Goldberg."

The women all started nodding and agreeing.

Brett shook his head. "I meant we can move the beds—"

"We'll need more than beds, and there isn't time to start moving everything she's going to need. She can't stay at the doctor's place all day," Martha said. "He might need the space for another emergency."

Shaking his head again, Brett said, "There aren't that many emergencies—"

"There might be," Martha insisted. "We'll go get things ready at your place. When Doc says she can be moved, Otis will help you bring her home. You should use your freight wagon so she can lie down. When Russ Perkins got bit last month, he couldn't walk for more than a week. I imagine it will be that long for her too."

The women started talking among themselves, and Brett figured interrupting wouldn't get him anywhere. He turned to Wally.

"You do have four bedrooms," Wally said.

"And a fine stove," Angus offered.

Brett sighed. "Josiah won't like it." He sure wouldn't if the tables were turned.

"We'll have a chance to hear what he thinks," Angus said. "He and the sheriff are walking this way."

As impossible as it seemed, Brett felt a bit sorry for Josiah as the group of women started heckling him even before he and the sheriff arrived.

"Ladies! Ladies!" the sheriff shouted. "Calm down! Just calm down."

"Have you seen the house he put that woman and her children in?" Martha asked. "It's deplorable. Simply deplorable! It's empty except for one bed."

"It was only for a few days," Josiah said. "Until they move in with me."

"And where will they all sleep at your place?" Jules asked. "You ain't got but one bed yourself."

"I do declare, Mayor," Angus said in his gentlemanly way, "that you should have made arrangements for Mrs. Goldberg and her children to stay at the hotel, like you did the other brides."

"Yeah," others agreed.

"Why didn't you?" someone asked.

"Because the hotel was full. The brides were still staying there," Josiah said.

"How long has this woman been here?" Jules demanded as he stomped forward to stand directly in front of Josiah.

Brett stepped between the two of them. "Mrs. Goldberg arrived the day of the weddings."

"So the hotel wasn't full," Jules said.

"I wasn't exactly sure of when she'd arrive."

"And I'm thirty-four," Angus said drily.

Brett had to agree with Angus's sarcasm. Josiah was lying. He'd known exactly when

Fiona would arrive. "Well, what's done is done," Brett said. "Mrs. Goldberg and her children need a place to stay now. One that will fit their needs as she heals."

"They can stay at my place," Josiah said.

"No, they can't," Martha insisted, pushing both Brett and Jules aside. "The quilting club members will be taking care of her, and we aren't going to be trekking up and down the steps at your place. Furthermore, as Mr. Carmichael just said, you only have one bed at your place. That's not enough room. Now, it's already been settled. She'll be brought to Mr. Blackwell's place. By the time she's fully recovered, I...we...everyone in town... expect you to have appropriate accommodations fully prepared for Mrs. Goldberg and her children."

As if her word finalized everything, Martha waved a hand. "Follow me, ladies, we need to get Mr. Blackwell's house ready."

As the women started to follow his wife, Otis stepped forward. "I believe a council meeting is in order, Josiah, don't you?"

"I already told—"

"Things have changed, Josiah," Otis interrupted. "Unless you're prepared to take on several angry men on your own, I suggest we call a meeting posthaste."

"I agree with Otis, Josiah," the sheriff said. "You need to get this issue under control before I have to take action."

After much mumbling and many snide remarks, Josiah agreed, and when Otis stated the meeting was open to any community members, the men followed him up the street. Wally and Angus lagged behind.

"Aren't you going?" Wally asked Brett.

"No," Brett answered. "Wyatt and Rhett need looking after."

Wally nodded and glanced up the road. "Care if I go?"

"Go ahead," Brett answered.

"Thanks, boss. I'll fill you on everything that's said."

Brett figured as much but wasn't sure he wanted to know what was or wasn't said.

Angus walked over to a bench by the door. "I retrieved these things from the river. I'll walk over and give them to the ladies."

Glad someone had thought of Fiona's boots and laundry, Brett said, "Thanks, Angus."

"Then I'll mosey over to the hotel for that ham I was going to get earlier. Would you like me to bring some back for you and the lads?"

Lunch had been the last thing on Brett's mind, but figuring the boys were hungry, he replied, "I'd appreciate that, Angus. I'm sure Rhett and Wyatt are hungry."

"Young lads always are," Angus answered, already on his way toward Brett's house.

There was a steady line of women carrying things from Fiona's house to his. Brett let out a long slow sigh as he watched the stream. Fiona would need a place to recuperate, but having her in the house would be tough. He already cared more about her than he should. Soon she and her sons would be Josiah's family, not his.

She deserved better than Josiah. Practically every single man in town would marry her given the chance. And they'd have made sure she'd had what she needed right from the start. Like a washtub so she wouldn't have been down at the river.

He could have prevented that himself. Forced her to use his washtub rather than go to the river. He should have insisted more firmly when she refused this morning. Hadn't because he respected her answer and her reason for not wanting to use his things. That he could understand.

What he couldn't understand was this whole

new level of frustration inside him. Why he'd taken to someone so quickly. Or wished so hard things were different.

Chapter Eleven

It might have been the snake bite, or the bitter medicine, causing the odd sensation of being separated from her body. Fiona heard people talking, asking her questions, and she even answered them. It was almost as if she was in some sort of dream. That was what she wanted. To dream. Actually, to sleep. She was so tired. And dizzy. Everything spun, even when she didn't open her eyes. Spun until she couldn't tell where things began or ended.

It was nice to no longer be lying on the hard table at the doctor's office. The mattress beneath her now was soft and so comfortable she didn't want to move. Her leg hurt and throbbed, but not as strongly as before. Or maybe her sleepiness dulled the pain.

How Brett kept appearing before her, telling her the boys were fine was a great relief.

He'd make sure they were taken care of, fed and watched over. For the first time ever, she wasn't the only one caring about them. Brett was so kind and thoughtful. And handsome. So very handsome.

Maggie was near too. As were other women. Fiona couldn't remember all their names. Didn't even try.

When Brett appeared again and told her to go to sleep, she trusted him so much she gave in and, even with the room spinning around her, let the sleepiness overcome her, knowing he would be in her dreams.

He was. The four of them were fishing. He and the boys were laughing. When something attempted to draw her out of a slumber she didn't want to leave, she tried to ignore it until she realized the laughter wasn't only in her dream.

She pulled her eyes open and then shut them again when nothing was familiar. Other than the laughing. She pulled her eyes open again and scanned the surroundings more thoroughly.

Nothing was recognizable, other than the gray-and-black plaid shirt hanging on a hook. It was Brett's. The one he'd worn during their picnic. Examining the room more closely, she questioned why she appeared to be in his bedroom. How? The throbbing in her leg registered then.

The snake bite. Brett had carried her, but it was to the doctor's house. Josiah had been there. Yelling. Then a wagon, and women. Several women. And Brett telling her to sleep.

The fading sunlight filtering in through the window said it had to be evening. Surely she hadn't slept the entire day away. Yet she couldn't remember more than bits and pieces, and pain.

She tried harder, and harder, until the snippets formed a full memory, that of the doctor digging a fang out of her leg and then applying a poultice.

Now fully awake, she pulled aside the blanket. From the knee down, her leg was twice the size it normally was. The poultice was held in place by loose gauze. That was when she noticed the nightgown. Her nightgown. She'd been wearing a dress this morning. Her heart started to race. How? When? Who?

The door opened slightly, and a vaguely familiar face peered around the edge.

"Oh, you are awake," the redheaded woman said. "I was afraid all that laughter might wake you. Those boys of yours are so delightful. They've had us in stitches."

Fiona waited until the woman walked closer before she whispered, "How did I get here? What am I doing here?"

"Oh, sweetie, the men brought you here. Brett and my husband, Otis." Patting her hand, the woman continued, "You don't remember?"

Fiona shook her head.

"That's because you were sleeping off and on. It's the medicine. I'm Martha Taylor. I own the dress shop here in Oak Grove, and my husband, Otis, owns the barbershop. Here, let me help you sit up a bit."

With the other woman's assistance, Fiona soon had two pillows propping her into a sitting position. She was still groggy and sore, but more aware.

"I'm sorry," Fiona said, still trying to make sense of things. "But why am I here? At Brett's house?"

"Because we couldn't take care of you at that house you were staying in. There was only one bed."

"I know, but—"

"I belong to the quilting club, and all of the members, well, those who live nearby, will be taking care of you until you are up and about again. We couldn't do that in the other house.

Brett has plenty of room for you and the boys, so here we are."

"Are you feeling better, Ma?"

Fiona smiled as Rhett sheepishly slipped into the room. "Yes, I am."

"Good!" He bolted across the room. "We played with Kade and Wiley today, and I rode a horse and fed it carrots. Birch really likes them. Hickory likes apples better. And we ate the fish we caught. It was good. And we're gonna spend the night here with Brett. We'll each have our own bed. Kade and Wiley each have their own bed. They live at the hotel. They ate fish too. We showed them where Brett buried the fish guts, but we didn't dig them up. Brett said he didn't think we should do that, on account that they might stink or something."

"I'm sure they might, and I'm glad that you didn't dig them up," Fiona said as he stopped to take a breath. "It sounds like you had a fun day." Her gaze went then to the doorway, where Wyatt was pushing the door open a bit wider.

"We kept checking in on you," Wyatt said. "Mrs. Taylor kept watch over you all day."

Fiona smiled at him and at Mrs. Taylor,

who'd waved him to walk closer. "There was nothing for you to worry about."

"That's what Brett kept telling us," Rhett said. "Didn't you, Brett?"

Air snagged in her throat as she glanced to the open door. Brett filled the entire doorway. Fiona pressed a hand against her chest, at how hard her heart beat. The sight of a man had never affected her the way he did.

"These two are a couple of hard workers," Brett said, gesturing at her sons. "With their help, I got twice as much done as I usually do."

Perhaps that was why. He was the kind of man who only lived in dreams.

"They are very good boys," Martha Taylor said. "Very well behaved. No squabbling or fussing whatsoever."

"And the fish they caught yesterday was as delicious as Rhett said," Maggie Miller said as she stepped into the room.

Brett had walked farther into the room in order for Maggie to enter. Fiona focused on getting her mind back in order as Maggie came closer to the bed, carrying a tray.

"I told them they'll have to catch more so you can eat some once you are up to it," Maggie said. "In the meantime, Sadie made you some chicken soup, per Dr. Graham's orders."

Fiona's cheeks burned as Martha smoothed out the blanket for Maggie to set the tray holding a bowl and a vase with a flower on the bed. "Goodness, you're all going to so much trouble. I—I don't know—"

"Oh, pish," Martha said. "It's no trouble. Why, we had a party while you were sleeping. Sadie and Rollie Austin cooked the fish Brett had taken there and brought it over here for supper, along with their boys. Maggie and Jackson joined us, and so did Otis and Dr. Graham." Her green eyes glittered as she continued, "We haven't had such a fun evening in ages. I was afraid our laughing would wake you long before it did."

"I wouldn't have minded," Fiona said honestly. If that was what it took to see her sons so happy, she'd get bit by a snake any day. Knowing the snake bite didn't have much to do with it, she shook her head. "You are all being so kind. I don't know how to thank you."

"There's no need to thank any of us," Martha said. "This is how things are done in Oak Grove. We look out for one another. Now, you eat this soup Sadie made before it gets cold. Dr. Graham said he'd be back in an hour or so to put a fresh poultice on your leg. You've slept through the last two he's put on. He wants one kept on your leg for at least twenty-four hours."

Having never been ill or waited on, Fiona tried to think of something to say, but her mind was blank. For a reason she couldn't explain, she looked at Brett.

He smiled as he placed one hand on Wyatt's shoulder and the other on Rhett's. "We'll leave so you can eat. Tell your ma you'll see her later."

The boys did as he asked, and as the room cleared out, he too told her to eat. Grinning, she picked up the spoon. Although it was very tasty, she could only eat a small amount of the soup. Then, with the help of Maggie and Martha, Fiona took care of relieving her bladder and getting back into bed. That wore her out. She couldn't put any weight on that leg, it was completely useless and throbbing painfully.

"I'm sorry," she said while lying back down. "I've never been so weak."

"You've never been bitten by a rattlesnake before," Martha said. "And that is exactly why we are here. To take care of you." Covering her with the blanket, Martha added, "You rest now. Doc will be here soon."

"I'll go get things ready," Maggie said. "Do you want a glass of water or anything?"

"No…thank you, though," Fiona answered.

"Dr. Graham showed us how to make the poultice," Martha said. "Just in case he has an emergency and can't get back. So don't worry—we have it all under control."

"I'm not worried," Fiona replied. "I just don't want to be such a burden to anyone."

"I won't hear any such talk," Martha said. "We are happy to help. All of us."

"But Maggie was just married the other day," Fiona said. "And you have a husband, a family who need you."

A sadness filled Martha's eyes. "It's just me and Otis." She sighed. "We had two babies. Girls. Millie and Beth. They would have been about the ages of your boys. Our Millie only lived for a few hours. Beth was born the next year and was a little over a year, fifteen months, when she died."

Fiona laid her hand on Martha's arm. "I'm so sorry."

"So am I," Martha said. "But I've accepted it. Things happen, and sometimes they are bad things. That's just how it is and dwelling on it doesn't help. A person needs to learn to put the past behind them and move on. That's what we did. We packed up and moved on. And we are glad we did."

Although she couldn't imagine one child would ever replace another, Fiona also assumed Martha wasn't much older than her. "You could have more children."

"Yes, we could. God willing." Martha smiled brightly. "Until then, we've decided Oak Grove is our family. Everyone here. Old and new. Now, you just rest while I go help Maggie see that everything is set for when Doctor Graham arrives."

Brett stood in the bedroom doorway doing little more than watching the two boys sleeping. It warmed his heart to see them resting so peacefully. They'd both wanted their own room, until it came time to go to bed. Then they'd decided to sleep together. He could understand why. They'd been worried about their mother all day and still were. He was too and had spent plenty of time thinking about what would have happened to Rhett and Wyatt if her injury had been worse.

Josiah wouldn't do right by these two boys. Others recognized that too. The town council meeting had been heated. Granted, that had kept Josiah busy for hours, but the meeting had broken up midafternoon. Josiah should have stopped by to see how Fiona was healing and how Rhett and Wyatt were doing.

Brett sure would have. Even with all the women in and out, he'd checked on her several times. He'd also thanked Martha several times. He was very thankful Fiona was here. His heart had nearly dropped to his feet when he saw her shaking so hard back at Nelson's place.

Wyatt stirred and rolled over. Brett quietly pulled the door shut. He then glanced down the hall toward the other bedrooms on the second floor before turning toward the staircase. Fiona was downstairs—in his room. He liked that and wished it could stay that way. If things were different...

Maybe that was what he needed to do. Make things be different.

Brett followed the hallway to the stairs and was halfway down when he paused at the sound of women's voices. Martha was talking to someone, but it wasn't Fiona.

He discovered who when he stepped into the kitchen.

"Oh, Brett, there you are," Martha said. "Joyce is here now. She'll spend the night with Mrs. Goldberg. I've already explained everything to her."

"Mrs. Chadwick," Brett said in greeting. He didn't know the woman well, but her husband, Chester, worked at the hardware store and filled in as a deputy whenever Sheriff Baniff needed one. Chester also was a member of the town council. "How are you?"

"I'm fine, Mr. Blackwell, thank you, and do call me Joyce. It is so kind of you to open your home to Mrs. Goldberg and her sons. All of us women appreciate that. It makes our job of taking care of her that much easier." She lifted a basket off the table. "I brought along some quilting to do while Mrs. Goldberg is sleeping, and I promise, I'll be as quiet as a mouse. You won't even know I'm here."

Quiet or not, his house was full, and that was noticeable. "It's right kind of all you ladies to take care of Mrs. Goldberg as you are."

"It's the least we can do," Joyce said. "How Josiah imagined he could sneak a woman into town and keep her hidden is beyond me. He didn't have permission from the council to put her in that house, you know."

"No, I didn't know," Brett answered.

"Of course he didn't," Martha piped in. "And making her and those boys live over there with nothing. Why, he should be ashamed of himself."

"Yes, he should," Joyce agreed. "I plan on telling him so next time I see him."

Brett flinched a bit deep inside on behalf of the mayor. If Josiah thought the men had been hard on him, wait until the women of Oak Grove caught up with him. That could explain why he hadn't stopped to check on Fiona. But if that was the reason, Josiah was even less of a man than Brett had thought. Adversaries should never keep a man from his woman.

As that thought settled deep inside him, a thump sounded on the back porch.

"That's Otis. He's come to walk me home. Will you be a dear and let him know I'll be ready in a few minutes?" Martha asked him. "I just want to introduce Joyce to Fiona."

Brett nodded and made his way to the door. Outside, he visited with Otis for a few minutes about the weather, crops and a few other things that didn't have anything to do with Fiona or Josiah.

Brett remained outside after Otis and Martha left, in order to have a bit of thinking time.

Not that he needed it. He just wasn't sure how comfortable he'd be sleeping with a strange woman in his house. Joyce wasn't exactly a stranger, and she was nice enough, it was just out of the ordinary for him. He certainly didn't feel that way about Fiona being in his house, though.

He was still sitting on the stoop when the door opened some time later. Instantly jumping to his feet, he asked, "Is something wrong?"

"No," Joyce said quietly. "Mrs. Goldberg is sleeping. So are the boys. I just wanted to let you know that I'm going to lie down on the sofa in your parlor. I'll hear if Mrs. Goldberg needs anything."

Brett reached over and held the door open. All his thinking was only making his mind go in circles. "I'll head on up to bed too."

They bid one another good-night and Brett climbed the stairs. After checking on the boys one last time, he entered one of the extra bedrooms. There he pushed his suspenders off his shoulders, removed his shirt and boots, and lay down, expecting sleep to be a long time coming.

Evidently it wasn't, because the next thing he knew, he was pulling himself out of a deep sleep and wondering why. Stars shone outside the window and the house was quiet. He listened carefully to the silence. Something unusual had to have woken him, so he climbed out of bed.

Down the hall he discovered Rhett had

flipped around in the bed, was now lying with his legs across Wyatt. After easing him around, Brett covered them both with the sheet again and then left the room.

The snores he heard walking down the stairs were coming from the parlor. Without glancing into that room, he continued into the kitchen. A muffled grunt had him moving faster toward the closed door of Fiona's room.

He found her sitting on the floor beside the bed. A sheepish smile said she wasn't hurt, so he knelt down. "What happened? Did you fall out of bed?"

"No." She leaned her head against the side of the bed and sighed. "I feel so bad having everyone wait on me. I thought I could do it myself."

Not sure what she meant, Brett reached for her arm. "Let me help you get back in bed."

"No, I think I'll just sit here a little longer."

Concerned, he asked, "Should I go get Doc?"

"No. The throbbing will ease in a minute."

The smart thing to do would be to get her back into bed and go fetch Joyce Chadwick, but he'd been doing what he'd thought was the smart thing a lot lately, and it hadn't all worked out very well, so he sat down beside her instead. "How bad does it hurt?"

"Not that bad. It's just the throbbing." She sighed again. "And the weakness. My leg is numb from the knee down."

"It'll get better soon." He lifted a brow. "If you follow Doc's orders."

The soft moonlight shining through the window made her slight smile appear even more hidden. "Following the doctor's orders is what put me on the floor." She gestured toward her shin. "The wrap came loose and the poultice fell off. I thought I could retrieve it myself."

Noting the bandage tied around her leg, he said, "It appears you did."

"Once I was on the floor."

"I'll go get Mrs. Chadwick." Brett started to push off the floor, but the warmth of her hand grasping his wrist stopped him.

"No. Please don't disturb her. I'll be able to get up in a few minutes."

Understanding all she'd been through, how she'd taken care of herself and her sons during some very rough times, he could see why she didn't like being beholden to anyone. Yet she had to know that there were times when everyone needed help. Not wanting to badger her, he leaned back against the bed and crossed his ankles. "I didn't spend much time in Oak Grove while working for the railroad. The tracks in this area were laid down fast and we moved westward at a steady pace, but this town had a better feeling than many of the others along the line and wasn't anything like the tent cities that followed the tracks. Oak Grove had a solid foundation. I knew it was a place I could call home. As soon as the line reached Denver and my commitment was up, I came back here, built my businesses and haven't regretted it for a moment since."

"I wondered how you ended up here."

"It wasn't my plan," he admitted. "Denver was my destination. I'd heard it was a bustling city and was considering starting a lumber company out there, but I quickly discovered it was already too big for me. Seemed like everyone was a stranger there."

"Settling in new places isn't easy," she whispered thoughtfully.

"No, it's not, and that's why I like Oak Grove. We don't have any strangers. Newcomers become a part of the community the minute they arrive. If they want to, that is."

The back of her head rested against the bed, and keeping it there, she turned slightly to look at him. "I want to become part of the community. I just…well… None of this has turned out like I expected it to."

"That's not your fault." Unable to stop himself from placing blame, he added, "Josiah should have told others of your arrival. If he had, you'd have been welcomed from the moment you stepped off the train."

She turned away from him and stared toward the window. "I'm afraid I've made a mistake, Brett. A big one that I can't change."

The sorrow in her whisper made his chest burn. "Everything can be changed, Fiona."

She shook her head. "Sam," she said heavily. "My husband. Wasn't a bad person. He'd lost jobs before and always found a new one, but after the refinery closed, rather than looking elsewhere for work, he and the Morgan brothers sat around complaining about how Rockefeller had forced the refinery to close. Sam and the Morgan brothers blamed Rockefeller for all their troubles, and that's why they tried to rob the train. They knew he was on it." She pinched her lips together and drew a deep breath.

"I pretended I didn't know that. Said I couldn't imagine why Sam had tried to rob that train. But as soon as I heard he'd done it, I knew why. He and the Morgans had been talking about getting back at Rockefeller for ruining their lives for months."

Brett had heard of John Rockefeller and

how his newly formed Standard Oil Company was forcing small oil refineries out of business across the nation. People needed lamp oil and Rockefeller wanted to be the only one to sell it. Even Abigail White had written an article about it in the newspaper. Telling people to stock up on oil now because the price was sure to go up again. "People don't always think about how their actions affect others," he said quietly.

"No, they don't." After another long sigh, she said, "Sam made so many promises. Things will be different next month, or next year. They never were. That's all Wyatt and Rhett know—broken promises." She closed her eyes and laid a hand against her forehead. "And I'm afraid I'm following in his footsteps."

"How so?"

"I promised them things would be different here. Our lives would be different. But it's not turning out at all like I imagined."

The sob she'd smothered had him twisting toward her. He gently grasped her elbow to remove her hand from her forehead and then wrapped both of his hands around her much smaller one. "You've only been here a few days, and what happened, your getting bit, was an accident. A pure and simple accident that certainly wasn't your fault."

"I'm not talking about the snake bite, Brett."

He'd assumed as much and was inclined to tell her his thoughts on her situation. "Not all the men in Oak Grove are like Josiah, Fiona. Matter of fact, I'd say none are. Most every other man in this town would have done things differently." Broaching what he really wanted to say was harder than he'd thought it would be. "Josiah may have invited you to come here to marry him, and you may have agreed to that, but you have the option of changing your mind."

They were facing each other and the way she was looking at him was making it hard to breathe. And to think. The desire to pull her close and promise her he'd change her life for the better was the strongest he'd ever known.

"May I ask you a question?"

His heart was pounding so hard he barely heard her. Giving his head a quick shake to clear it, he answered, "Of course."

"How many bottles of tonic did you buy from Maggie?"

The question was so strange, it was a moment before his thoughts cleared. "Is your leg hurting that badly?"

"No," she said. "I'm just curious if—"

"If what?"

"If you are a drinking man."

"Not so much," he answered. "I have a beer over at the Wet Your Whistle now and again, but to be honest, I've never even tasted Maggie's tonic. I bought several bottles from her just so I had a reason to talk to her." It was odd how he hadn't realized certain things before. Things he did now. "She's nice and all, but I couldn't see myself being married to her, so I didn't buy any more after that. The bottles were still full when Josiah confiscated them."

Her brows knit together as she frowned. "Josiah confiscated them?"

"Yes. He claimed she couldn't sell them because she didn't have a permit, so he rounded up all the bottles he could that she had sold. Can't say what he did with them. I never asked, but I suspect he destroyed them."

Her fingers squeezed his as she closed her eyes and shook her head.

Sensing she was thinking about Josiah, Brett had to let her know what he thought. "No one would blame you if you didn't marry him. They—"

"I can't go back on my word," she whispered. "I can't. I've told Rhett and Wyatt too many times that a person has to make good on their promises."

"In most instances I'd agree with you," he admitted. "But not in this one. At some time or another we've all made a choice we thought was the right one, only to discover we were wrong. Admitting that is just as important as making good on promises made."

Several things had been happening inside him while they'd been sitting on the floor next to each other, whispering in the dark. Things he'd been ignoring. Not only how his heart drummed so hard it almost hurt to breathe, or how parts of him were fully aware she was wearing little more than a nightgown and he had on only a pair of britches. But it was the sadness in her voice that made him want her to understand she did have a choice to not marry Josiah. No one should ever be forced to do something they didn't want to do.

Still holding her hand, he leaned forward, and though his intent had been to place a small kiss upon her forehead, a stronger desire inside him took over. A blaze of fire shot through his veins as his lips brushed against hers.

She gasped, and just when he'd convinced himself he should pull back, her lips moved against his.

The way they pressed against his was a perfection he'd never experienced. A powerful instinct had him leaning closer, demanding and receiving more. He'd never concentrated so hard on a connection, or the revelations created by a single kiss. Deep inside, he knew this kiss had the ability to change his life.

Her hands were grasping his shoulder and his were holding her waist when their lips parted. She'd been the one to pull back. She then pushed him farther away before she covered her mouth with one hand.

"I—I shouldn't have—"

Not willing to listen to her regrets, Brett said, "I'm going to lift you into bed and then go get Mrs. Chadwick to put on a fresh poultice."

Without giving Fiona a chance to protest, he hoisted her off the floor and gently laid her on the bed, being extra careful to not jostle her leg.

"Brett, I—"

He pressed a finger against her lips. "I'm going to go get Mrs. Chadwick."

Chapter Twelve

The fresh poultice hadn't seemed to cause any additional stinging or throbbing. It may have, but Fiona had simply been beyond feeling it. Her mind and body had been too focused on other things. Like kissing Brett.

How had that happened?

She knew how, and she knew why. Brett was everything she'd been hoping to find in a man. If she didn't know better, she'd say she'd fallen in love with him the moment she'd found him feeding her children.

Which was ridiculous. A person didn't fall in love that fast. Learning to love someone took time. Only, he was just so likable. So easy to like. And so easy to love.

Of its own accord, a smile pulled on her lips as she thought of watching the sunrise with him, and sitting on the floor in the dark whispering to him.

She'd known he wasn't a drinking man and had sensed that even before asking him. The fact Josiah had deliberately lied about that erased her smile.

"How is your leg feeling this morning?"

Having been lost in thought, Fiona pulled her gaze off the window and turned to the man standing in the doorway. "Much better, thank you, Dr. Graham."

"That's good," he replied while setting his bag on the foot of the bed. "I just ran into Martha. She said to tell you she'll be along shortly."

"That is kind of her," Fiona said, "but I'm sure I won't need to be waited on today. The boys and I will go back to the other house."

"Not yet, you won't. That leg may feel better while you're lying down, but that will change if you try to put any weight on it. I've seen plenty of snake bites and, take my word, you need to stay right here for at least a couple more days." Pulling back the sheet, he started to untie the bandage holding the poultice in place. "How did you sleep last night?"

Before Fiona could answer, Mrs. Chadwick, who'd followed the doctor into the room, said, "I didn't hear a peep out of her all night. I changed the poultice around two or three, but she slept right through it."

Fiona hadn't slept through it but had pretended to. She'd feared Brett had returned with Mrs. Chadwick and hadn't wanted to face him. In four days she was to marry another man, and that had her stomach churning worse than the bitter medicine had made it yesterday.

"That's good to hear," the doctor said. "The first night is usually the roughest."

"She slept like a baby," Mrs. Chadwick insisted. "I'll be more than happy to come back tonight."

"Oh, I'm sure that won't be necessary," Fiona said. Another night of sleeping in Brett's house had her heart racing. "Really, I won't need—"

"Now don't talk nonsense," Mrs. Chadwick said. "Martha will be here today, Maggie this evening, and I'll be back tonight. We have it all scheduled. There are others who want to help too. Martha will see to scheduling them in for an hour or so."

"Yes, I will," Martha said, poking her head in the doorway while removing the calico bonnet covering her red curls. "You must have already fed Brett and the boys, Joyce, I saw them as I walked past the feed store."

"Brett was up with the sun," Mrs. Chadwick

replied. "And those boys weren't far behind him. They didn't want to wake Fiona, so Brett took them all down to the hotel for breakfast."

"That's Brett," Martha said. "I do declare there isn't a more generous man in this town. Some woman's gonna be mighty lucky to marry him." Martha stopped next to the bed. "You too, Dr. Graham. You'll make a fine husband. Why, this town is just full of men who will make good husbands, isn't it, Joyce?"

Nodding, Mrs. Chadwick agreed, "Most certainly. Less one or two of course."

"Of course," Martha agreed. "But one bad apple doesn't spoil the whole crop."

The undercurrent between the two women was so obvious Fiona would have had to be unconscious to not feel it, or to understand who they were talking about. She'd tried to explain to Brett that she didn't have a choice when it came to marrying Josiah. She'd not only given her word, the man had paid good hard-earned money for her and Wyatt's and Rhett's train fares.

Furthermore, admitting a mistake wasn't the same thing as going back on your word. Mistakes could be fixed, but going back on your word couldn't.

And so she wouldn't.

Even if her heart wasn't in it as deeply as it should be.

She'd have to fix that.

Learn to love Josiah.

The sinking feeling inside her said that would be hard. Very hard.

Her mind continued to bounce about, causing the little voices inside her head to keep talking until they gave her a headache. Upon discovering that, the doctor insisted she take a few more teaspoons of the bitter medicine.

Joyce Chadwick left at the same time the doctor did, and Martha, who it was impossible to say no to, insisted Fiona put on a fresh nightgown. One Martha had brought with her this morning, claiming it was a gift.

The gown was sky blue with layers of white lace sewn onto the neckline, cuffs and hem.

"It's too lovely to sleep in," Fiona said.

"That's what I thought," Martha said, "which is why I want you to have it. You'll be receiving plenty of company today."

"Company? Who?" The thought was enough to make her throat go dry. Lying in bed, whether dressed in the beautiful nightgown or not, was not how Fiona wanted to greet company.

"Members of the quilting club will be stopping by on and off today. I'm setting up a schedule of who will assist in your care for the next week."

"I—I'm sure I won't need care for that long," Fiona insisted.

"Yes, you will," Martha replied matter-of-factly. "Some are bringing meals. Others have volunteered to wash bedding and such. Everyone wants to help. That's how it is around here. I've brought along some tea to serve while you're meeting the ladies. There's not a one of them you won't like. I promise." At the doorway, she ordered, "Now you rest up, you hear?"

Despite all her misgivings and the guilt swimming about inside her stomach, Fiona had to smile. If all the women in Oak Grove were similar to the ones she'd met so far, she would indeed like them.

Fiona's mind was about to settle in on that thought and what that might mean, when a knock sounded. The murmur of voices said Martha had answered the back door, and Fiona smoothed the bed covers and the lovely blue gown in preparation of meeting another woman from the quilting club.

The disappointment that knotted her stomach when the bedroom door opened had her questioning her ability to do several things. Including not losing her temper.

Red-faced and pulling his suit jacket across his chest, Josiah stomped into the room. "I would have provided you with a washtub if you'd said you needed one."

Thrown by his statement, Fiona didn't have a response. Except to realize learning to love him would come a close second to learning to love the snake that bit her.

"Now, Josiah," a tall and slender woman said. "I'm sure Mrs. Goldberg isn't worried about a washtub."

The woman's voice was so high-pitched it made Fiona's spine quiver.

"I'm sure she's sorry she didn't ask for your assistance. Everyone in town knows you are always more than happy to oblige when asked." The woman's features were as narrow and thin as she was, including the fingers on the hand she held out. "I'm Abigail White. My brother, Teddy, and I own the *Oak Grove Gazette*. I write all the articles for the newspaper and Teddy prints it."

Fiona shook the woman's hand, which was oddly cold in comparison to the temperature of the room. "Hello."

The woman then pulled the pencil out from

behind her ear. "I'm here to write a story about you."

"Me? Whatever for?" Fiona asked with a good amount of fear settling into her stomach. She was too full of secrets, of things she didn't even want to admit to herself, to talk to any reporter. The ones who'd written about Sam—all over Ohio—had cast very unfavorable images of anyone who had been related to the robbers.

"Because a snake bite is a serious accident," Josiah said. "Readers need to be informed."

"Oh," Fiona said while nerves still danced in her stomach. "Well, there's not much to tell."

Abigail poised her pencil over the top of a pad of paper. "It's my understanding you and Brett Blackwell were at the river when it happened."

"No," Fiona said. "My sons and I were at the river. They were playing in the grass and I was washing clothes. The snake—"

"Where was Mr. Blackwell?"

"I don't know," Fiona answered. "I heard him shout out a warning just before I was bit. He hadn't been there until then."

"What happened then?"

The memory made her heart skip several beats, which made her uncomfortable thinking about explaining how Brett had picked her up and carried her, therefore Fiona simply said, "He took me to the doctor's house. I'm sorry, but it all happened so fast, it's a bit fuzzy in my mind, but the snake was in the wat—"

"So Mr. Blackwell could have been at the river with you and you don't remember?"

"Abigail," Martha said, walking into the room. "I don't believe people care if Brett was there before she got bit or not. We are all just glad he got her to the doctor's house in time. Which is what your article should focus on. How people should respond after being bit. Dr. Graham can answer that better than either I or Mrs. Goldberg, but in his absence, I will state the best action is to seek his assistance immediately. One of the snake's fangs had broken off in Mrs. Goldberg's leg and needed to be removed. He then set a poultice on the injury to draw out the poison. We have changed that poultice regularly and will continue to do so until the doctor advises otherwise. You can quote me on that."

The sneer Abigail gave Martha was chilling. The one she settled on Fiona wasn't any warmer. "I'm assuming you are being well taken care of by the people of Oak Grove."

"Yes," Fiona answered. "I'm overwhelmed by their generosity."

"And why is that?" Abigail asked. "Did you not have any friends back in Ohio?"

Once again, Fiona was speechless.

Martha, however, had plenty to say. "How many friends she had back in Ohio is none of your business, Abigail. It has nothing to do with a rattlesnake bite." Grabbing the reporter by the arm, Martha continued, "I've made tea, which I was going to offer you a cup of, but considering you have all the information you need, I'm sure you'll want to get back to your newspaper office to write the story."

Abigail twisted against Martha's hold. "Why did you insist upon being brought here, Mrs. Goldberg, to Mr. Blackwell's house?"

"She didn't," Martha said, pulling Abigail toward the door. "I insisted. Just as I'm insisting you leave now. I've told you before that poking your nose where it doesn't belong is going to get you in trouble."

Once she had the woman over the threshold, Martha reached back and closed the door. Their exchange could still be heard but was hushed enough that Fiona couldn't make out the words.

She didn't need to. The beauty of the sky

blue gown she wore seemed to suddenly become stained with a bright red *A*. Fiona had to swallow the lump that formed in her throat as Josiah stepped closer to the bed. She'd sat on the floor beside Brett last night in nothing but a thin nightgown, yet she felt far more exposed now than she had then.

The image of him, of his bare chest, that formed in her mind didn't help the inner guilt assaulting her.

"You've created quite a scandal, Fiona," Josiah said.

She'd willingly accept her own shame, put that blame on herself, but she wasn't about to let him overlook his responsibility for what had happened. "Do you think I don't know that?" she asked. "Do you think any of this is what I wanted? Well, if you do, let me tell you how wrong you are. I expected to come here and be welcomed by the man who had invited me. Invited me and my sons to move here and become his family. That's what I expected, Josiah. Instead, we were shunned by that very man. You may not see it that way, but I do. You acted as if you didn't want anyone to know why I'm here. Why? Why would you invite us here and then act as if you were ashamed of us? I didn't lie. I didn't pretend to be someone I'm not."

He sighed and with a plop sat down in the chair beside the bed. "No, you didn't."

Flustered, she had one more point to make. "You knew what you were getting. That we were penniless. Yet you behave as though we are too big of an embarrassment for you to own up to." That was exactly how she felt, and that was also one of the reasons she'd wanted to leave Ohio so badly.

"I apologize if that is how I have made you feel," he said.

She couldn't help but notice how humbled he appeared with his head hung low. Another splattering of guilt filled her stomach. She didn't want to demean him. Knowing how that felt, she'd never want to impose that upon someone else. "I'm sorry, Josiah. I don't mean to put all the blame on you, but to be honest, I'm not sure what to do. If you've changed your mind about marrying me, just tell me. I'll figure out a way to reimburse you for the train fare. Figure out something for the boys and me. I—I just can't keep doing this—living as if it's all a farce."

"I can't either," he said. "None of this is how I'd planned things."

"Then what is?" she asked, sensing his frustration might be as thick as hers. "What did you want? What *do* you want?"

He stood and walked to the window, looking out through the opening with his back to her. Fiona held her breath. A part of her, a large part, wanted him to say he didn't want to marry her. That was wrong. She shouldn't feel that way. But couldn't deny she did.

"I want a wife, Fiona," he said. "I need a wife. A politician, a businessman, should be married. That's why I encouraged the Betterment Committee to bring marriageable women to Oak Grove. I instantly recognized that none of the five women who arrived would be suitable for me, but then your letter arrived. A widow with two children. That seemed perfect."

"Until you met us," she said.

He turned about, and for the first time, honesty seemed to fill his eyes. "No. I'm sorry if it appears that way, and I understand that it might. I am ashamed of how I handled things. And I realize that is just an excuse. The truth is, I started having doubts before you arrived. I'd even hoped you'd changed your mind."

"Why? What had happened?"

"A whole lot of nothing and everything put together, my dear."

As odd as it was, his endearment didn't irritate her. He was clearly distressed and sorrowful.

He paced the floor between the bed and the window. "The other brides caused a bit of a fiasco. Especially the McCary sisters. Neither one of them married men who had contributed to the cause. The men did in the end, but that upset the others, and they blamed me. To be honest, I didn't know if all five of those girls would be getting married as they'd agreed or not. People were pounding on my door at all hours of the day and night, wondering what I was going to do about it. I had half a notion to scrap the entire idea, except I had five women in town, over two dozen men vying to marry them and an acquaintance back in Ohio scrounging up more to send out here."

She thought of Brett, of him vying to marry one of those women, and she thought of what he'd said last night, that we all make mistakes.

"I'd had every intention of putting you and the boys up in the hotel like the town had the rest of the women, but that morning before you arrived, before the others got married, I got scared. I knew your arrival was going to start the ruckus all over again, and I just wasn't ready for that. So before the weddings, I hauled the extra bed that was in the back room at my house—I slept down there more often than I did upstairs in the summer—over to the house the town built. It wasn't right, but I thought I could hide you there for a few days. Only until things calmed down. It was foolish thinking on my part. An eligible bride in Oak Grove is more sought after than money or gold."

He'd stopped near the edge of her bed. "So, you see, it's nothing you've done. It is truly all my fault, and it's something I need to correct."

"How?"

"I can start by no longer pointing a finger at you for every little thing, can't I?"

He was acting so sincere, so kind, she could see that underneath his pompous attitude, he was human. A man who had made a mistake and was genuinely sorry for it. "Yes, you could," she agreed, "but will it help?"

"It will help you."

"I won't pretend that your attitude or behavior has made me like you very much."

He chuckled. "It shouldn't have." Patting her hand, he said, "I am sorry for the way I've acted."

Being a touch skeptical after all that had happened, and having heard that the men had demanded a meeting yesterday, she asked, "Did the town council point all this out to you?"

"Some of it, yes, but some I've known since you arrived." He crossed the room and then pulled the chair closer to the bed before he sat back down. "And some I didn't realize until I heard Abigail question you. I'm afraid I let my frustration out on her this morning. Tried pointing the blame at you and Brett."

Fiona's heart shot into her throat so fast. She almost choked and held her breath to keep from coughing. Yet she knew she had to ask one more thing. "Why did you tell me Brett was a drinking man when he's clearly not?"

He shook his head. "Fear again. That is my only excuse. I've known Brett Blackwell for years, and he is a good man. Well respected. I owe him an apology too." He sighed. "Brett had purchased several bottles of Maggie Miller's tonic. Her sister, Mary, was brewing it out at Steve Putnam's place and Maggie was selling it. I can't even begin to tell you what sort of problems that was causing. As the mayor, I had to put a stop to it. And I did. I confiscated all the bottles and dumped them in the river. But having Maggie arrested—"

"You arrested Maggie?" Fiona hadn't meant to interrupt him, but the idea of Maggie being arrested was unfathomable.

"I didn't. The sheriff did. She was selling her tonic without a permit. Things are different out here than they are back east. A town needs law and order. If not, it'll fill up with ruffians pretty quick. Some people don't understand how much work, how much time and effort, it takes to make sure Oak Grove remains the solid, respectable town we've created. I take my job as mayor very seriously."

Coming from a place that wasn't as friendly or generous as Oak Grove, she had to admire his dedication. It was honorable and dissolved many of the misgivings she'd unjustly labeled him with.

Leaning forward, Josiah took a hold of her hand. "I do still want to marry you, Fiona."

It was as if a waterfall of disappointment washed over her. "You do?" Despite all he'd said, or perhaps because of it, she'd thought he'd say he couldn't marry her. An outlaw's widow.

"That is the reason I invited you here. I've already spoken to Connor Flaherty, and he's agreed to perform the ceremony this Saturday. And upon speaking with Jackson Miller, I've decided the attic of my place will not be suitable for the boys to sleep in, so I will make arrangements to purchase the house next door and have the furniture from my house moved there—"

Fiona pulled her hand out of his as the idea

of living next door to Brett for the rest of her life hit her. "No!" The startled look on Josiah's face had her saying, "I mean, won't that be extremely expensive?"

"Don't worry about that," he said, taking a hold of her hand again. "A man needs to take care of his family. That's what you and Wyatt and Red are. My family."

"Rhett," she corrected and then repeated something Rhett has said over a dozen times the past couple of days. "It rhymes with *Brett*."

"Rhett." Josiah laughed and shook his head. "I thought he said it rhymed with *bread*. Well, I won't make that mistake again. I'm afraid I wasn't listening any clearer than I was thinking. I do apologize for that too." Squeezing her hand, he asked, "You do accept my apologies, don't you, Fiona?"

Her throat constricted so tight, she couldn't speak, or even nod.

Chapter Thirteen

Brett hadn't gotten much work done. He'd been too busy watching his house, and counting the number of people going in and out. They were all familiar, mostly ladies from Martha's quilting club. Abigail White had entered too, but she'd left soon afterward. Josiah hadn't. He'd been there for over an hour before leaving.

A number of thoughts as to what might have transpired between Josiah and Fiona crossed his mind, but not a one stayed put. If Fiona had told Josiah she didn't want to get married, the mayor would have stomped right over to the blacksmith shop.

He hadn't. When Josiah had finally left, he seemed in good spirits and had merely waved while walking past. Brett had returned the gesture. Only because he had to. There was no one else in the vicinity that Josiah could have been waving at.

Brett had ventured to the house then, to question Fiona, but hadn't made it past Martha, who had been rolling out dough on the kitchen table and said Fiona was resting. He'd considered coming up with an excuse to go into the bedroom, but something in Martha's eyes, a knowing glint, had said that was exactly what she'd expected. Therefore, he'd simply said he needed the shovel out of the shed and left again.

He had enough shovels at the feed store, but in light of the excuse he'd come up with, he'd gotten one out of his shed, taken it back to the shop and sharpened the end of it. It had needed that. And standing at the workbench had given him a direct view of his house.

"Quite a pickle, wouldn't you say?"

Setting down his sharpening file, Brett stood the shovel next to the bench before turning around. "What are you doing here?" he asked Teddy. "I'd think you'd be cranking on that old press of yours, getting out the news about the meeting yesterday."

"So you heard what happened?"

"From just about every bachelor in town." The feed store had been packed with men first thing this morning, but nothing that had been said had been news to him. Wally had filled him in on how the meeting had gone yesterday. Josiah had stuck to his story, that Fiona wasn't one of the brides brought to town for the Betterment Committee and that, being the mayor, he'd made an executive decision about letting her stay in the house. There had been lots of grumbles and arguments, but according to Wally, it had all remained peaceful and had broken up with no real changes made about much of anything.

"Josiah says the wedding will be this Saturday," Teddy said. "I confirmed that with Reverend Flaherty of course. I can't have any misprints."

"Did you confirm it with F—Mrs. Goldberg?" Brett asked.

"No." Teddy had crossed the room and leaned one hip against the workbench. "How long is she going to be at your house?"

"I don't know," Brett answered, tossing a log into his firebox just for something to do. "Until she's healed. Martha Taylor has women lined up to take care of her day and night for the next several days."

"And that puts you in a pickle, doesn't it?"

"Why do you keep saying that? I'm not the

one in a pickle. I've got plenty of room." He was trying to sound dismissive about the entire situation and hoped Teddy wouldn't see through that.

"Because…" Teddy said, stretching the word out much longer than necessary.

"Because…" Brett copied his friend but also shrugged.

"Don't tell me you've forgotten."

Brett hoisted his leather apron over his head. "Forgotten what?"

"That your new wife is due to arrive soon," Teddy said. "Could be tomorrow, could be the next day. Could be…"

Brett stopped listening as his insides turned cold. He hadn't forgotten. Pulling enough air into his lungs to fill a set of bellows, he silently cursed himself. When he'd sent that telegram, he'd thought any woman could become a wife. His wife. He knew differently now.

"*Midweek* means—"

"I know what *midweek* means," he told Teddy.

"Think she'll like another woman staying in your house?"

As his gaze settled on Teddy, an understanding formed. The excitement in Teddy's face was there for a reason. "You're hoping she won't," Brett said.

Teddy shrugged. "An unmarried woman in this town will make several men happy."

"Including you."

"I asked you to have your mother send two. You said no."

Brett was wishing he'd said no to one. That was a secret he needed to keep. "Hand me that poker, will you?" After Teddy did and Brett had stirred the coals into flames, he said, "I'm sure she'll understand once she hears the circumstances. Besides, with so many women at my house, she can move right in."

"Damn," Teddy muttered. "I didn't think of that."

"That, my friend," Brett said with a grin, "is why your sister writes the newspaper and you only print it."

Teddy laughed. "Could be. Abigail says I never think things through."

"I never thought I'd agree with your sister on anything."

"You heading over to the hotel for lunch?"

"No," Brett answered. "Martha said she'll have lunch ready by noon. I do have to go collect Rhett and Wyatt soon. They're over there playing with Rollie's boys. Let me finish this brake handle I'm repairing for Jules and I'll walk with you."

"Good enough," Teddy said. "I'll go visit with Wally for a few minutes."

It didn't take Brett long to straighten out the handle and pound it back in shape, then he dipped it in water and set it aside to cool. All the while, his mind had been making full circles. From Fiona to Hannah Olsen and back again. Teddy was right. It was a pickle. And not a sweet one.

That conclusion didn't help at all. How could he go from having no wife to having two? One he wanted to marry and one he'd promised to marry. That was the gist of it. He wanted to marry Fiona and had to find a way to make that happen.

A short time later as they walked toward the hotel, Teddy, who obviously had been researching the subject, explained how many days a train ride from Wisconsin should take, given the variable routes. Brett knew how long it should take. He'd traveled there and back a couple of time over the years. By his calculation, and Teddy's, Hannah could very well arrive on the train tomorrow. That was, if she got on the train on Monday morning. Thursday if she didn't get on the train until this morning.

That didn't give him much time. Along with everything else circling his mind this morning, he'd decided to talk to Hannah about marrying one of the other men in town. Teddy was an option. He was a good guy. But then there was Abigail. Brett couldn't imagine she'd be very welcoming to any woman Teddy took up with.

Brett collected the boys, and not even their chatter about how much fun they'd had playing with Kade and Wiley could get his mind off the situation at hand. Not marrying Hannah would upset his mother, and that didn't settle inside him any better than everything else.

Seeing the grass stains on Rhett's and Wyatt's pants and the dirt on their faces made him think even more of his mother. And theirs.

Stopping at the well in his yard, Brett told the boys to wash up before going into the house. They did so without complaint, which didn't surprise him. Fiona had done a good job teaching them to mind their manners and listen when spoken to.

It didn't surprise him to see Otis in his kitchen either. The barbershop always closed over the lunch hour and it was his wife cooking lunch for the lot of them.

"I remembered what good eaters you boys are," Martha said as they entered the house. "I made enough chicken and dumplings to fill you up clear to your eyeballs."

The boys laughed at that, and then Wyatt grew serious. "How's Ma doing, Mrs. Taylor?"

Martha grinned as she walked over to kneel down in front of Wyatt. "She's doing mighty fine, young man. Mighty fine. You can run on in and see her before we sit down to eat if you'd like."

"Thank you, ma'am," Wyatt said, sounding like he was seventeen instead of seven. "We will. But we won't stay long enough to tire her out."

"You go on ahead, then," Martha said, patting his head before she stood up. "That woman has done a right fine job with those boys. But that doesn't surprise me none. She's a hard worker."

"Worker?" Brett glanced at the door. "She should be resting."

"Don't go getting all flustered, Brett," Martha said. "She's been in bed all day. Since I knew I'd be here all day, I brought along some sewing and Fiona insisted upon helping me." Martha walked to the stove while continuing, "She's sewing the lace on the new dress I'm making for Patty Owens. It's a secret, though, so don't tell anyone. Gayle Owens asked me to make it for Patty for her birthday. It's a replica of the one Charlotte Larson bought for her daughter Violet while in Denver last month. I'm sure you saw it. Violet wore it to the weddings last Saturday."

Brett hadn't noticed any dress on any of the women at the weddings on Saturday. He'd been too focused on not being one of the grooms. He didn't have that problem now. A tiny tingle coiled itself around the base of his neck, in the exact spot his mother would take a hold of when she wanted him to listen to what she had to say. It had almost always been important, and over the years, he'd come to admit that her advice while gasping his neck had been good, something he'd needed to hear.

He should have remembered that on Saturday. His mother had always told him to be careful of what he prayed for in case, someday, he got what he asked for and it turned out to be more than he'd bargained for, more than he was ready for.

His gaze returned to the bedroom as his spine stiffened. One kiss didn't mean Fiona wanted to marry him, but he sincerely wished it did.

"How those two girls, Patty and Violet, can be best friends is beyond me," Martha was saying as she elbowed him aside to set plates around the table. "They're as different as toads and frogs. This will be Patty's first party dress, a long one. All the way to the floor." Martha slapped his shoulder and then gestured toward the bedroom. "Go on, take a look yourself. And tell those boys I'm about to put the food on the table."

Brett crossed the room but stopped just outside the doorway. Rhett had climbed up on the bed and sat with his arm around Fiona's neck. Wyatt stood at the side of the bed, listening intently to whatever she was saying.

Brett hadn't seen her since last night, when he'd kissed her, and for a moment he couldn't move. She was by far the prettiest woman he'd ever seen. Smiling and speaking softly to her boys, her face glowed and her eyes shone, and his heart started drumming all over again. He was looking at exactly what he wanted. Not just a wife. Not just a family. Love. That was what he'd been missing since leaving home, and that was what he longed for.

"Hey, Brett," Rhett said. "Ma said we could ride Hickory and Birch, so long as it's all right with you."

He stepped into the room. "I wouldn't have offered if it wasn't all right." His eyes shifted to Fiona, and he hoped she felt that same way. That she wouldn't have kissed him back last night if it hadn't been all right.

She closed her eyes for a moment and licked her lips before she told the boys to go eat lunch while it was hot. As Rhett climbed down, she said, "You too, Mr. Blackwell, go eat while it's hot."

"I will," he said, ruffling first Wyatt's and then Rhett's hair as they walked past him. "First I want to know why you're sewing when you should be sleeping."

"Because I slept all night," she said.

He knew that wasn't true yet nodded. "How's the leg?"

"Hardly hurts," she said. "We'll be out of your hair in no time. I promise."

"You aren't in my hair," he insisted quietly while stepping up beside her bed.

She glanced around, almost as if she didn't want to look at him. "Well, I feel as if we are."

"You sure seem to have a lot of feelings about things," he said. "And none of them are good ones."

The click of the door made them both glance that way. Glad Martha had thought of giving them some privacy, Brett continued, "Why is that?"

Not meeting his gaze, she said, "Perhaps because they're the only feelings I've known for a long time."

"Then isn't it time you changed that?"

"We can't all be like you, Brett," she said. "Every woman who's walked into this room today has told me how kind and generous you are. What a big heart you have. How you've helped them out, one way or another, at one time or another."

"What's wrong with that?"

The frown on her face could have been laughable, if she didn't look so mad.

"There were over half a dozen of them," she said.

He knew that. He'd watched them all come and go. "Life gets tough sometimes. A person needs a helping hand. I don't mind helping anyone out. That doesn't make me any better than anyone else. Especially those women. They're doing the exact same thing, and none of that is cause to make you angry."

"I'm not angry," she protested.

"Could've fooled me."

She leaned her head back and took a deep breath. "Why do you have to be so kind? So—so happy?"

"Well, if a person can't learn to be happy, can't learn to laugh at things when they go wrong, they aren't going to amount to much. They might very well end up lying around feeling sorry for themselves."

She sat up straighter. "I'm not lying around feeling sorry for myself."

"I didn't say you were. I said a person might be if—"

"I heard you," she said. Then with a sheepish grin that reminded him of Wyatt, she added, "And I'm not angry. I'm just frustrated."

"Want to tell me why?"

"No." She shook her head. "I can't."

"Can't or won't?"

"In this case, there isn't any difference."

He could accept that, but only because he'd already figured out what was bothering her. "Josiah came by to see you."

She nodded.

"If he said something to—"

"He didn't," she interrupted. "Well, he did, but it wasn't bad. He said he's buying the house next door from the city and that we'll all move in there on Saturday after we get married."

The flare of anger that assaulted his insides shocked him. "You don't have to marry him, Fiona. You have other choices."

"No, I don't, Brett." She wouldn't look at him again. "I made a promise and I'll keep it."

He'd never been in this predicament before. It was as if he was trapped. Having seven brothers, he'd fought for what he wanted before, and would again. However, it wasn't the strength of his arms he had to use. Leaning forward, he lifted her chin so she had to look at him.

"Do you know what I want to do right now?"

"What?" she asked quietly.

"Kiss you. Kiss you long and hard. Kiss you so you'll understand that the promise you made to Josiah isn't what you truly want."

She closed her eyes and swallowed visibly before saying, "It doesn't matter what I want, Brett. I have to stay true to my word."

He leaned closer, ready to do just what he'd said he wanted to, but she pressed her fingers against his lips. "Please don't, Brett. Please. And please don't be angry with Josiah either. We've talked. He's sorry about how he's treated me and the boys. He's a busy man. Taking care of so many, the entire town… I understand that. Understand why he wasn't able to be as welcoming as I wanted him to be. We're going to…"

Anger filled him so completely, Brett stopped listening and spun around. The door opened just as he reached for the knob.

"Your lunch is getting cold," Martha said.

"I'm not hungry," he said flatly.

The worry in the two sets of little boy's eyes that landed on him put a good dousing on his anger.

"It's really good," Rhett said pleadingly.

Stopping next to their chairs, he said, "I'm sure it is. I have to get back to the shop so Wally can go eat. I'll see you two over there later."

"Do you want to take a plate with you?" Otis asked.

Brett shook his head and then headed out the door. Whatever yarn Josiah had spun around Fiona had taken hold. As impossible as that seemed. She should be smarter than to fall for his lies.

Brett stopped long enough to swing around and stare at the house the town had built. There weren't more than fifty yards between that house and his. There was no way in hell he was going to let her move in there with Josiah. No way in hell he was going to let her marry Josiah.

Spinning back around, he started forward.

The best way to meet trouble was head-on, and being that it was noon, that meant the meeting would take place at the hotel. Where Josiah always took lunch.

Chapter Fourteen

She'd shed more than a bucket of tears since Sam died, and at least that many long before then, but none of them had been like the ones burning her cheeks now. This time it was as if her heart was breaking in two. Which was not only impossible, it was ludicrous.

There was no way she was in love with Brett. No way asking him not to kiss her could hurt her so deeply. The only sane reason for her condition was the snake bite. She must be so full of poisonous venom, she was going insane. Becoming a lunatic.

A lunatic who couldn't stop crying.

Or stop feeling. The moment she'd heard the back door open, she'd known Brett had arrived home for lunch, and though she'd known Rhett and Wyatt would be with him, it had been the sound of his voice that had sent her heart racing. The sight of him standing in the doorway had taken her breath away. He'd stopped there, watching her talk to her sons, and she'd had to force herself not to look at him.

She'd also tried not to remember how glorious it had been to kiss him. She'd kissed Sam a hundred times over, and never once had her insides gone so soft and warm she'd thought she was melting from the inside out. But that was what had happened last night.

It had to have been the venom inside her. Because, even now, hours later, those sensations were still there, and every time she thought of Brett, she craved his touch. His lips. Even while fully understanding that he was mad at her.

Her mind, being under the influence of rattlesnake poison, was trying to justify how easy it would be to break her promise to Josiah. How tempting it was to tell the boys that she wasn't going to marry Josiah, but Brett instead.

They'd be overjoyed. They worshipped Brett and he would certainly be a father they could be proud of. One who would teach them right from wrong, praise them and even punish them when they did wrong. Which she doubted would happen very often because they would want to make him happy. She saw that already and could appreciate it.

So what was holding her back? Her conscience? Her stubbornness? That deep-down bottom-of-the-gut reasoning that she could be wrong about Brett? Because he seemed so wonderful now, but so had Sam in the beginning. With Josiah, she knew what she was getting. He'd already explained everything to her clearly and simply. Assured her there would be no more surprises.

A life without surprises would be awfully dull.

Good heavens, what was wrong with her? Josiah had apologized. She'd accepted it.

But only on the surface. Deep down, she didn't want to like him. And that was a serious problem.

"Knock, knock," Martha said while opening the door. "Feeling better?"

Fiona wiped the moisture off her cheeks with both hands. "I don't know what's wrong with me, Martha. I truly don't. I'm not prone to crying, and yet..."

Martha set the tray she carried on the dresser and then dipped a cloth in the water basin next to it. After wringing out the water, she carried the cloth across the room. "Here, wash your face—it'll make you feel a bit better."

Fiona washed her face and her neck and hands before handing the cloth back. "I don't know that I've ever been more confused. It must be the rattlesnake venom."

Martha hung the cloth on the edge of the basin before picking up the tray again. Crossing the room, she shrugged. "I don't rightly know. It very well could be. I've never been bitten by a rattlesnake, but I have been bitten by other things."

"Like what?" Fiona asked as she shifted her legs while Martha set the tray on her lap.

"Oh, the occasional bee sting, other bugs, flies and mosquitoes." Martha nodded to the tray as she sat down in the chair beside the bed. "A rabbit."

"A rabbit?"

"Yes. Right on the tip of this finger. It got infected, so my father scraped it clear down to the bone. The tip has been numb ever since. Which is a blessing for a seamstress. I've never needed a thimble."

Fiona grinned as she picked up the spoon. "How do you do that? How do you find the good in everything?"

"Because I want to. I don't want to be sad.

I don't want to be miserable. No one does."
Martha's green eyes took on a watery sheen
as she said, "I told you our Beth was only fifteen months old when she died?"

Fiona nodded.

"It was a fire. Early in the morning. We
lived with Otis's parents. He and I were down
in the barn milking cows when the fire started.
It could have been a lamp, it could have been
the fireplace, we don't know. By the time we
smelled the smoke, the whole house was in
flames. None of them got out. Not his mother,
his father or Beth. We found all three of them
in the front parlor, almost to the door."

Unable to eat after hearing that tragic tale,
Fiona set her spoon down. "Oh, Martha."

"I'm not telling you this to make you sad,"
Martha said, wiping a cheek. "I'm telling you
because, one, you are a friend, and sometimes
it's good to talk about things, no matter how
badly it hurts, and two, because I want you to
know, that even though I miss them, will miss
them forever, I don't dwell on losing them. I
don't dwell on them being in heaven while I'm
still on earth. I remember the times I had with
them, and the months I spent carrying our little Millie inside me, next to my heart where
she too lives on along with Beth and all the

other loved ones I've lost. We have to go on, not despite our losses and pains, but because of them. They've made us stronger, wiser, and, more important, made us not take things for granted. Tomorrow holds no promises, today is where we are."

Smiling, Martha shook her head. "I know that sounds like a bunch of gibberish, but it's not. We aren't the same people today that we were yesterday. We're a bit older. A bit wiser. What seemed like a good idea can be looked back upon as a foolish mistake, or one of the most amazing things that ever happened to us. Trouble is, we won't know which it is until tomorrow."

It was Fiona's turn to smile. "I'm trying to make sense of that."

"Me too," Martha said. "But it's true, isn't it? It happens to everyone. What we thought we wanted one day isn't what we want the next. But it would be a dull world if everyone did the exact same thing today that they did yesterday simply because they were afraid to try something else. There would be no new inventions. No new people to meet. No new recipes to try."

Fiona nodded. "That would certainly be dull."

"We don't like being hurt," Martha said.

"Being wronged. Or wrong. But we can't stop living today because of yesterday. The most wonderful part is, we have that choice. Everyone makes mistakes, but the happiest people learn from them and go on. They don't let their mistakes consume them. They admit their failures or shortcomings and say, I won't do that again. So to answer your original question from before I started babbling, I find the good in things because I want to. I want to be happy. Regardless of the losses we've shared, I want Otis and me to laugh, to have fun and, most important, to not be afraid to love. Just like the good book says, that's the most important thing. Love. No one should go without that. No one."

Fiona picked up the spoon again as Martha's words settled in her mind. There was a lesson in Martha's ramblings, she was sure of it, and she probably would have grasped it if her mind hadn't kept wandering to Brett. Once again, she attempted to blame her scattered thoughts on the rattlesnake bite, for surely Martha's words meant she should accept Sam's death and move on, but she and the boys were already here, so there was no reason for Martha to tell her that. And there was no way Martha could know that marrying Josiah seemed like a terrible mistake or that she'd fallen in love with…

A shiver zipped up her spine as Fiona turned to look at Martha. The shiver crossed her shoulders and consumed her entire body as a knowing smile appeared on the other woman's face.

Going with her gut instinct, Fiona asked, "How did you know?"

Martha clapped her hands together as she giggled. "How did I know? I may be married and love my husband dearly, but I'm still a woman." She held up one hand. "Josiah Melbourne." She held up the other hand. "Or Brett Blackwell." The hand she'd fictionally put Josiah into fell back to her side, while the other one, representing Brett, rose even higher. "It's a pretty easy choice."

Fiona had to laugh at Martha's antics. And then groan.

"Oh, Martha, what am I going to do? I've given my word to Josiah."

"And the president promised there would be no more Indian attacks." She huffed. "Granted, he's a politician, so his promises are meant to be broken right from the start."

A battle continued on inside Fiona. "But it's not right to break a promise."

"What's not right is that you made a promise before you met either man. You had no idea what to expect."

"Neither did Josiah."

"That's right, and please believe me, if he thought it wouldn't suit him, he wouldn't think twice about not marrying you. I'm not saying that's right, but I am saying this is one of those times when people will completely understand."

Fiona still wasn't convinced and shook her head. "It's not other people, Martha. It's me. Deep inside I know it's wrong not to keep my word to someone when I've given it."

"Because others have broken promises to you."

"Yes. Practically from the day I was born."

"So you've vowed to never break one."

"I can't. I just can't."

Martha nodded. "Because you don't want to hurt anyone the way you've been hurt."

"Yes," Fiona admitted. "My father promised he'd come back from the war and didn't. My mother promised we'd be fine—we weren't. She died. My aunt and uncle promised to take care of me." She shook her head. "They couldn't wait for me to leave. My husband—" Having already said enough, she ended with "died."

"There is this thing about being hurt," Martha said gently. "It teaches us how to forgive. Let me ask you something. Which one do you think will be easier for Rhett and Wyatt to forgive you for—your telling them that you made a mistake, or making them accept Josiah Melbourne as their father?"

Fiona knew that answer yet wasn't sure she should admit it. "Josiah's trying," she persevered. "He apologized."

"I'm sure he did. Half the town is mad about what he's done." Martha shrugged. "He's done a lot of good things for this town, and can be friendly at times, but I definitely wouldn't want him being the father of my children. And I sure as heck wouldn't want to sleep next to him at night."

Fiona gulped. She didn't either. "Oh, Martha, what am I going to do? The wedding is this Saturday."

Martha shook her head. "You, my dear friend, will not be allowed out of this bed by Saturday. I personally guarantee that."

Excitement had started to build inside Fiona, as well as determination. "Thank you, but I can't do that. I can't pretend to be ill."

"You aren't pretending," Martha insisted. "It may seem like a little bite, but your leg is still swollen to twice the size it should be, and it could very well still be that way come Saturday."

Fiona's thoughts had grown so much clearer. She had forgiven others in the past. Her parents. Her aunt and uncle. Their promises hadn't been broken on purpose. Not even Sam's had. It was time she forgave herself. Admitted her mistakes and didn't let them hold her back. A smile formed as she told Martha, "Brett is a good man."

"One of the best."

Her heart sank. "Who was very mad at me when he left."

"That man can't stay away from you for more than a few hours at a time. A nod in the right direction from you and he's going to be putting horseshoes on upside down." Martha waved her arms in a clumsy fashion. "Poor horses won't know if they are coming or going."

Fiona laughed so loud she covered her mouth with both hands. "Oh, Martha, I've never met anyone quite like you."

"Good. That's how it should be, because I've never met anyone like you either." Jumping to her feet, Martha grasped the tray. "I'll go warm this up, and this time I'm going to leave you alone so you'll eat it."

"Thank you," Fiona said, meaning it with

all her heart. "I don't recall a time when I've been so full of joy, so happy."

"I tend to do that to people." With a wink, Martha carried the tray out the door.

Fiona leaned her head against the pillow and drew in a deep breath, filling her lungs as full as her heart was feeling right now. She couldn't wait to talk to Brett. To explain she'd been wrong. Of course she'd have to talk to Josiah too. That wouldn't be easy, but not much in her life had been easy.

Up until now.

It was only going to get better too. She knew it. Just knew it.

Chapter Fifteen

⟶⟶⟶⟶⟶⟶

Brett had found Josiah at the hotel, but his anger had taken a good dousing when Josiah apologized before Brett had even opened his mouth. Josiah's long-winded apology had gone on…claiming Fiona was exactly what this town needed. How her life up until now hadn't been easy and he would make sure that changed. The whole town would.

Unable to deny any of it, Brett had been searching for something to say when Wayne Stevens, the depot agent, had approached him. It appeared his new wife had broken the key off in the lockbox and Wayne needed it opened before the train arrived.

Brett collected a few tools from his shop, went to the depot and got the box open just as the train whistle sounded.

Stepping out of the depot, he noticed Josiah driving a buggy away from the livery. It was just as well that he hadn't said anything to the mayor. Josiah had seemed sincere, and it certainly wasn't his place to tell Josiah that he couldn't marry Fiona. Not while she kept insisting that she had to marry him.

Rubbing his chin, Brett decided that was what he had to do first. Convince her otherwise.

The whistle sounded again, and Brett huffed out a breath. He didn't have a lot of time either. Things needed to be worked out with Fiona before Hannah arrived. That would make explaining things to Hannah, and eventually his mother, easier.

Easier on him maybe. Hannah was expecting to become his wife. The most he could hope for was that she'd be open to marrying someone else.

That wasn't as simple as he'd once thought it was. The idea of just marrying anyone no longer appealed to him. Perhaps because now he saw past the act to the life that it could turn into. A life full of watching sunrises in the morning and whispering in the dark come nightfall.

Brett returned to his shop but didn't get a whole lot accomplished for the rest of the afternoon. He was glad to lock up when the time came. He owed Fiona an apology for the way he'd left her this afternoon and was ready to give it.

"Supper isn't quite ready," Martha said as he and the boys walked into the house. "I was hoping these young men would visit the barbershop with me to see how much longer Otis will be." Smiling at the boys, she added, "I know where he keeps some peppermint sticks."

The shine that appeared in Rhett and Wyatt's eyes was almost as bright as the one in Martha's.

"You'll keep an eye on Fiona, won't you, Brett?" Martha asked. "We won't be long."

"Sure," he said, glancing at the closed bedroom door.

"I knew you would," Martha said. "Come along, children."

As soon as they shut the door, Brett crossed the room, set upon taking advantage of the chance to speak to Fiona privately.

His rehearsed apology and his explanation of how hard it is to break a promise but that at times it had to be done left his mind as soon as he opened the door. Fiona was sitting up in bed and the gentle, welcoming smile that covered her face had him grasping the door frame to keep himself steady. She was, without a doubt, the most beautiful woman he'd ever seen. Would ever see.

"Hello," she said brightly.

"Feeling better?"

"Yes. And I'm sorry I made you angry earlier."

She hadn't looked away from him and he didn't either. "I'm sorry I got mad earlier. I shouldn't have."

"Yes, you should have," she answered. "I was being stubborn. I can be like that sometimes."

He grinned to make sure she knew he was teasing and winked. "You don't say?"

Her cheeks turned pink as she giggled. "Yes, I say." Shaking her head, she continued, "I—well, nothing was as I expected, and I didn't know what to do about it. I thought I could make it work, thought I had to, when in reality, I should have been willing to admit I was wrong."

"Sometimes that's the hardest part," he said, stepping into the room.

"Yes, it is, or can be." She bit her bottom lip before saying, "I believe you donated to the Betterment Committee in order to obtain a wife."

"Yes."

"Are you still interested in obtaining a wife?"

For a fraction of a moment he wondered if she knew about the telegram he'd sent his mother, but then he noticed her cheeks were turning red. He shrugged and tried to keep his smile from growing too large. "That depends."

"On what?"

"On who is interested in becoming my wife."

She didn't blink or hesitate before saying, "I'm interested."

The excitement that shot through him was like none he'd felt before, yet he contained it while pulling the chair up to the side of her bed. "I thought it would be harder than this. That I'd have to convince you."

"You had me convinced the moment I met you, when you insisted we eat supper with you. And again when you showed me the sunrise. And then the picnic. And then there was that monster fish."

"All of that was before. What changed your mind today?"

She shrugged. "I guess you could call it a reckoning. In this case, I had to weigh out exactly what keeping my word would do, and what not keeping it would do. Rhett and Wyatt already adore you."

Brett took a hold of her hand. "I'm mighty fond of them too, but I want to know about you. Do you want to marry me for yourself, and not just for Rhett and Wyatt?"

She wrapped her other hand around his. "Yes. I want to marry you for me too. I want that more than anything."

Happier than he ever remembered being, Brett wanted to shout to the heavens. He settled for kissing the back of her hand, both hands. "I'll make you happy, Fiona," he vowed. "I swear it."

"I have no doubt you will because you already have," she said quietly. "Just by being you. Your actions, how you live your life, are—well, it's exactly what I'd wished for. Prayed for. I can't wait to become Mrs. Brett Blackwell."

Unable to contain his enthusiasm any longer, Brett did give out a happy whoop and then kissed her.

Immense joy filled Fiona. If there had been any lingering doubts that she wasn't doing the right thing, they completely disappeared when Brett's lips met hers. There was no room inside her for anything but bliss. And pure contentment.

She returned his kiss with an open heart. Kissing him was as natural as the sunrise they'd watched together. As if it was meant to be. Had always been meant to be.

When the perfection of his lips eased off hers, she smiled and sighed. He was exactly what she'd dreamed of finding. "Maybe I should pinch myself," she told him. "To make sure I'm not dreaming."

"Then pinch me too," he said. "Or maybe just kiss me again."

They did kiss again, several times, before he pulled her closer and gave her an enormous and wonderful hug.

He then leaned his forehead against hers. "I promise to be the best husband possible, Fiona, and the best father too."

"I know you will," she answered. "And I promise to be the best wife I can be."

After yet another quick kiss, he sat back down in the chair and took a hold of her hand. "When?" he asked. "When do you want to get married?"

A sliver of regret washed over her. She should have told him she had yet to speak with Josiah, but once she'd made up her mind, she hadn't been able to wait. "I have to speak to Josiah first. I haven't told him that I won't marry him."

The way Brett nodded eased her concern. "Do you want me to talk to him?"

It would be easy to say yes, so she shook her head. "No, I need to do that." With a hint of shame, she asked, "Would you mind if we didn't tell anyone, especially Rhett and Wyatt, until after I talk to Josiah? I owe him that much." She squeezed his hand, truly wanting him to understand. "I planned on telling him first, but I don't know when he'll stop by again, and then I saw you standing in the doorway." She shrugged. "I'd been lying here, hoping you wanted to marry me, but I wasn't sure and I just—"

"I want to marry you, Fiona. I spent most of the day trying to figure out a way to make you see that." He kissed the back of her hand again. "And keeping all this excitement to myself is going to be hard, even for a little while."

"For me too. If I wasn't confined to this bed, I'd walk over and tell Josiah right now."

"You're not getting out of this bed until Doc Graham says you can," Brett said. "Furthermore, I saw Josiah head south in a buggy earlier today and he hasn't come back yet. Leastwise, he hadn't before I left the shop."

Fiona was about to say that Josiah hadn't mentioned anything about going anywhere today when the back door of the house opened. She sighed and leaned back against the pillows, accepting their alone time was over.

For now.

Knowing there would be many more times like today, she couldn't control the smile on her face.

Brett gave her hand a final squeeze before he released it. He stood up and crossed the room but stopped in the doorway to ask, "Who are you?"

Instantly concerned, Fiona sat up, wishing she could see past him.

"It's me... Rhett. Don't you recognize me, Brett?"

"Well, you sound the same," he said. "You best come in here and see if your ma recognizes you."

Even more concerned, Fiona leaned toward the edge of the bed. "What's happened?"

The way Brett glanced over his shoulder and winked eased her concern but increased her curiosity. Rhett was the first through the doorway, closely followed by Wyatt. Their hair had been trimmed and was parted down the side and slicked back. They both looked adorable.

"Hey, Ma."

"Well, hello, young man." Following how Brett had reacted, she said, "What is your name? You sound like my son Rhett, but you don't look like him. And who is that with you?"

Wyatt laughed while Rhett frowned as they walked closer. "It's us, Ma. Me and Wyatt. Mr. Taylor cut our hair."

Enjoying the game, she pressed her hands to her chest. "Well, my goodness, it is you. Just more handsome than I remember."

Brett picked up Rhett and set him down on the bed beside her. "They're so handsome, I hardly recognized them," Brett said.

"Mr. Taylor even put shaving cream on our faces," Rhett said, preening as he turned his face for her to see both sides.

"I declare," she said. "It shines likes it's been freshly shaved." She hooked a finger beneath Wyatt's chin and examined his face. "Yours too. I don't believe I've ever seen two more handsome young men."

"He didn't really shave our faces," Wyatt said. "He just let us know how it will feel when we're old enough and need that done."

"I suspect that's something it's good to get

used to," she said, seeing how much they'd enjoyed the experience. Her heart couldn't grow more full. The entire town of Oak Grove was proving to be exactly what she'd hoped to find.

"That's what Mr. Taylor said," Wyatt explained. "He said it won't be long and we'll be regular customers, just like Brett."

"I'm sure it won't be long at all," she answered while her mind was thinking about how excited they'd be to learn she was marrying Brett instead of Josiah. They would be happier than she'd seen them in ages. Perhaps ever. It was hard not to tell them right now, and the shine on Brett's face said he knew exactly what she was thinking.

Never silent for long, Rhett started telling her about his day. How he'd played with the Austin boys all morning and then ridden Brett's horses in the afternoon. Fiona listened and asked questions, all the while taking note of how Brett had sat down and lifted Wyatt onto his lap. Her older son had plenty to say too. Good things. Events he was excited about. They'd changed over the last few days. Had gone from solemn and silent to happy and excited. She knew exactly why and she'd forever be grateful to Brett.

It wasn't long before Martha entered the

room, carrying a tray. "I have your momma's supper here and yours is on the table," Martha told the boys. "Run on into the kitchen and sit down so we can all eat before it gets cold."

After Brett and the boys left the room, Fiona reached out to take the tray from Martha.

"I believe I see an extra sparkle in your eyes," Martha whispered.

Fiona bit her lip as she set the tray on her lap but then couldn't help but whisper back, "He said yes."

"Of course he did." Martha laughed quietly. "Did you expect differently?"

Fiona shrugged. "I hoped not."

"I knew not," Martha replied before she turned about. While walking toward the door, she said loudly, "Eat up. We'll have you up and about in no time."

Fiona ate and found herself wishing she was already healed. Or that the snake had never bitten her. But if that hadn't happened, she wouldn't have been brought here. Everything would be different. Or back to how it had been, with her planning on marrying Josiah instead of Brett. Smiling, she gratefully accepted the fact she was glad to have been bitten by that snake.

Maggie and Jackson Miller arrived as

soon as supper was done. Martha and Otis left shortly afterward, with Martha insisting she'd be back in the morning. Maggie had brought along a pie that the men and boys enjoyed while she removed the poultice on Fiona's leg.

"Doc had to go see to a patient," Maggie explained, "but before he left, he told me we can now just put a damp cloth on your leg to ease the swelling and to tell you he'll be over tomorrow. He went out to the Baker place. They're expecting a baby any day now."

"I sincerely appreciate everything that everyone is doing for me," Fiona said. "I just hope I can someday repay you all."

"Your friendship is all the repayment we want," Maggie said. She sighed then and shook her head while draping a cloth over the snake bite. "I've never seen a town like Oak Grove, and trust me, I've seen a lot of towns. My sister, Mary, and I traveled a lot. Our da was a traveling man. And I assumed this place would be like so many others. Where strangers weren't welcomed. I was wrong. I've only been here a little over a month and truly can't imagine living anywhere else. You'll feel that way soon too."

"I already do," Fiona admitted.

"Good." Maggie gently replaced the sheet. "I can't wait for you to meet Mary, my sister. We're twins."

"I heard that." Unable to imagine two women being as beautiful as Maggie, Fiona asked, "Do you look alike?"

"Most people think we look exactly alike, but not Jackson. He claims I'm prettier." She giggled while gathering the discarded poultice and bandage. "Mary says Steve says she's prettier. That's how love is. I know there isn't a man more handsome than Jackson in my eyes. Or one who is more loving or generous. Two months ago, I would never have imagined I'd have a husband who treats me like a queen." She shrugged and her blue eyes twinkled as she said, "I always thought of myself as a queen but didn't truly believe I'd ever find a king like Jackson. He's so wonderful and amazing and, well, he's everything to me. He's driving me out to see Mary this weekend—" She held up a hand. "I just thought of something."

Maggie's face had lit up even brighter, while a chill rushed over Fiona. Josiah had probably told others they were to get married this weekend.

"Mary has two pet raccoons. They are still

babies and so adorable—I'm sure Rhett and Wyatt would love to see them. Would you allow them to ride with Jackson and me out to the Circle P? We'd keep a close eye on them."

Taken aback by the request, Fiona said, "That's kind of you to offer, but—"

"Please?" Maggie said. "They are such good boys, and I know Mary wouldn't mind."

"Thank you," Fiona said. "But maybe Jackson wants to be alone with you. You are newly married."

If possible, Maggie's smile grew as her blue eyes glowed with happiness. "Yes, we are, and it's wonderful. But we won't be alone. Angus is going with us. He wants to see the raccoons, and he told me to tell you hello. So two more won't be a problem. Please say yes. And please let me ask them. I want them to know they are welcome in Oak Grove too."

"Oh, dear," Fiona said. "You make saying no impossible."

Maggie laughed. "Jackson says the same thing." Holding up the items she'd gathered, she added, "I'm going to get rid of this stuff. The boys are outside with the men, so I'll ask them about Saturday. Do you need anything when I come back? A piece of pie?"

"Thank you, but no, I'm still full from supper," Fiona answered. "Lying around doesn't work up an appetite."

"I'll be back in a little bit, then." She stopped at the doorway. "It is all right that I ask the boys, isn't it? I can tell them they have your permission to go?"

"Yes," Fiona answered. "You can ask them and tell them they have my permission."

"Thank you."

Fiona laughed as Maggie scurried out the door. My, how her life had changed since yesterday morning.

"Hey, there."

She twisted toward the open window. Brett was bent down so he could rest his arms on the sill in order to poke his head through the opening. "Hey, there yourself," she replied.

"So Rhett and Wyatt are going to the Circle P on Saturday?" he asked.

Fiona laughed. "Were you eavesdropping?"

"No. Playing hide-and-seek and just happened to hide under the window."

She couldn't remember hearing of a grown man playing hide-and-seek, but if there was one who would, it was Brett. "Who's it?"

"Rhett. He's looking for Wyatt, who's hiding under the front steps."

"What about Jackson?" she asked, assuming he was still there.

"He's behind the shed." An excited squeal had Brett pulling his head out. "Gotta go!"

Fiona laughed aloud. She truly couldn't believe she could be more happy. Closing her eyes, she said a quick prayer of thanks and then laughed again at the squeals of delight coming in through the window.

Chapter Sixteen

Brett couldn't remember a time he'd been so antsy. He couldn't stop his toe from tapping the floor or the tips of his fingers from drumming together. Joyce Chadwick had arrived shortly before dark and he could still hear her moving around downstairs. It had to have been more than an hour since he'd said he was going to bed and come upstairs.

If not more. Rhett and Wyatt were sound asleep. He'd checked on them twice.

Fiona was probably asleep too. He'd let her sleep if she was. He just wanted to see her one more time before he crawled into bed. But he didn't dare sneak downstairs until he knew Joyce was asleep in the parlor.

He hadn't thought about sneaking around after dark for years and years. Back then it usually had been to snatch something to munch on out of his mother's kitchen.

Pushing off the bed, he walked to the window. The big yellow moon filling the night sky hadn't moved much since the last time he'd looked out, and he smiled at his own impatience.

And his happiness. He almost couldn't believe Fiona would soon be his wife. He could look far and wide and not find a finer woman anywhere. Or a prettier one. The way her eyes changed colors amazed him. They could be gray one minute and hold an entire rainbow of colors the next. He's seen that this evening when she'd agreed to marry him.

That was what he wanted to talk to her about, if she was still awake. He needed to tell her about Hannah Olsen. Fiona already had enough on her mind, having to admit to Josiah that she wouldn't be marrying him, yet not telling her about Hannah would be wrong. He didn't want her to think he wasn't being completely honest with her.

He'd reassure Fiona that as soon as Hannah arrived, he'd apologize and tell her that he couldn't marry her, and that he'd help her find someone else more suitable. Or pay for her passage back home or somewhere else. Whatever she wanted. Hannah might have changed her mind too. That was always a possibility. Which could be reason enough to wait before talking to Fiona about it, he pondered. There was no sense bringing up something that might never happen.

There was no sense standing here either.

Brett made his way down the hall and the staircase. Joyce was stretched out on the couch in the parlor. He couldn't tell if she was sleeping or not and decided he didn't care.

A few steps later, the moonlight shining in the bedroom revealed Fiona definitely wasn't sleeping.

"Not tired?" he asked while shutting the door behind him.

She shrugged. "I haven't done anything to make me tired."

He picked up the bottle Dr. Graham had left with Martha yesterday off the top of the dresser.

"I don't want any more of that," she said.

"Don't blame you." He put the bottle down again. "But it does help with the pain."

"There isn't a lot of pain anymore. It's just uncomfortable because it's still so swollen."

"Anything I can get for you to help with that?"

"No, but thank you for offering. Joyce put a cool cloth on it earlier, so it's not so bad right now. What are you doing still up?"

He sat in the chair next to her bed. "Not tired either."

"To hear Rhett and Wyatt talk, you should be as tired as them."

"They were asleep as soon as their heads hit the pillows," he said.

"I can believe that."

The softness of her voice, whispering with her in the dark like this, made him smile.

"It was kind of Maggie to offer to take them out to see her sister," she said. "To see the baby raccoons. They're very excited at the prospect."

"They'll enjoy it," he agreed. "And you have nothing to worry about. Steve Putnam owns the Circle P. He's a good man. So is Jackson. They'll all keep a close eye on Wyatt and Rhett."

"I have no reason to believe otherwise," she said. "The entire town of Oak Grove is full of good people."

A tinge of guilt splattered his insides, and Brett sighed. "I have something to tell you, Fiona. It's nothing bad, just something I think you should know."

She shifted, pushed herself up in the bed. "Did the boys do something?"

"No, the boys haven't done anything."

"Then what is it?" she asked.

"You know I've been looking for a bride for

a while, that I contributed to the Betterment Committee?"

"Yes."

This was more uncomfortable than he'd thought it would be. He stood and walked to the window. "Well, when all of those brides chose others and I had doubts whether Josiah's plan would bring any more to town, I sent a telegram back home and ordered one for myself."

"A bride?"

He turned around. The muted darkness obscured the expression on her face, but he could tell she was looking at him. "Yes. She could be arriving any day. Or she might have changed her mind—I can't say for sure."

"What do you mean? Didn't you exchange letters?"

"No, I wired my mother and asked her to find someone. She wired back saying I should expect someone to arrive this week." He crossed the room and sat down in the chair again. "It doesn't change anything between me and you. I'm going to tell her I can't marry her. That I'm marrying you instead."

Fiona's heart was sinking faster than a rock tossed in a pond. Her happiness had been short-lived, yet the loss was one of the greatest she'd ever known.

"I'll tell her as soon as she arrives, and I'll help her find a suitable husband or pay her way back home or—"

Shaking her head, Fiona had to force herself to say, "You can't do that."

"I know it doesn't sound very nice," he said, taking a hold of her hand. "But I've thought about it. Long and hard. I can't marry her."

Though it hurt, Fiona had to point out the facts. "She's coming all the way out here expecting to marry you."

"I'll help her find someone else. Someone who will want to marry her, and whom she'll want to marry. I promise."

Fiona's throat burned. Compared to him, the other men in town didn't hold a candle, and wouldn't to this other woman either.

"When Mary McCary arrived, she didn't plan on marrying Steve," Brett said, "but that's who she married. Same with Maggie, who married Jackson. Neither Steve nor Jackson had donated to the Betterment Committee."

She wanted to pull her hand out of his, but it was as if her muscles wouldn't work. "That doesn't matter. She's coming here intending to marry you—"

"You came here to marry Josiah."

"That's differ—" She couldn't finish the sentence. It really wasn't different. If he was wrong, so was she.

"I can't marry someone else, Fiona," he whispered fervently. "Not when I love you."

Her insides buckled. She loved him too. Had already admitted that to herself. It was amazing how fast it had happened. Unbelievably fast. She figured it was because he was exactly what she'd dreamed would happen. That she'd find a man she could love. One Rhett and Wyatt could love too. She'd let herself believe she deserved that. Deserved to be happy.

"I wasn't going to tell you," he said. "Thought I'd just wait and see if she even showed up, but in case she does, I wanted you to know about it. Wanted you to know that I will always be honest with you."

Fiona wanted to tell him she wished he hadn't said anything. Then she could go on believing in her short-lived happiness. Go on believing that for once in her life things were happening just as they were supposed to. Maybe they were. Maybe she wasn't ever supposed to be happy. Truly happy.

"No one else knows," he said. "Other than Teddy White."

Fiona bit her lips together, wishing she could come up with something to say. The only thoughts racing around in her head were ones she didn't want to say. Ones she didn't want to hear or believe. She was comparing Brett with Josiah again. Despite all that had happened, Josiah had fulfilled his promise. He'd offered to marry her and was fully prepared to do just that.

She couldn't help but think about this other bride, of her hopes and dreams and how devastating it would be to arrive only to be told the man who'd invited her to Oak Grove was marrying someone else.

Fiona pulled her hand out of Brett's and scooted down in the bed. "I'm tired. I need to rest."

It was a lie. She might never rest again. Her entire being felt broken. Right down to her soul. She couldn't knowingly crush someone else's dream, not while realizing exactly what that felt like.

His silence filled the room for several long moments before he whispered, "All right."

The warmth and softness of his lips touching her forehead was almost her undoing. Willing every muscle to remain still, Fiona held her breath and squeezed her eyelids together more tightly to combat the tears.

"Good night," he murmured.

She didn't trust her voice to work. Once the door was shut, she let out a shaking breath and then let the tears fall.

When the sun finally rose, Fiona wondered if that had been the longest night of her life. She'd contemplated many things while lying there, staring into the darkness. Her life. Her sons. Brett. Josiah.

Staying up all night hadn't done any good. None whatsoever. Neither was trying to convince herself that she could still marry Brett. It was all her fault. Hungry or not, she should never have agreed to have supper with him that first night.

The anger inside her grew so ugly and consuming she couldn't stay in the bed any longer. She needed a way to release it.

Tossing aside the covers, she flipped her legs over the edge of the bed, and not really caring how badly it might hurt, she stood. The first step sent a river of pain all the way to her hip, but she ignored it—the best she could—and took another. By the time she arrived at the window, the throbbing was so intense, she stuck her head out the opening and sucked in air, praying for a way to ease the pain.

"What are you doing out of bed?"

"I can't lie around any longer," Fiona growled against the pain to answer Joyce's question.

The woman grasped her arm. "But your leg's still too swollen and walking will only make it worse."

"I can't—" She had to suck in more air to continue. "I just can't."

As sweet and kind as all the others, Joyce said, "I know it's hard, but it'll be harder if you don't let that leg heal properly."

Fiona refused to move, even turning to look at the other woman was beyond her.

Joyce left her side, but only for a moment.

"Here, the chair is right behind you," Joyce said. "Let me help you sit down."

With few options, since her good leg was trembling as badly as the injured one, Fiona sat.

"Stay right there," Joyce instructed. "I'll be right back."

Fiona leaned her head back and closed her eyes to block out some of the pain in her leg. What was in her heart might never ease. Which was all her own fault. She wouldn't be hurting, wouldn't be disappointed, if she'd used some common sense the past few days. Making a mistake was one thing, as was breaking a promise, but she wouldn't shatter someone else's dream. Couldn't. That had happened to her too many times.

"Here," Joyce said as she arrived. "I have a stool and a pillow. Let's prop that leg up on it and I'll get a cool cloth. It's hard to be laid up. No one likes it."

Fiona didn't trust herself to speak.

The understanding smile on the other woman's face slowly dissolved. "Goodness, you look like you haven't slept a wink. Why didn't you wake me?"

With renewed tears threatening to fall, Fiona just shook her head.

"I'll send Brett for Dr. Graham and—"

Fiona grabbed Joyce's arm. "No, I'll—"

"I'm already on my way."

Fiona covered her face with both hands at the sound of Brett's voice.

Brett ran at full speed to Nelson Graham's house. Why hadn't he asked Fiona what was wrong last night? He'd assumed she'd grown quiet after he'd told her about Hannah because she was upset—the one thing he hadn't wanted to happen. He hadn't thought that her leg might be hurting. Might be full of infection.

He was almost to the stoop when Nelson opened the door.

"What's wrong?" the doctor asked. "I saw you coming out my kitchen window."

"It's Fiona," Brett answered abruptly. "She's hurting. Been up all night."

"I'll get my bag," Nelson said, already heading into his examining room.

Moments later when they started toward his house, Brett wanted to fling Nelson over his shoulder and run as fast as he had earlier. The man was full of questions. None of which Brett could answer.

"I don't know. Maybe she tried walking and fell again."

"Again? When did she fall?"

"Night before last. She tried getting out of bed without help."

"I declare, Brett, a sick woman is worse than a sick man. They just can't stay down. No matter how much I insist."

"What's happened?" Martha asked as she ran across the field. "Is it Fiona?"

"Yes," Brett answered.

"Well, hurry," Martha said, passing them both as she ran toward his house. "Hurry, I say."

Both he and Nelson picked up their speed and Joyce met all three of them at the door. While the others asked questions, Brett brushed past and hurried into the bedroom. Fiona was sitting in the chair and didn't appear to be injured or hurting. Relief washed over him as he walked closer.

"What happened? Did you fall again?"

She shook her head.

He knelt down beside her chair. "Then what happened?" he pressed, concerned. There were bags beneath her eyes and no color in her cheeks.

"I just couldn't lie there any longer," she said, turning to look out the window. "There was no need to fetch the doctor. There's nothing he can do. There's nothing anyone can do."

"Yes, there is," he said.

"I can't do it," she whispered. "I can't take someone else's husband."

Brett's stomach fell. "I'm not—"

"She believes you are."

"Brett," Dr. Graham said from the doorway. "Wait out in the kitchen, please."

It went against his better judgment, but Brett did as Nelson requested. Partially. He walked through the kitchen and out the back door. What he'd seen on Fiona's face gutted him. There was no shine in her eyes. In fact, she appeared to be as sad and dismal as when she'd first arrived in town.

It was all his fault. He wasn't any better than Josiah.

Flustered and needing to release it, Brett headed over to feed his horses. It wasn't long before Nelson found him there.

"She'll be fine," Nelson said. "Once she stops worrying about others taking care of her."

"She's not used to that," Brett explained.

Nelson nodded. "You doing all right?"

"I'm fine," Brett answered, although he knew he might never be fine again.

Nelson laid a hand on his shoulder. "I can't say I envy you, Brett. Going from being a bachelor to having a houseful overnight, but I do admire you."

"No reason to."

"Yes, there is, and I'm not the only one." Taking a step, Nelson added, "I'll be back around noon to check on her."

Brett nodded and walked around the side of his building. The house was too full for any time alone with Fiona, not that it would do any good. He'd seen her eyes.

An hour or so later Maggie Miller stopped at the shop with Rhett and Wyatt in tow.

"Brett, is it all right if Rhett and Wyatt go with Jackson and me to see Mary today? Jackson needs to speak to Steve about a cabinet he's building. Angus is riding with us."

"What did Fiona say?"

"She's sleeping," Rhett said. "Can we go? We'll be good."

Knowing they'd be well watched, Brett said, "I don't see why not."

Rhett wrapped both hands around his leg. "Thanks, Brett. You're the best."

As Brett patted the boy's back, he told himself it wasn't over yet. He'd find a way for them to be together. Fiona and him, and these two little boys. He'd make Fiona see that.

Chapter Seventeen

She'd had a few close friends over the years, but Fiona had never known any quite as dedicated as the ones she'd acquired since arriving in Oak Grove. Especially Martha, who was pacing the room and fluttering her arms.

The commotion that had awoken her earlier had been a heated discussion between Josiah and Martha. One that had ended with Josiah leaving. "Did he say what he wanted?"

"He said he needed to speak to you and I informed him you were sleeping. Which you still would be if he hadn't been so loud." Martha planted both hands on her hips. "He told me it's my fault the town expects him to pay for the house next door. It seems Josiah drove around the township yesterday attempting to get people to sign a decree that he'd written, and no one else had approved, that states the town will give him that house just because he's the mayor. When Otis told me that last night, I put my foot down. That's not why the house was built. Half the people in Oak Grove made donations of money and supplies to build that house with the understanding that once it is sold, the profits will go to build another house, and so forth. Giving this first one to Josiah won't benefit anyone but him."

"Why would he expect the house be given to him?" Fiona asked curiously.

"I don't know," Martha said, "but I can tell you, he's expected an awful lot since he became mayor, and the more he's given, the more he wants."

The regret washing over Fiona was piling up so high, she soon wouldn't be able to breathe. "It's my fault. Josiah said he'd buy it and move his furniture in there before the wedding." Fiona buried her face with both hands. "I've made such a mess. Such a mess for everyone. I should never have come here."

"This isn't your fault. You didn't make a mess."

"Yes, I did. I'm the one who wrote first. I asked Josiah to marry me." Flustered, Fiona placed both hands against her temples. "Then after he agreed, after he paid for me and the boys to come here, I turn around and nearly beg Brett to marry me instead. Now I have Josiah attempting to buy a house he clearly can't afford and Brett ready to send back the bride he ordered."

"Bride? Brett? What bride?"

Fiona slunk farther down into the bed, wishing she could completely disappear.

Brett was in his shop, taking his frustration out on a hunk of iron, when someone slapped him on the back.

"You ready?" Teddy asked.

"Ready for what?"

"To meet your bride," Teddy answered. "By my calculations, she should be on today's train."

Hannah Olsen could very well be on today's train. Brett had already deduced that.

"Figured I should meet her with you," Teddy said. "Make her feel welcome."

"I don't need anyone—" Brett stopped. Maybe Hannah would take one look at Teddy and think he was more to her liking. If she was on this train. There was a chance she wouldn't be.

The chances she was were more likely. His mother would have sent a telegram if Hannah had changed her mind. That was more of a certainty than the sun rising in the east and setting in the west.

"You're going to at least take off your apron, aren't you?" Teddy asked. "You sure don't seem as excited about this as I expected."

Brett removed his apron and swallowed a good ball of guilt as they walked to the train station.

They were on the depot platform when the train rolled in. The metal-on-metal brakes screeched as the wheels were forced to stop rolling and steam hissed out of the smokestack as the fire was dampened down.

"What do you think she'll look like?" Teddy asked, eyes glued to the metal door that had yet to open.

"I don't know," Brett answered. It had been a long time since he'd seen any of the Olsen sisters. Not that it mattered. There wasn't a woman prettier than Fiona in all of this world. Nor one he could ever love. Not like he loved her. Shortly before Teddy had arrived, Dr. Graham had walked past the shop on his way to the house to check on her again. He'd wanted to follow the doctor right into her bedroom, and tell her that together they could work this out.

Teddy let out a slow whistle before he asked, "Is that her?"

Brett glanced toward the train door and the young woman holding on to the metal banister with one hand and a brown tapestry bag with the other. She was tiny with blond curls poking out beneath a flowered bonnet.

Teddy elbowed him. Brett stepped forward.

"Brett Blackwell?" the woman asked.

He nodded. "Hannah Olsen?"

She nodded at the same time as her eyes rolled inside her head.

Brett shot forward and caught her before she hit the stairs.

"I've seen people afraid of your size before," Teddy said, "but I've never seen one faint dead away."

"Grab her bag," Brett said, carrying Hannah into the shade of the depot awning.

"What happened?" Wayne Stevens asked as he hurried out of the depot. "Did she trip on the stairs?"

"I don't think so," Brett said.

"Who is she?" Wayne asked. "Do you know her?"

"She's a friend of my mother's." The answer had come out of nowhere, yet it was the truth and Brett decided to stick with it. "She was scheduled to arrive today for a visit."

Her head was drooped against his shoulder,

and Brett shifted slightly to look upon her face when she let out a little moan. A second later along with another moan, she opened her eyes.

She pressed a hand to her head. "What happened?" Before he could answer, she said to herself, "I must have stood up too fast."

"I'll get Doc," Teddy said.

"Bring her into my office," Wayne said.

Brett shook his head. "Nelson's at my house. I'll take her there."

For the second time in less than a week, Brett found himself carrying a woman to see the doctor.

Hannah was fully awake by the time they arrived, and apologizing and insisting he let her down. Brett didn't need her fainting a second time, so he carried her all the way into his parlor. There he set her down on the couch.

Martha was beside him, asking all sorts of questions, and Nelson wasn't far behind, with just as many questions.

"She's a friend of my mother's," Brett said. "Arrived on the train, but fainted as she was stepping off."

"A friend of your mother's?" Martha asked.

"Yes," Brett answered while looking at Teddy with a glare that said no one needed to know more than that.

"Brett's mother sent a telegram the other day." Looking at Hannah, who was staring at her feet, Teddy added, "And she fainted all right. Right there on the train steps."

"I'm sorry," Hannah said quietly as she lifted her head. "I think I stood up too fast. The train ride made me queasy and—" She slapped a hand over her mouth.

Martha's response was to grab the ash bucket near the fireplace. Brett took a clue from Teddy and headed for the doorway at the sound of Hannah emptying her stomach into the bucket.

"I, uh, got some work to do," Teddy said, rushing toward the back door.

Brett considered following him, but the open door leading into Fiona's room snagged his attention instead and changed the entire direction of his thoughts.

"Are you feeling better?" he asked her, once standing in the doorway.

"I'm fine," she replied dully.

Searching for something else to say, Brett rubbed his chin. "Rhett and Wyatt went out to the Circle P with Maggie and Jackson."

"I know."

He stepped into the room and closed the door. "I didn't have a chance to say anything to her yet."

Fiona shook her head.

"She fainted."

Her expression grew soft and a touch sorrowful. "You can't say anything to her, Brett. She's here to marry you, and that's what needs to happen."

"She's awfully young, Fiona, and isn't a whole lot bigger than Wyatt." He'd been afraid he'd squish her just carrying her to the house. "I think she's sickly."

"Which could be why your mother sent her to you," Fiona said. "Because she needs someone to look after her. Take care of her. That's part of being married too."

He hadn't thought along those lines when thinking he wanted a wife but understood it once Fiona had been bitten. Seeing she was being taken care of had been the easiest thing he'd ever done. Not because Martha had overseen her care and Dr. Graham her recovery, but because in his heart seeing her well cared for had become very important to him right from the start. From that very first night when she and the boys had been so hungry.

"I'm assuming your mother is a lot like you," she said softly. "Willing to help anyone at any time."

He nodded but then shook his head, out of frustration, not denial.

Fiona held a hand out and he took it while sitting down in the chair next to her bed.

"That girl is your responsibility, whether you want her to be or not."

His mind was as cluttered as a log jam, yet she was right. Hannah was his responsibility and he'd take care of her. At the same time, he wanted to take care of Fiona. "We can work this out."

Fiona shook her head. "There's nothing to work out. You'll marry her and I'll marry Josiah."

His frustration hit a new level and Brett shot to his feet. "No."

Fiona's heart was breaking at the same time it was welling with love for this man. He wouldn't be in this predicament if it wasn't for her. She couldn't become his wife. Couldn't expect him to break promises he'd made to other people on account of her. Couldn't shatter dreams. "What's her name?" she asked quietly.

"Hannah Olsen," he said. "Our families have known each other for years. Her family owns a logging company that supplies my family's lumber mill with logs. My oldest brother,

Hue, is married to her sister Gretchen, and another one of my brothers, Norman, is married to her sister Laurel."

"So you've known her for a long time," Fiona supplied, hoping that would ease some of her own pain.

"I can't even say if I've met her before." He sighed heavily and sat back down. "I'm assuming I did, but I never paid much attention to any of them. I was always working. Sharpening saw blades or repairing equipment. Even as a youngster I liked working with metal and knew I'd leave home someday so I could do that. There were a lot of us boys, and Hue and Norman, being the oldest, would be the ones to take over the lumber mill. The rest of us knew that and didn't mind. It was fun talking about where we'd go and what we'd do when the time came. Furthermore, the last thing most of us wanted was to hook up with one of the Olsen girls. Their father is as mean as a bear woken up midwinter. He dang near killed Hue when he and Gretchen were caught kissing."

A good portion of empathy formed inside Fiona for the young woman she had yet to meet. Her father had died long before she'd met Sam, so she had no idea how a father would react to catching his daughter kissing someone.

A knock sounded and Martha opened the door a second later, "Brett, Dr. Graham would like to speak with you."

"How is she?" Fiona asked Martha.

The smile Martha provided looked strained, as did her voice when she said, "Feeling a little better."

Because it had seemed so natural, Fiona had forgotten she was holding Brett's hand until his fingers squeezed hers before he pulled his hand away. She watched him leave the room and considered calling for Martha, but she could see the other woman was busy in the kitchen.

Being confined to the bed had annoyed her all along, but right now she was beyond annoyed. Martha was making too much noise for her to hear any of the conversation that might be taking place in the parlor. It wasn't any of her business, but Fiona wanted to know what was being said.

The clatter that came from the kitchen had Fiona leaning over the edge of the bed. It appeared as if Martha was purposely being as loud as she possibly could. She wasn't slamming cupboard doors, but she wasn't exactly gently closing them either.

"Martha," Fiona said. "Could you come here, please?"

"In a minute, I'm making tea."

Despite the noise, Fiona's ears, tuned in to such sounds from being a mother, picked up on someone crying. Not loud sobs, more of a sad whimpering.

"Martha," she said, this time with more insistence.

The other woman appeared in the doorway. "I can't say anything, so don't ask me to." With a shake of her head, Martha shut the door.

Fiona couldn't say that she'd ever felt more isolated. She flipped the covers back and was lowering one leg to the floor when the door opened.

"Don't you get out of that bed," Martha said. "I mean it."

When the door shut again, Fiona smothered a growl as everything inside her festered up good and tight. Her stomach grew so tied in knots that not even long deep breaths eased the frustration making her insides tremble.

Her ears were still tuned in to what was happening outside of the room. The creaks of the stairs as someone went upstairs and then the muffled sound of people talking in the kitchen aggravated her even more.

When the time came for her to finally get out of this bed, she'd pack up Rhett and Wyatt

and they'd leave town for good. She had no
idea where they would go, but—

The opening of the door stopped her thoughts,
and the sight of Brett had her asking, "Is Hannah all right?" It was odd to speak of the girl
as if she knew her when they'd never even met.

He was ashen and shook his head as he shut
the door and then walked over to the chair beside the bed. She watched his every move, not
realizing she was holding her breath until her
lungs started to burn.

She let the air out and, after refilling her
lungs, merely said, "Brett?"

His elbows were propped on his knees as he
held both sides of his head.

"Brett, talk to me. What's wrong?"

He lifted his head slowly and his eyes were
full of grief as he said, "I'm gonna have to
marry her, Fiona. I have to."

She'd been saying that all along, so the
shower of regret that rained down upon her
was completely unnecessary. "Of course you
are," she said quietly. "You asked her to come
here for that reason."

He sat up and leaned his head against the
back of the chair for a moment before he
looked at her again. "She's pregnant, Fiona.
That little gal is pregnant."

Stunned and at a complete loss of words, it was a few quiet moments before Fiona was able to ask, "Who is the baby's father?"

"His name was Eric Olson," Brett answered.

"Was?"

"He died last month in a log jam in the bay."

Empathy filled her. "Oh, the poor thing. How long had they been married?"

"They hadn't been married," he answered. "Eric Olson was from across the lake, in Minnesota. We called them the Minnesota Olsons and Hannah's family was the Wisconsin Olsens. They both own logging companies. The Minnesota Olsons spell their name with an *o* and the Wisconsin ones with an *e*. That's what they stamped their logs with in order for everyone to know the difference—*o*'s and *e*'s. My father used to say the two families were related at one time, until a feud separated them. And they've been feuding ever since. That's why she's here. When Eric died and his father, and hers, found out she was pregnant, they cast her out. She went to her sister Gretchen, and Hue took her to our mother. Old man Olsen would have found out if she'd stayed there, and who knows what might have happened then. That was on Sunday. My mother arranged for her to get to the train station on Monday without anyone knowing."

As bad as Fiona had thought things were for her, Hannah clearly had it worse. "Oh, Brett, the poor girl."

"Doc says the baby will be here around the end of the year." Brett stood and walked to the window. "That is if she gets her strength back up. She doesn't want to eat because she says nothing stays down."

"She'll need to eat little bits at a time and several times throughout the day," Fiona said. "And drink tea made with ginger. That helped me when I was carrying Wyatt and Rhett."

He turned around and walked back to the chair. After sitting down, he took her hand. "I feel bad for her, Fiona, I sincerely do. I can imagine how mean her father and Eric's father were to her. I've seen those two men go at it. They want to kill each other. It's bad. Really bad."

"That's why your mother sent her to you," Fiona said, "knowing you'd take care of her."

He lifted her hand and kissed the back of it. "I love you, Fiona. I want to marry you, and—"

She pressed a finger to his lips, and although it was heart-wrenching to admit, she said sadly, "It's out of our hands now, Brett."

"No. There are a lot of men, good men, in this town who want a bride and—"

"Stop, Brett." She couldn't take much more. Just couldn't. "You've already said you have to marry her, and you do. You know that as well as I do. Hannah is young and scared, and if she's put under much more pressure, she could lose her baby."

The look on his face told her she'd struck a chord. "Dr. Graham already told you that, didn't he?"

"Yes, that's what he said." He closed his eyes. "He said it could take her life too."

"He's right." She swallowed at the lump in her throat. "Your mother knew all that, and that's why she sent Hannah here. A mother knows her children. Just like I know Rhett and Wyatt, your mother knows you. She knows you'll do right by Hannah. No matter what sacrifices you have to make, you'll do right by her."

Chapter Eighteen

For the first time in his life, his muscles weren't enough. They couldn't carry the load he'd been given. Because this time, the load was inside him. Fiona was right. Hannah Olsen needed to be taken care of, and whether he wanted it or not, he'd been given the job of seeing it happened. A man wasn't much of a man if he turned his back on his duties. He'd never done that before and wasn't about to do it now.

A man didn't begrudge what he'd been chosen to do either. That was something else he'd never done—begrudged anything he'd had to do. Accepting all that, he still wished there was another way.

"How's she doing?"

Brett turned away from the window he'd been staring out of, watching his house for no real reason. Doc Graham had left some time ago. Shortly after Martha had sent him back to his blacksmith shop. "Doc says she'll be fine," he told Teddy. Nelson wasn't one to share his patient's ailments, but Teddy had a way of getting information out of people. Not as cleverly as his sister, but he still could muster up a good story when he wanted to.

"This isn't a story for your paper, Teddy. I don't need—"

"Hey," Teddy said, holding up a hand. "I'm your best friend, remember? I sent the telegram to your mother."

"I know," Brett admitted as guilt sliced across his stomach. "I just, aw, hell, I guess I'm second-guessing the whole notion about being married."

Teddy shook his head. "I don't believe that, not coming from you, not for a minute. There's something else brewing here." Leaning closer he whispered, "And she's in your house."

Brett crossed his arms, a sign most men took to mean that he'd had enough.

Teddy wasn't most men.

"If you're trying to irritate me, you're doing a damn good job."

"I'm not trying to irritate you," Teddy answered. "I'm trying to get you to admit that you like Fiona."

"What good would that do anyone? And why do you care?"

Teddy shrugged. "Because I consider you my best friend, and if you do like Fiona Goldberg, I have some information you might like to know about. And because I'm second in line if you don't want to marry Hannah. You do remember that part of our deal, don't you?"

Homing in on the one thing that mattered, Brett asked, "What information do you have on Fiona?"

"It's not specifically about Fiona," Teddy said.

"What is it?"

Teddy leaned against the workbench. "Josiah spent yesterday visiting folks and asking them to sign a piece of paper stating the town should give him that house we built as part of his salary."

"Why should the town give him that house? If he wants it, he should buy it, just like anyone else would."

"That's what everyone told him, and he's not happy about it." Teddy grinned. "I took it upon myself to do a bit of snooping. Josiah didn't pay for the tickets for Fiona and her sons to come here out of his own pocket. The money came from the Betterment Committee."

"How do you know that?"

"I can't reveal my sources, but I don't doubt it's one hundred percent true." With a shrug, Teddy continued, "I'd say Fiona Goldberg can marry any man who donated to the committee, including you, and there's nothing Josiah can do about it."

There had been a time that news would have elated him. Now it distressed Brett further. Especially as another thought formed. "Who knows about this?"

"You and me, and my source, who I can't divulge."

"Make sure it stays that way," Brett said. He may have accepted Hannah was his responsibility to take care of, but he hadn't completely lost hope of marrying Fiona and he sure as hell didn't need a crowd of others making her offers.

As if the man knew they'd been talking about him, Josiah barreled into the shop. Without a single hello, he spouted out, "What's this I hear about a woman staying at your place, Mr. Blackwell?"

"Which one?" Teddy asked.

"I'm not speaking to you, Mr. White," Josiah said with a glare. "I'm speaking to Mr. Blackwell."

Unaffected, the smile never left Teddy's

face. "Well, in that case, I'll let you two have your conversation." Tipping his flat-brimmed hat, Teddy walked out the door.

"Is there or is there not another woman staying at your place?" Josiah asked. "One who arrived on the noon train?"

"I don't see how that's any of your business," Brett replied. "But I'll tell you this, I donated a large portion of the lumber that went into the house the town built, and I didn't do that in order for you to live there for free." What Teddy had revealed ate away at Brett. If Josiah was mishandling the committee's money, and lying about it, folks around here wouldn't stand for it. If Fiona did end up marrying him, where would that leave her and the boys? Out in the cold, that was where, and he wasn't about to let that happen. Brett pointed a finger at Josiah. "You better get your own business in order before you stick your nose in someone else's."

"My business is in order," Josiah spat. "You're the one sticking his nose in where it doesn't belong. Have been ever since Fiona arrived in town."

"I wouldn't have had to if you'd treated her fairly."

"She's my bride-to-be and I'll treat her as I see fit!"

Brett took a step forward before he stopped himself, realizing his temper could get the best of him this time. Holding back as much as possible, he bellowed, "Get out! Get out before I throw you out so far it'll take you two days to walk back to town."

As Josiah ran for the door, a truth struck Brett like a two-by-four. He couldn't marry two women. Oak Grove was mostly made up of good people, but Josiah would see that poor little Hannah was eaten alive if he found out she was pregnant and unmarried. Fiona was older and stronger, but he couldn't stomach the idea of her marrying Josiah. Truth was, he'd strangle the little pipsqueak before letting that happen.

Brett wasn't in any better of a mood two days later. Fiona was healing quickly, even up and about a little more each day. He was happy about that. It also made him worry that she'd be gone each time he walked in the house. Martha insisted Fiona still had a lot of healing to do, but he knew how stubborn she was.

She'd barely spoken to him. Granted, he'd kept his distance. Seeing her every day and not having a way for things to work out made him feel as if he'd let her down. Broken a promise. If only he could come up with a way to take care of Hannah while marrying Fiona, but try as he might, he couldn't. And for the first time since he'd left home, where he'd had cause every now and again to charge his brothers for something they'd done—not him—he'd started to blame others. Namely Josiah. The mayor had been making noise about Hannah and her arrival, partially because his own hornet's nest was about to explode.

Whoever had been Teddy's informant had a larger circle than just Teddy. The whispers about Josiah spending the Betterment Committee's money for his own good had reached far beyond the outskirts of town. Steve Putnam and his wife, Mary—who was indeed identical to her sister, Maggie, including how happy they appeared with their newfound marriages—had ridden up to the blacksmith shop a short time ago.

Steve had hung around the shop while his wife, along with Maggie, went to see Fiona and Hannah.

That seemed to signal other men to mosey on over, and they did. Two at a time in some cases. Brett was glad that Rhett and Wyatt, along with Rollie's boys, had gone fishing with Joyce Chadwick's son, Charlie. Otherwise the boys would have been playing in the corral and seen the men heading this way like braves on the warpath.

Brett's musings faded as the men crowded around.

"Sounds like Josiah's bit off more than he can chew this time," Steve said after the rounds of greetings and talk of weather and horseflesh had diminished.

"He sure has," Otis said. "The town council is considering impeaching him."

"I didn't think it was that serious," Steve said.

"It is," Rollie Austin said. "We can't have a mayor misappropriating the town's money. Now, I'm happy he came up with the Betterment Committee idea and for the first brides that arrived."

"Of course you are," Jules said. "You married one of them."

"And it's six brides," Don Carlson said. "Don't forget about Fiona Goldberg. He paid for her passage with committee funds."

Brett's jaw tightened as others agreed with Don's statement.

"As I was saying," Rollie continued, "I'm

happy about the brides, but there was a lot more money donated than what it costs to bring in five or six brides. I flat out asked Josiah what he did with the money and he refused to answer me."

"Me too," Otis agreed. "As a member of the council, I requested a statement from the bank for both the committee's account and the town's account. The town's account balances, no monies are missing, but the committee's account has less than fifty dollars in it." Otis pointed toward Steve. "You donated more than that much yourself, Steve."

"I did," Steve said. "And I'd have paid double that. You all remember that when you're looking at my wife. She's mine."

After a round of good-hearted laughter and joking, Wally said, "I heard Josiah gambled it away down in Dodge."

"I heard that too," Bill Orson said. "I'll admit, I've lost a dime or two at the gambling tables, but it's always been my money. Not someone else's."

Brett figured he had more reason than some to be angry at Josiah but couldn't wrap common sense around Josiah being that crooked. It just didn't fit, but something was askew, he couldn't deny that.

"Well, gentlemen," Teddy said, "I believe the question is, what is the town going to do about it? Josiah provided us with half the number of brides he promised. Are we going to hold him to the fire, make him produce the other six?" Looking at Otis, Teddy said, "If you impeach him, that's not going to happen."

"It's not going to happen if Josiah's gambled away all the money either," Jules said.

"I happen to believe Josiah has the money to repay the committee," Teddy said. "The rest of you should too. Don't you read the paper? Josiah's a lawyer for the railroad. Every time there's a notice about a new acquirement of land by the railroad, Josiah processed it, and he gets paid for every transaction. Abigail gets the information for those notices directly from Josiah. I think he doesn't want to spend his own money, that's all. He's like a tree rat, squirreling away his nuts for winter. Well, I say it's about time it freezes in July."

The roar of cheers and agreements nearly rattled the rafters.

"Teddy's right!" someone shouted. "It's time Josiah answers to us!"

Mumbling among themselves and egging each other on, the men started up the street, making a beeline for Josiah's office.

"You joining them?" Steve asked.

"No," Brett answered.

"Don't agree with them?"

"I agree that Josiah needs to pay the money back. I just don't need to be part of that," Brett answered, pointing toward the crowd.

"I've always admired that about you," Steve said. "With your strength and size, you could knock a man out without even trying, yet I've never even seen you throw a punch."

"I learned long ago I don't like seeing people hurt, so why would I want to hurt anyone?" Brett shrugged. "I'd rather put my efforts to good use, work toward something good than fight against something bad."

"Some men live their whole lives and never figure that out, Brett." Steve then tipped his hat. "I have to head over to Jackson's place and look at a cabinet he's building me. If you see my wife leave your house, I'd be obliged if you'd tell her where I went."

"I will," Brett answered. As Steve left, Brett walked to the edge of the lean-to and watched the men barrel into Josiah's office.

It was hard to feel sorry for someone who'd brought so much grief onto himself, but having had plenty of his own recently, he felt a touch sorry for Josiah.

He was still standing there, watching, when someone tapped him on the shoulder. Turning about, he couldn't stop the smile from rising on his face. He'd never forget the first day he'd met this tiny dark-haired woman, or how she'd thrown together a meal for eight hungry men in a matter of minutes. "Hello, Mary. Steve asked me to tell you he went over to Jackson's."

"I guessed as much." Her grin turned a bit sheepish. "I watched him leave. I wanted a chance to talk to you."

"What for?"

"I'll never forget what you did for me," she said. "How you gave me a ride out to the Circle P and stayed, helped me. If not for you, Steve would never have hired me as his cook."

"Oh, yes, he would have," Brett assured her.

She shook her head. "The Steve I know now would have, but that first night, he'd rather have had a rattlesnake in his kitchen." She laid a hand on his arm. "I owe my happiness to you, Brett Blackwell, and I'll never forget that. If there is anything I can do for you, and I mean anything, you let me know."

His cheeks grew a bit warm at her offer. "Thank you, but there isn't anything I need."

Curling a finger, she gestured for him to lean down. When he did, she stood on her tiptoes and kissed his cheek. "Your heart must be as big as you are, Brett."

She might be right about that. The way it dragged along behind him, making him stumble at times, said it had to weigh about as much as he did.

"Opening your house to Fiona and her sons," she said with a sigh, "and then to poor little Hannah. She is so young to be a widow."

What started out as a shiver turned into a warm tingle as it shot up his spine and hit his noggin hard enough to ring a bell. He spun about to take a good long look at his house. Why hadn't he thought of that?

He grabbed Mary by the shoulders, picked her up and planted a quick kiss on her cheek. "Thank you." Setting her back on the ground, he headed for his house with his heart thudding inside his chest right where it belonged.

Chapter Nineteen

"The seed's been planted," Maggie said, holding the curtain aside.

Peering over Maggie's shoulder, Fiona pressed a hand to her chest, where her heart pounded so hard she wondered if she should sit down. The seed had been planted all right, but she had to wonder if it was a bad seed. "I don't know about this."

"Trust me," Maggie said, her blue eyes twinkling. She and her sister were indeed identical twins, and Fiona had taken an instant liking to Mary as much as she had to Maggie. Perhaps even held a bit of envy for these two black-haired women. They were not only beautiful, she could well believe they'd pulled a fast one over on more than one person over the years.

Nothing harmful, she'd bet, simply fair turnabout when needed to even out the odds. Like what was being suggested now. No one would be harmed, and it was a good solution.

She withheld a sigh, wishing she had more of Maggie's gumption.

"And trust Brett," Maggie whispered.

"I do trust him," Fiona admitted. "But—"

"If you want to be treated like a queen, you have to act like one," Maggie said with a wink. "I'll leave out the front door and tell Martha and Hannah that Brett's on his way."

A part of Fiona wanted to grab Maggie's arm and ask her to stay, the other part of her told her not to. That Maggie was right. If she was ever going to get what she wanted, she had to be bold enough to do something in order for it to happen.

She loved Brett. Loved him with all her heart, and wanted to see him happy. To see his eyes light up when he walked through the doorway. These past couple of days, though he was still as big and strong as ever, a part of him had been missing. A part she dearly loved. It had been what made him whole. She could give that back to him. Had to give that back to him. That was how love worked. Both parts gave and received.

A thud sounded on the back step and for a moment Fiona wondered if she'd just been caught in a Kansas tornado. Some claimed those fierce wind twisters popped up out of nowhere, and that was exactly what it felt like. As if she'd been lifted up, twirled around and set back down again so fast her head was still spinning.

Then she started to panic. Brett would walk through the door in a second. Drawing a deep breath, she braced herself. It was time. Time to let go of the past. Time to do things differently in order to secure a better future for herself and the boys.

She was standing next to the table, holding on to it with one hand, when he opened the door. Her heart took a tumble, a wonderful one, at the sight of him. He was smiling.

Then a frown formed as he glanced around. "Where is everyone?"

She swallowed and had to clear the frog from her throat. "Martha and Hannah went for a walk."

He nodded, but his frown remained. "Should she be doing that? Hannah," he clarified. "Shouldn't she be in bed?"

"No, she's already doing much better." Having gotten to know the young woman over the past couple of days, Fiona had already formed a protective feeling for Hannah. The girl had been through so much and was so young. Barely eighteen. "She's managing to keep food down now and the fresh air will do her good."

"What about you? Shouldn't you be in bed, or at least sitting down?"

"No, Dr. Graham was here this morning and said the swelling is almost gone. Thank goodness, I thought I might get frostbite from all the ice Martha kept packing on my leg. That or the hotel would run out of ice."

"Let me see."

This was Brett and he wouldn't take no for answer, so she hoisted the hem of her skirt high enough for him to see her calf. After a few moments of his thorough scrutinizing, she asked, "Satisfied?"

"It does look good." His eyes met hers. "You look good too."

Her breath snagged in her lungs. The shine was back in his eyes. "So do you."

He took her hands, both of them. "We need to talk."

No longer needing the table for support, not with him near, she curled her fingers around his. "Yes, we do."

He shuffled slightly and shook his head as if unsure where to start.

"I've missed you the past couple of days," she said.

He shrugged. "I tried to keep my distance. Seemed like the last few times we've talked, I ended up putting my foot in my mouth and my teeth were getting sore."

She shook her head, trying to hold in a giggle, but it still escaped. He was so…so charming. "You didn't put your foot in your mouth. I'm the one who messed it all up." Letting out a sigh, she said, "There has to be a way we can make this all work, Brett. Work for everyone. I love you. These past couple of days have made me realize that even more."

"I love you too, Fiona." Stepping forward, he let go of her hands to pull her into his arms.

His hug, his solid, strong, wonderful hug, filled her completely, right down to her soul, which came to life, knowing this was where she belonged. Encircled by him, loved by him.

"There is a way, Fiona," he whispered. "If you'll hear me out, I'll try to explain it so it makes sense."

A knock sounded on the door just then. More than a knock. A pounding that wouldn't stop.

Fiona stepped back as Brett turned about and pulled open the door, and a passel of good old-fashioned disgust washed over her as Josiah barreled into the room.

Poking a finger at Brett's chest, Josiah said, "I'm the only one ordering brides around here, Brett Blackwell." He poked Brett again while adding, "The Betterment Committee was my idea, not yours."

The breath Brett took made him look even taller, even broader. "What are you talking about, Josiah?"

Josiah wobbled slightly as he stepped back. "Hannah Olsen. I have it on good authority that you received a telegram informing you of her arrival."

Fiona squeezed her hands into fists. If Josiah learned the truth behind Hannah's arrival and her condition, he'd make the girl's life miserable. Fearing that might be exactly what happened, she scrambled around the table to place herself between the two men. It was time for her to stand on her own two feet. In more ways than one. She was at the base of this mess and it was time she cleaned it up.

Brett, however, had moved, as well. He'd crossed the room and now opened the cupboard. Taking something out, he said, "I did. The telegram's right here. It's says I'm to expect Hannah Olsen midweek. What your 'good authority'—no doubt Abigail White—forgot to mention was that this telegram was from my mother, and that my family has known Hannah all of her life."

Ready to fight for Hannah's secrecy as strongly as she'd fought for her own, Fiona said, "The other thing that Abigail doesn't know is that Eric Olson died last month. Take it from me, until they live through it, no one understands a widow's agony. How all they want to do is get away from it. From the pain. From the misery. From the memories. Brett's mother knew he'd provide Hannah with a safe haven to adjust to Eric's death without everyone reminding her of it on a daily basis."

Josiah frowned and shook his head. "I wasn't aware of that. I— Abigail…" He shrugged but then pulled on the lapels of his jacket. "I should have been informed."

His pompous attitude tugged Fiona's mind in another direction. He was so self-centered, so focused on who he was, that nothing else mattered to him. It blinded him to the point he didn't even see what several others had. That she and Brett had fallen in love.

The hand Brett rested on the small of her back not only filled her with warmth, it filled her with courage. She glanced over at him and the look they shared was full of understanding and support.

Drawing a deep breath to preserve her courage, she turned to face Josiah. "I can't marry you, Josiah. Can't and won't."

"What do you mean you can't?" he spouted, spraying spit. "Yes, you can and you will. You agreed to it."

Fully understanding his ego meant that this had to be about him, not her, she said, "You're a smart man, Josiah." As he nodded, she continued, "You know I'm not the kind of wife a mayor needs. I'd rather go fishing than embroider flowers on napkins in order to impress houseguests."

"Yes, well, you could change," he said.

She bit her lip for a moment. "I could, but I wouldn't expect my sons to. Rhett and Wyatt can get dirty just walking across the street. Little boys are like that. And they like to dig worms and collect bugs, and chase frogs and climb trees. They can be loud and rough, and all that would anger you. And with your busy schedule, you wouldn't have time to see to all the things they'll need while growing up."

He let out a loud sigh and then planted a hand on the table. "I suspect you're right, Fiona. I am extremely busy, and all of that would anger me." As if understanding how shallow he sounded, he added, "Only because I am such a prominent figure and it's expected my family will behave appropriately at all times."

"Exactly," she added and held in a grin at the muffled guffaw behind her. The fact he seemed to agree so readily surprised her, but it shouldn't have. Josiah hadn't truly wanted to marry her right from the start, she'd just been too stubborn to accept that. Or to focus on making it not happen. "I am sorry, Josiah, and will find a way to repay you the money it cost—"

"You don't owe him anything," Brett said. "The Betterment Committee paid for your train tickets out here. Didn't it, Josiah?"

Josiah plopped down on the nearest chair. "Yes, but I was willing to reimburse the committee if it all turned out." With a smirk, he added, "As you see, it didn't. So I was smart not to use my own money." He then held up a hand. "Before you ask, let me reassure you, just like I did every other man in town a short time ago, I did not gamble away any of the town's money, or the committee's. My contact in Ohio requested more money. It seems brides are harder to come by than we first thought. Shortly before Fiona contacted me, I'd sent Alfred Winsted—he's the mayor of Bridgeport, Ohio, and we grew up together—the rest of the committee's money, except for fifty dollars, which we needed to keep here for any additional expenses that might arise. When Fiona agreed to come, I told Alfred to pay for her passage out of that money." Pulling on the lapel of his suit coat, he added, "But there will be six more brides, Alfred guarantees it."

The hand Brett had on her back slid around to her side as he stepped closer beside her. "Six more?" he asked.

"Yes, we'll get the full dozen," Josiah said. "I gave my word to this community, and I'll see that it happens."

"Make it seven," Brett said, looking down at her. "I'll reimburse the committee for Fiona's passage."

"Why would you want to do that?" Josiah asked.

"Because I'm marrying her," Brett said.

Fiona was afraid her heart would beat right out of her chest. Or that she might turn around and beg Brett to kiss her, right here in front of Josiah.

"What about that other gal you brought to town?" Josiah asked. "Don't you plan on marrying her?"

Brett shook his head while his eyes never left hers. "Hannah doesn't need a husband, not right now, she just needs some looking after. Fiona and I will do that."

If possible, her love for him grew tenfold. She nodded, letting him know she was in full agreement. And she wanted him to kiss her. Lord, how she wanted that. She'd missed him so much the past couple of days.

"Well," Josiah said, pulling his jacket across his chest, "I suspect it will all work out just fine, then." He stood and offered Brett his hand. Brett took it, and as they shook hands, Josiah said, "I must say I'm relieved. I'm a bit set in my ways and wasn't looking forward to having a full house." Turning slightly red in the face, he glanced at her. "No offense, Fiona."

"None taken," she answered, leaning a bit closer to Brett, craving his touch beyond all else.

"And I'm glad to hear you'll be seeing to that other gal," Josiah said. "When Abigail suggested she must be another mail-order bride, I almost had a heart attack. If I'd known the fiascos bringing single women to town would cause, I'd never have let Donald Swift convince me that it was a good idea." He turned about.

"Speaking of that, I must go see Micah at the bank. I don't want him transferring money over for me to buy that house now, and…"

Fiona stopped listening to Josiah's mumbling as he made his way out the door.

Brett's eyes were once again locked with hers and knowing what was about to happen had her body tingling as an entirely feminine warmth spread throughout her system.

When his lips touched hers, nothing had ever felt more right. More perfect. And for the first time in her life, there wasn't a single regret for her to harbor.

Looping her arms around his neck, she held on as he kissed her, and she kissed him back. Everything that had been empty inside her was suddenly so full she was overflowing with happiness. It was as if she was a completely new person. Healed from the inside out.

Brett's lips left hers at the same time as he scooped her into his arms.

"What are you doing?" she asked as he walked around the table.

"Taking you back to bed so you are good and healed for our wedding."

"I am good and healed," she insisted. "Now

put me down, I'm too heavy for you to be carrying around."

"You'll never be too heavy for me to carry," he said, kissing her as they entered the bedroom.

He'd kicked the door shut. It was the desire inside her, the love she wanted to share with him right now that made her pull out of his kiss. "Put me down, we aren't done talking."

He didn't just set her on the bed. He laid her on it and stretched out beside her. "You're amazing," he said softly while running a finger along the side of her face. "Letting Josiah think you couldn't marry him for his sake."

"I didn't want to make him angry." It was hard to think of others when he was touching her. It had her heart racing, and her mind. It was imagining how wonderful it would be to become his wife in every way. To be his wife every day for the rest of her life.

"We have Hannah to think of," she managed to say.

He kissed her softly before he asked, "How did you know I planned on letting folks believe Hannah is a widow?"

She rolled onto her side so they faced each other and cupped his cheek with her hand. "Because I know you. I knew you wouldn't stop until you found a way to take care of Hannah and to marry me at the same time. That was exactly what I wanted too, and I finally realized the only way it could happen would be for me to be open to suggestions."

He lifted a brow. "Suggestions? I didn't—"

"I know. Maggie did, and she can be very convincing when she has her mind set on something."

"So can you."

He was running a hand up and down her side and it was so enticing, her thoughts fluttered. It took determination to get them back on track. "Hannah and Eric would have been married if their families had allowed it," she said. "They were awful to her, and she's so scared, so heartbroken over his death. She truly does need looking after."

Brett's thoughts and desires grew stronger each moment he lay on the bed beside her. She was so beautiful. Her eyes held every color of the rainbow and sparkled like drops of dew catching the morning sun. He almost couldn't believe he was this lucky. That she was going to be his wife. His to love forever.

A bout of seriousness overcame him. It wasn't enough to quell his happiness or his desire, but enough to admit he wouldn't shirk his other responsibilities. His mother had sent Hannah to him to take care of, to provide for, and he would. But that didn't mean he had to marry her. "Hannah will stay here with us, as long as she needs. We have plenty of room. We'll be the family she didn't have back home. No one needs to know she and Eric weren't married. It's no one's business, and if they think it is, they'll answer to me. She'll have that baby right here, and we'll provide for her and her baby and love them just as much as we love Rhett and Wyatt and any other baby that comes into this family."

He wiped at a tear that trickled out of her eye. "I was hoping that would be all right with you."

Her smile was soft and sincere. "Of course it's all right with me."

"Will you talk to her about it with me?" he asked. "She cowers every time I walk past. I think I scare her."

"It's not you per se. It's what she's been through. How she's been treated. She just needs time to heal, and to learn there are people who care about her."

"You're the perfect person to show her that," he said. "You have more goodness and kindness inside you than anyone I've ever known. That's just one of the things I love about you."

"It's one of the things I love about you too," she answered softly. "I'd never have imagined I could love someone as much as I do you. It's amazing, and so wonderful I can't stop smiling."

"Please don't ever stop smiling," he said. "The first time I met you I thought if there was one thing about you that I could change, it would be to see you smiling all the time."

She scooted closer. "You, Brett Blackwell, are absolutely the most amazing man."

Grasping her hip to press her tight against him, he kissed her soft lips. Not one to gloat, he figured this time he could. "I can't wait to show you just how amazing I am."

Chapter Twenty

"I didn't expect so many people," Fiona said, twisting to scan the wagons parked on all sides of the church.

"No one would miss Brett Blackwell's wedding," Martha said.

"We just agreed to get married yesterday," Fiona said, still in awe.

"And I spread the word as soon as you said yes," Martha said with a laugh. She sighed then. "It's all worked out so perfectly. It just couldn't be better. And Brett couldn't be marrying a more perfect, more beautiful woman than you."

"It's the dress," Fiona said, referring to the gorgeous violet-colored gown that was trimmed with yards upon yards of white lace. "I can't believe you had this hanging in your shop."

"Well, I did, and now it's yours." Pausing as

they neared the church steps, Martha fussed with the collar. "I am a wonderful seamstress, if I do say so myself. This fits you like a glove. Just as I knew it would."

Martha had not only nursed her back to health, she'd become the best friend Fiona had ever had. Thinking about how fast her life had changed, Fiona shook her head. "I can't believe that just a week ago I stepped off the train in Oak Grove, wondering if I'd made the biggest mistake of my life."

"He might be big," Martha said. "But he's not a mistake." With a wink, she nodded toward the church. "There's your handsome groom, and two of the finest-looking young men this town has ever seen."

Brett—with Wyatt on one side and Rhett on the other, all wearing matching black suits—stepped out of the church doorway. The three of them looked striking together. And proud. And happy.

"The women in the quilting club sew more than just quilts," Martha said before she gently kissed her cheek and rushed off to scurry up the steps.

Brett walked down the steps and took her hand. "I figured the four of us would walk up the aisle together, if that's all right with you?"

"That will be perfect," Fiona answered, lifting the edge of her skirt. "Absolutely perfect."

"We picked these for you, Ma," Rhett said as she and Brett arrived on the top step.

Both boys handed her several sunflowers.

Even in their wilted state, they were the most beautiful flowers she'd ever seen. "Thank you," she said. "They're lovely."

She and Brett had talked to her sons last night, and as she'd imagined, they were ecstatic about her marrying Brett rather than Josiah. But it had been later, after everyone had gone to bed, that she'd discovered just how happy it had made her sons. Especially Wyatt. He'd sneaked into her room, climbed up onto the bed and, while lying in the crook of her arm, told her how he'd prayed that she would marry Brett. In the dark, he'd whispered other things, telling her how scared and worried he'd been about their future, but how that was all gone now because he knew Brett would never let them down. He'd then talked about becoming a blacksmith, or a feed store owner, and shared a dozen other things he'd do before he'd finally dozed off.

Blinking back the tears that memory created, she knelt down and kissed both Rhett and Wyatt on the forehead. "Are you two ready?"

"This means we get to live with Brett forever, right?" Rhett asked.

"Yes, that's exactly what this means," Wyatt agreed happily. "Forever and ever."

"That's right," Brett announced, kneeling down beside her. "Forever and ever."

"Then I'm ready," Rhett said.

"Me too," Wyatt added.

"Me three," Brett chimed in.

Fiona laughed. "Me four."

A hush fell over the pews full of people as the four of them walked into the building. Rhett and Wyatt, side by side, led the way to the altar. Fiona, holding on to Brett's arm, really didn't need her feet. It was as if she floated along beside him, riding on the wings of happiness and love.

She may have been in Oak Grove only a week, but familiar faces smiled at her the entire way forward. Right to the front row, where Martha and Otis, Joyce and her husband, Chester, and their two children, Charlie and Betty, along with Josiah, sat on one side. On the other side sat Maggie and Jackson, Steve and Mary, Hannah, and Angus O'Leary. He'd arrived at the house this morning to say he was Hannah's escort for the day.

The old man winked at her, and Fiona

winked back. Josiah might be the mayor of
Oak Grove, but there wasn't a more prominent
citizen than Angus O'Leary.

The preacher provided a flawless service, Fiona was sure of that, but in truth, she
couldn't remember exactly what he'd shared
during the sermon. She was too focused on the
man she was marrying. In all the world there
couldn't be a more perfect man than Brett, and
more than once she'd pinched herself just to
make sure she wasn't dreaming.

When at last the preacher proclaimed, "You
may now kiss your bride," Fiona was holding
her breath, anticipating the action that would
tie her to Brett forever.

That happened all right. After Brett shouted,
"Yee-haw!" he picked her up, twirled her
around, set her back down and planted a kiss
on her lips that lasted so long she could have
fainted for lack of air.

Or she may have been out of air because she
was laughing as hard as everyone else in the
church. Life with this man was going to be fun.
She was ready for fun, and laughter. The life
she'd always known was out there, just waiting for her to break out of the past and step up
to claim it.

She laughed again as Brett scooped her into

his arms and carried her out of the church as the people in the pews all cheered and clapped.

On the steps he kissed her again before saying, "As much as I want to carry you straight home, I can't. We have to attend the party in the meadow first. I wouldn't want to hurt anyone's feelings."

Fiona wouldn't mind being carried straight home either, but this was Brett. He cared about people's feelings, their needs, and she wouldn't have it any other way. "Me neither, and there's food."

"This may be the only time you ever hear this, but I'm not hungry," he said while carrying her down the steps.

"I did hear that once before," she reminded him lovingly.

He winked at her. "I was a bit grumpy that day."

"And I was a bit stubborn," she said, kissing his cheek as he finally lowered her feet to the ground.

He held out his arm for her to hook her elbow with his. "This way to the food, Mrs. Blackwell."

"Why, thank you, Mr. Blackwell," she answered.

He winked at her again. "Eat fast."

She laughed. And laughed her way through most of the afternoon. It truly was a glorious wedding day by all accounts.

When Brett arrived at her side, she not only knew he was ready to leave, she was too. Rollie and Sadie Austin had invited Rhett and Wyatt to spend the night with them at the hotel, and Hannah had informed them with a shy smile that she'd stay the night at Martha's. Therefore it was just she and Brett who entered the house shortly before evening.

No words were needed. Barely any were spoken other than whispered *I love you*s as they closed themselves in the bedroom and, with mutual consent, slowly undressed one another.

Fiona told herself there was no reason to be shy. She certainly wasn't a virgin, yet she felt like one. Like a part of her was untouched. Maybe it was because she was untouched by Brett. Something she craved so intensely it made her slightly nervous.

She was breathless too. But that was caused by the sight of Brett. He was a handsome man, but unclothed, he was a magnificent being. His body was so sculpted, so defined; he was like some superior male specimen that God had only been able to create once. She truly couldn't believe he was hers. But he was, and she was going to enjoy him for the rest of her life. "Are you ready to fulfill that promise? Show me how amazing you are?"

With a self-assured grin, he gestured toward his waist. "What do you think?"

She laughed as she sauntered toward him. "I do think that's pretty amazing." Reaching out, she grasped his shoulders and gave him a shove, making him land on the bed. "Now show me what it does."

He did all right, but he took his time, treating her like a queen the entire way. The way he touched her, caressed her, kissed her with such tenderness she truly felt worshipped. She'd never imagined there was so much more to coupling than the final act.

When they ultimately came together as husband and wife, it was beyond comprehension. He took her further than anything she'd known existed and kept her there, riding wave after wave of immense pleasure. She'd never considered herself greedy, but in this instance, she was, and relished every second of it, and rejoiced in the ultimate freeing reward.

The aftermath left her suspended in an unearthly place too beautiful to describe. Surrounded by splendor, by peace and happiness, she snuggled against Brett's side, loving the feel of his heart beating beneath her palm.

"That was so amazing, I'm going to have to pinch myself again," she whispered. "To make sure I'm not dreaming."

"Welcome to my world," he said, kissing the top of her head. "I've been pinching myself for the last twenty-four hours."

"You have not," she said, giggling. His humor would always delight her. As would his love, and his amazing body.

"Want to see the bruises?" he asked.

"Yes," she challenged.

He rolled over, trapping her beneath him as he balanced on his arms. "Only if you promise to kiss them."

A thrill shot through her. "All right," she agreed. "I promise."

* * * * *

If you enjoyed this story, you won't want to miss these other great reads from Lauri Robinson

SAVING MARINA
HER CHEYENNE WARRIOR
UNWRAPPING THE RANCHER'S SECRET
THE COWBOY'S ORPHAN BRIDE

And make sure you look for Lauri Robinson's short story "Surprise Bride for the Cowboy" in our MAIL-ORDER BRIDES OF OAK GROVE anthology!

MILLS & BOON®

HISTORICAL

AWAKEN THE ROMANCE OF THE PAST

A sneak peek at next month's titles...

In stores from 5th October 2017:

- **Courting Danger with Mr Dyer** – Georgie Lee
- **His Mistletoe Wager** – Virginia Heath
- **An Innocent Maid for the Duke** – Ann Lethbridge
- **The Viking Warrior's Bride** – Harper St. George
- **Scandal and Miss Markham** – Janice Preston
- **Western Christmas Brides** – Lauri Robinson, Lynna Banning *and* Carol Arens

---

0917/04

MILLS & BOON®

EXCLUSIVE EXTRACT

Spy Bartholomew Dyer is forced to enlist the help of Moira, Lady Rexford, who jilted him five years ago. He's determined not to succumb to her charms *again*, because Bart suspects it's not just their lives at risk— it's their hearts…

Read on for a sneak preview of
COURTING DANGER WITH MR DYER

Bart longed to slide across the squabs and sit beside Moira, to slip his hands around her waist and claim her lips, but he remained where he was. If he could give her all the things the far-off look in her eyes said she wanted, he would, but he wasn't a man for marriage and children. To take her into his arms would be to lead her into a lie. Deception was too much a part of his life already and he refused to deceive her. 'I'm sure you'll find a man worthy of your heart.'

'I hope so, but sometimes it's difficult to imagine, especially when I see all the other young ladies.' She picked at the embroidery on her dress. 'I don't have their daring, or their ability to flirt and make a spectacle out of myself to catch a man's eye.'

'You may not make a spectacle of yourself, but you certainly have their daring and a courage worthy of any soldier on the battlefield.'

This brought a smile to her face, but it was one of embarrassment. She tilted her head down and looked up at him through her eyelashes, innocent and alluring all at the same time. 'Now I see why they only allow male judges on the bench. No female judge could withstand your flattery.'

'Perhaps, but a man is as easy to flatter as a woman, one just has to do it a little differently.'

She leaned forward, her green eyes sparkling with a wit he wished to see more of. 'And how does one flatter you, Bart?'

He leaned forward, resting his elbow on his thigh and bringing his face achingly close to hers. He could wipe the playful smirk off her lips with a kiss, taste again her sensual mouth and the heady excitement of desire he'd experienced with her five years ago. Except he was no longer young and thoughtless and neither was she. He'd experienced the consequences of forgetting himself with her once before. He had no desire to repeat the mistake again, no matter how tempting it might be. There was a great deal more at stake this time than his heart.

Don't miss
COURTING DANGER WITH MR DYER
By Georgie Lee

Available October 2017
www.millsandboon.co.uk

MILLS & BOON®

Why shop at millsandboon.co.uk?

Each year, thousands of romance readers
find their perfect read at millsandboon.co.uk.
That's because we're passionate about
bringing you the very best romantic fiction.
Here are some of the advantages of
shopping at www.millsandboon.co.uk:

* **Get new books first**—you'll be able to buy
  your favourite books one month before they
  hit the shops

* **Get exclusive discounts**—you'll also be
  able to buy our specially created monthly
  collections, with up to 50% off the RRP

* **Find your favourite authors**—latest news,
  interviews and new releases for all your
  favourite authors and series on our website,
  plus ideas for what to try next

* **Join in**—once you've bought your favourite
  books, don't forget to register with us to rate,
  review and join in the discussions

Visit **www.millsandboon.co.uk**
for all this and more today!